Dorset Libraries
Withdrawn Stock

Ophelia in Pieces

**Dorset Libraries
Withdrawn Stock**

Ophelia in Pieces

CLARE JACOB

First published in 2011 by
Short Books
3A Exmouth House
Pine Street, EC1R 0JH

A CIP catalogue record for this book
is available from the British Library.

ISBN 978-1-907595-14-1

Printed in Great Britain by Clays Ltd, Bungay, Suffolk

Chapter One

It had started over a jar of capers. She'd bought skate for dinner specially to go with the capers, capers she'd been given by a grateful deli-owning client some years ago. It was true that they'd sat untouched in the cupboard ever since and were probably long past their best-before date. But she hadn't thought of that as she had stood in the slush in the fishmonger's. She'd told herself that at last she was going to cook: she would stake a claim to a normal existence with a skate and caper dinner and she'd wear that red dress he said suited her. Or used to say suited her.

So far it had all gone well. Her idea had been cemented by the fishmonger.

'Skate, madam? Lovely with capers…' He had given the fish an extra toss in the air to express the joy of it. She'd bought a bottle of the driest Chablis, and some raspberries so fat you could fit a finger inside. They had seemed miraculous, these perfect plump fruits waiting for her to pluck them from the dirty astroturf display on Camberwell Church Street.

Ophelia stopped at the pub window to apply a fresh coat of lipstick, checking its outline and checking for something else too: that composed but open expression that she wanted to carry away with her. The air was warm, sustaining, and the late June sun would make it pleasant to eat supper in the backyard. Alex would be tired after his rugby, happy to go to bed and let his parents dine and talk properly for once. It was going to be a lovely evening.

But when she came in Alex and Patrick were eating ice cream together in the kitchen and scarcely raised their heads. Alex presented a mop of upstanding hair as he peered into the depths of his bowl. His arms had traces of mud. Patrick nodded but didn't raise his eyes. A frown-line bisected his forehead. Both Alex and Patrick wore jumpers with sleeves pulled out of shape. Neither said 'Hi!' or 'You're back!'

She put her shopping down noisily. 'I hope you aren't spoiling your appetite, Patrick. I'm cooking skate with Corvino's capers for dinner.'

Patrick looked up at her uncomprehendingly.

'You know, *dinner*? At least you'll remember Corvino, the murdering deli-guy who promised me a whole ham if he got off but just sent me a jar of capers?'

This wasn't how she'd meant it to be. Patrick was far away and her reiteration was bringing him no nearer. Alex was staring into his bowl. She thought of the stupid thing her client had said earlier: 'Venus isn't in the ascendant for you today.'

Patrick shrugged, as though he'd caught her line of thought and didn't particularly care for it. 'I'm not sure we've still got those capers. I had a clear-out to make room for my curries.' His voice was so cold it sounded like dislike.

She felt the floor lurch under her, felt he'd thrown her out with the capers and she didn't belong here any more, with her bony wing of a fish and her crisp black suit. The months of late nights in chambers, the struggling home to find Alex asleep and Patrick deep in his computer, the week-ends spent at her desk while Alex and Patrick giggled in the kitchen or played ball games in the churchyard, the snatched meals and perfunctory conversations all seemed to gather in a great growing wave which crashed over her, leaving her clinging to a chair back, full of despair.

Patrick exchanged glances with Alex. They were like teenagers resenting an adult presence. She didn't know how to join them so she swung herself round and walked quickly out of the room and up to her bed. For a while she sobbed into her pillow. No one came and she began to think perhaps *she* was the childish one, a grown woman having a tantrum.

She lay very still and listened. Alex and Patrick were upstairs now. Patrick was tucking Alex into his bed, wishing him goodnight with a cheerful ease in his voice, as though nothing had happened. She bit into her arm until it struck her as silly.

Patrick came in with his loose limbs and drooping eyelids. His lashes were longer than hers and hid far more. He sat down on the bed next to her, not touching her, not looking at her. They both stared at the carpet without speaking for a while, as though their conversation – her questions, his answers, the sorry conclusion – were all legible in the zigzags around the edge of the rug. Although they were close – she could see that his jeans were worn thin at the thigh – they seemed inexorably separate, like flies caught in adjoining webs, suspended in time and space, unable to have the conversation, or to refuse to have it. It was Ophelia who struggled into speech.

'What's going on, Patrick?'

'Nothing.'

It was so unfair, him forcing her to force this out of him. This was certainly not nothing.

'Come on, Patrick. Don't lie. I know it's not nothing. And the more you say it's nothing the bigger the thing seems.' How could it be nothing, the heaviness on her chest, the invisible wall that made it impossible to reach over and touch him, the atmosphere that chilled and slowed his responses? She balled her fists.

'Patrick!'

'OK.' He touched her knee and then moved his hand away quickly.

She relaxed her hands and put them palm down on the bed, on either side of her hips. Patrick was rubbing the top of his thighs. No wonder the jeans were worn there. How had she missed this new variation on his age-old fidgeting? It was new, this and so much else; and all the while she'd been running along with the old Patrick, with their old conversations keeping her company in her head.

And then: 'Yup. There is something going on.'

No, words were not better. She gripped her knees. She needed to get through this. It was a bit like giving birth.

He looked away, out of the window, and his body was still, as though he'd left it behind. 'I've felt, for a very long time, that you haven't been here. You haven't been available for anything, jokes, stories... even physically... You're always working and preoccupied. I need more than that. I need to feel loved. You know how it is.'

He still didn't look at her. It was this, even more than what he said, that made things clear to her.

Her shrill voice hurt her own ears: 'So, you are having an affair?'

He sighed, as if weary of himself, her, the banality of it all. 'If you want to call it that.'

She felt like she'd been dipped in icy water.

She got up and went to the window but she didn't look out. Instead, she looked back. She realised that she had known about this, deep down, for months, since Christmas.

A week before his office Christmas party, Patrick, whose

hair had always hung in thick, dirty curls down to his collar, had come home with a haircut. It was a number one at the back and sides and a number two on top, a cross between Grace Jones and an American marine.

'What the hell?' Ophelia had said, stopping dead on the stairs.

Patrick, just inside the hall and still in his coat, had run his hand over the pelt on his scalp and said, 'Soft and clean as a cat!' with a grin.

Ophelia had liked his Byronic look, and she'd loved twisting her fingers in his hair when they kissed. 'I'm not sure I want to be married to a cat,' she'd said, giving an exaggerated frown to hide a deeper misgiving.

He'd pounced forward and given her a winning smile. It almost worked, but not quite.

'What made you do it?' she'd asked, not coming closer. 'Won't you get cold?'

'Come on, Feely. It's good to have a change sometimes. I'm just sharpening up a little.'

'So long as you don't become uncomfortably pointy,' she'd said and given him the hug he'd been waiting for.

It suited him. You could see his high-cut cheekbones better, but she'd regretted the alien feel and look of it. Several times in the following week she'd caught herself staring at him as if he were a stranger.

The window reflected Patrick on the bed behind her. His face was turned towards their dresser, away from her.

'Are you having an affair?'

'If you want to call it that.'

What else could you call it? She didn't want any of this. All because she'd bought skate for dinner. Her throat burned. 'This is unbearable,' she said.

He turned to her with his mouth open, as though he had

something to say; but no sound came out. He looked at her beseechingly and she almost reached out to him. Then, to her disgust, he looked away.

She stood up, full of the vigour and righteousness of her anger, clinging to it.

'You can go. Go now. It is enough.'

And, to her amazement, he did. He got up unsteadily, stuffed some clothes in a bag and walked to the door. He gave her a horrified backward look and this time it was she who turned away. She heard the door shut, kedunk, and he was gone.

Chapter Two

The fundamental question had been settled then and neither of them sought to disturb it. She had thrown him out of the house and out of that comfortable place in her mind where she'd kept him, like a household deity, connected to her most vital thoughts. Into the vacuum old and new ghosts flooded, sometimes real people, sometimes nameless presences; sometimes she just felt the potent void itself, a space dense with all the absences in her life.

She fought back. In his hurry to go, Patrick had left almost all of his things. Ophelia waited until Alex was at school and then emptied the cupboards of Patrick's clothes. Every item of his clothing made her angrier; each epitomised his frailty in a different way. His underwear made her imagine his lover's nails reaching under the elastic, his cardigan had her fingerprints on the buttons. The socks were odd and holed. His jeans still held his shape. She added his pillow to the pile. It was so full of his smell it filled her bed like a censer, making the memory of him dwell in the chill side of the bed where he'd once slept.

She carried two full bin bags downstairs. She put them in the yard and looked at them.

Patrick would have gone to live with that woman. She'd be pampering him, feeding him lotus flowers. He wouldn't bother to take these bags away for months and she'd have to look at them, every day. She got a bottle of white spirit from under the sink and a packet of matches. This would get rid of the smell of Patrick in that pillow, she told herself.

She poured on the fluid and threw matches on top. Thick black smoke swirled and spread everywhere, making her cough. The plastic shrivelled away. Flames licked upwards and heat threatened the wooden fence. Gradually, the smoke turned greyer and in the end there were just two piles of ash in the middle of two black rings on the concrete. The surrounding plants were scorched. Ophelia swept away the ash but the rings stayed, staring at her. She didn't want Alex to see this and ask questions, so she got bleach and brushes and scrubbed till her hands were cracking and bleeding. It looked better, but not much.

Ophelia knew Alex was suffering too. When she told him about the split, darkness had descended on his face and he'd seemed to collapse inwards. He hadn't asked any questions or responded at all, except to say, laconically, 'Well, at least now we can move that umbrella stand.'

She'd smiled bitterly. Patrick's affection for the over-large umbrella stand was a family joke. None of them had umbrellas, or even liked them, and the stand took up over half the width of their narrow hall, but Patrick had always insisted it had 'character'.

'You can put it wherever you like,' she'd said, but when she found it behind Alex's bedroom door later she felt she'd been turned inside out.

Ophelia started going out as soon as Alex was in bed. She roamed the streets. She liked to walk in a straight line and she didn't care about direction. The regular motion of her feet seemed to keep some of her unhappiness at bay, but only while she was out.

Unwelcome thoughts drifted into her head all the time.

Conversations would replay themselves as she sat in the places where they had happened.

Just before the split, when she was defending a case with her friend and mentor Samuel, she'd come home straight from court one day and found Patrick drinking a beer in front of the six o'clock news. She was burning to tell him what had happened in court, but he'd scarcely turned to her as she entered so she hovered until the news finished and then switched off the TV. He scowled.

'Let me tell you about my day!' she'd said and started pacing in the small space between the furniture. 'We had the main prosecution witness in the box. He's the chief conspirator who's giving evidence against all the others to get a lighter sentence. He told the jury what bad things all the other defendants had done, but he never mentioned our guy, Alan, at all.' She'd paused and Patrick had stared at her without seeming to see her. Surely he wanted to know what they'd done? She couldn't imagine not being riveted.

'In his statement, the main guy gave the impression Alan was in on everything so it seemed weirdly deliberate, when he gave his evidence live, that he was silent about Alan. Anyway, we could have stayed mum and said to the jury, "Look there's not much against Alan here,' but Samuel wanted more than that. He stood up and stared at the witness for a minute and then said, "Would you say that Alan is, in so much as any of us ever are, an innocent man?"'

The phone had gone and Patrick had answered it. He hadn't said, "Hang on a moment, I've just got to finish a conversation;" he'd said, 'Hi, oh yes, hello *you*,' and he'd started an excruciating conversation about some lost keys in the office. Ophelia had walked out and poured herself a large glass of wine. After the call finished, he hadn't come to find her. All evening she'd waited for Patrick to say, 'And what happened? Did the witness say Alan was guilty?' but he never had.

––––––––

That was last week. Now, like the marriage, that trial was over. Alan was free but Ophelia couldn't concentrate on anything. She was supposed to be preparing for a short fraud trial starting the following week. She was being led by her head of chambers, on Samuel's recommendation. But however much she tried, she couldn't study the papers. She was supposed to correlate the dates on fraudulent invoices with attendance sheets for other suspects in the office, to make schedules showing how those suspects were just as likely as their client to be responsible for the lying documents. She was meant to look for new patterns and come up with fresh ideas. Usually she loved this sort of sleuthing but these days her eyes were awash and her mind drifting to places it shouldn't be. She risked disgracing herself in front of her head of chambers now.

She sat holding her head over a file, watching an invoice bubble up where a tear had landed, when her phone rang.

'Ophelia, I'm glad I got you. It's Paul here.' Paul Simms had always been one of her favourite solicitors and he knew her direct-dial number.

'I've had a last-minute transfer of a case with a hearing this Friday. Nice Sri Lankan woman charged with stealing thirty thousand pounds from her employer. I'm sure you'll like her. I thought she was charming. It's in St Albans, so you'll get one of those judges with beards.'

She laughed. It was almost like old times, talking to Paul. 'It certainly adds tone, having a judge who looks like an Old Testament prophet,' she said, and then, knowing that Paul was likely to grab the conversation and take it into all sorts of by-ways, she added quickly: 'Anyway, I'd be delighted to take on the case. Send me the papers.'

'It's in for pleas and directions on Friday. Something of a sticky wicket but I'm sure you'll get her off the charges in the end.'

'Right,' Ophelia said, struck by the optimism of his approach. Paul Simms was a man who understood risks but preferred not to acknowledge them when it came to his clients. His instructions always told you to 'defend vigorously' without giving any details of what you were supposed to say or how the client claimed to be not guilty.

'Anything I need to know about her defence?'

'She's pregnant.'

'Oh.'

The papers arrived on Thursday evening, bulky, heavy and hopeless. Samuel had borrowed and then left her wheelie case in the men's robing room at the Old Bailey so she had to pack all the files, her book on the law and her robes into a long sausage of a bag that crushed her shoulder.

On the Friday she wore stilettos, and by the time she got to Euston, the pressure on her left shoulder had dislodged her wobbling left heel and she was forced to hobble half on tiptoe. The cappuccino she bought to lift her spirits stuck like Pritt Stick to the roof of her mouth, and she still couldn't think how she was going to help Mrs Kalpanichandran.

The papers told Ophelia that Mrs K had run Mrs Letts' flower shop for three years. Before Mrs Letts had discovered the fraud, she'd had complete faith in Mrs K. In the first two years Mrs K had made a significant amount of money for Mrs L. Her accounts had always been impeccably clear. After that, Mrs K had started to record large purchases of lilies and Kenyan roses in the balance sheet but these were never sold. At the same time, the stock records showed no such lilies or roses. Still, Mrs K submitted both the accounts and the stock sheets together. Ophelia analysed the purchases and stock day by day and a not guilty plea looked doomed. There was no statement from Mrs K about any of this.

She got out her Archbold *Criminal Pleading, Evidence and Practice* and flicked through the rice-paper pages slowly so they stood upright for a moment in the air before flopping down again. Her eyes skimmed over the random pages. Diplomatic and international immunities from prosecution... unfortunately, Mrs K did not appear to be the Sri Lankan ambassador; Sovereign and State immunities, certainly not; children under ten, no way.

As soon as Ophelia got to the concourse outside the courtroom, she saw a woman she was sure was her client, surrounded by a large and gloomy-looking clan. Mrs K was young, pretty and neatly turned out in a navy suit. She had delicate bones and a swelling middle. She looked far advanced in the pregnancy.

When Ophelia called her name, she stood up quickly and stepped away from the others. The handsome young man she'd been sitting next to scowled.

Ophelia turned to the group: 'I need to speak to Mrs Kalpanichandran alone for a while but it's very helpful that you've all come.' She saw angry, disappointed looks flash between the members of the family. She looked down the concourse hoping to see the clerk whom Paul was meant to have sent to take a note. 'You haven't seen anyone from the solicitors, have you?' she asked, turning back.

A grey-haired, heavily jewelled woman shook her head. 'No and we have been putting out calls all morning.'

'Well, there've been problems on the trains,' Ophelia said and wondered whether she'd ever be free of this defence barristers' reflex of apologising for everyone's mistakes.

She led the way into a small room with a thick door and no ventilation, just off the main concourse. Mrs K sat and looked down at her manicured hands while Ophelia spread out her files.

Ophelia asked her question gently. 'So I just need to know, Mrs Kalpanichandran, how we deal with the discrepancy between the number of flowers you say you bought on the stock records and what you've put on the accounts, for the same day.'

Mrs K didn't look at her, but sighed, and played with her bangles.

'Because there is a distinct difference, as I'm sure you are aware.'

Mrs K took a deep breath and looked up at the fluorescent circle which lit the room with eerie evenness. 'I know,' she said, and then she looked at Ophelia, frowning. 'I put the pages together purposely. I wanted Mrs Letts to see everything, but I could not bear to tell her.'

'What was going on?'

'Well, it was for my husband. He did not want to lose face. His family adores him. He is their greatest achievement. He got the best degree in engineering at university.' She stretched out her ringed fingers and smiled to herself. Ophelia could see that she adored him too.

'He is still studying, but he started gambling. At first only a little, and then more and more. And when we couldn't get another mortgage he asked me for money. I took what I could, but I hated doing it. I made it so obvious...'

'You stole to pay the bills?'

'Yes, and to pay his debts. Sometimes he'd lose a thousand pounds in one night. It was terrible. And Mrs Letts didn't see for such a long time...' Mrs K hid her face in her hands and began to shake.

'Here, have a handkerchief,' Ophelia said, digging one out of her handbag.

'I'm so sorry. I didn't want to cry.'

'Don't worry. It's quite normal,' Ophelia said, drawing a flower on the corner of her notebook, waiting for Mrs K to calm down. 'You'll plead guilty to the theft and false accounting charges, then?'

Mrs K took her hands from her face and lay them face up on the table. 'What can I do? I am guilty, but my family, my husband's family, don't want me to say so. It is too much shame.'

Ophelia smoothed out the pages of her notebook. 'Well, if you plead guilty you get a much shorter sentence, a third less than if you are convicted after a trial. And we haven't really got anything we can say at a trial, so you'd be found guilty anyway, which would be more shame. So it is much better to enter your plea now. Tell me more about yourself, – things I could say to the judge to make him treat you leniently.'

Mrs K stared at her hands. 'So I will go to prison, then?'

'The Court of Appeal says you should go to prison for stealing that much from an employer, even on a first offence. It's the breach of trust they see as so serious. But tell me about yourself. Mr Simms has given me nothing to go on.'

Mrs K folded and unfolded her fingers as she told Ophelia about how she'd met her husband at university, how she'd given up her studies so she could support them, how proud they'd both been about money, and how they'd never asked his family for anything. Ophelia guessed that the family had not been that happy about the marriage in the first place.

Mrs K said she always hoped her husband would win back the money, and sometimes he had, but never enough. 'The last time was the biggest,' she said. 'He lost five thousand pounds in one night just after I told him I was pregnant. I think he wanted to provide for the baby. But now the baby will be a prisoner.'

Ophelia thought of the grey, jewelled matriarch outside. 'Is your husband's family wealthy?'

'Yes, very.'

'Could they pay back the money you stole, if that would help?'

'Well, they have the money,' she said, looking up anxiously at Ophelia.

'And could your husband get a job?'

'They'd give him some teaching at the university, I'm sure.'

'One last thing: what does your husband's family think about your pregnancy?'

Mrs K nodded and swallowed. 'We don't know if it is a boy.'

Ophelia sighed. Although clients were sometimes sorry to get a female barrister, at least girls were normally wanted, as babies. She looked at her watch. Only fifteen minutes until they'd be called before the judge.

'When are you due?'

'In two months.'

If Mrs K had wanted to, she'd have known if it was a boy by now. Maybe she did know and it didn't help.

'OK, Mrs Kalpanichandran, so you will plead guilty and I will do my utmost to get you a suspended sentence, yes? I'll ask for your sentence to be deferred, so you can pay back the money and have the baby. If you do what the judge says you might not go to prison. If you fight this you'll get two years at least.'

'Yes,' she said, very quietly.

Ophelia came out of the room. She concentrated all her efforts on the matriarch. Mrs K senior was unbending at first, muttering things like 'My daughter-in-law must pay for her crime,' and she stared at Ophelia's heel-less left shoe as if to say, 'Why should I listen to you? You can't even manage to wear a pair of shoes!'

Ophelia faced her down. 'Let me ask you something. How will you feel if your grandson is born in Holloway Prison, along with the children of drug addicts?' Ophelia could see the wave of shock passing through the group. The young husband looked particularly wretched.

The elderly matriarch started to shout, 'No, no, that's not going to happen!'

'Well, the only way it won't happen is if you pay the thirty thousand pounds into the court before the sentence is passed.' Ophelia felt the balance of power shift her way.

'It will be paid. We will arrange for this tomorrow,' said the matriarch, looking as fierce in her defence of her daughter-in-law as she had been at first in her rejection.

The young man from Paul's office arrived just as the case was called into court. He got everyone's names wrong, even Ophelia's. 'It's a guilty plea,' she whispered, and he nodded blankly. There would be no useful solicitor's note about Mrs K's change of plea, she thought ruefully as she went to give her name to the usher and prosecutor. Ophelia had failed to keep a proper record too. She ought to have got Mrs K to sign something about it. There just hadn't been time.

The clerk stood and read out the indictment in a stilted, indifferent voice and Ophelia turned to see Mrs K looking very small and frail in the dock behind her. After every count the clerk said, 'How do you plead, guilty or not guilty?'

Ophelia had to strain to hear the whispered: 'Guilty'.

After that everything was very quiet and solemn, like a moment of prayer. Ophelia stood up to start her mitigation and she felt a wave of sympathy for Mrs K, which made her wobble even more on her unstable feet.

She told the judge how Mrs K had almost wanted to be caught, how she'd done this for her husband, whom she loved too much, too uncritically, how now she would lose everything. To her horror, Ophelia heard her voice crack.

She tried to rally herself. She needed to elicit emotion, not show it. A lachrymose barrister was a disastrous one.

'The discovery of the fraud and the pregnancy have brought the family together at last. The family want to pay back the money, her husband is getting a job, and she, in two months, will give birth to their child. Love and responsibility have replaced the secrets and guilt. They hope most fervently that this child may not be born in prison.'

Ophelia felt tears pricking and a blush rising from her neck. Luckily, the judge was not looking at her. He was studying her client, comparing Ophelia's account of things with his own hunch about Mrs K. Judges usually believed they could know everything, given sufficient scrutiny of the papers and defendant.

'Please, Your Honour, give Mrs Kalpanichandran a chance to prove her remorse and rehabilitation. I'm asking you just to defer her sentence for three months so they can do everything I have set out. If they fail, they know prison awaits.' There was a catch in her throat, damn it, and the judge was staring at her.

'Miss Dormandy, would you like a break?' This was too bad. She squeezed her hands together behind her back and swallowed.

'Thank you, Your Honour, but that is all my mitigation.'

She bit her tongue.

The judge stared at Mrs K, who was crying quietly. At last he said very slowly, 'Right, Mrs Kalpanichandran, I think in your case I can, unusually, defer sentence as your counsel suggests. I've been told you can pay back all the money, with the help of your family who are here to support you, and your husband will find work.' He stared at the group in the public gallery. 'I need to hear that all of these things are done when I see you again, otherwise, as I'm sure Miss Dormandy has told you, you must expect an immediate term of imprisonment. This offence is so serious that only custody is appropriate. I will wait to see whether I can suspend that term of imprisonment in your case. I'll see you again on the first of October. You can have bail on the same terms as before.'

Ophelia felt her tears well up with a vengeance now. This wouldn't do. If she got a reputation for crying in court she'd never be briefed again. She seemed no more able to control herself in front of a judge than when she was working at her papers. Those files for the following week's trial still sat unscheduled and crinkled with tear-stains on her desk.

Chapter Three

As she walked along the narrow pavement to St Albans Station, past dusty antiques shops and cleaner barbers', she turned on her telephone. It started to ring almost at once. She stared at the bright screen and her heart constricted. Alex's school. Had he been hurt?

'Hello?'

'Miss Dormandy, it's your son's headmaster here. Alex is in detention next door.'

Ophelia's first feeling was relief. 'Oh… Mr Brett. Is there something I can do?'

'As you know, Miss Dormandy, we have a strict anti-theft policy at this school and a deliberate theft leads to immediate suspension. Alex was caught using a very valuable gold pen another boy had lost. He says he found the pen, which may be right, but he knew it was valuable and that it wasn't his.'

'I don't think –'

'Everything is in hand. He has written the boy a note of apology but I should tell you that any repeat of this behaviour will be viewed very seriously indeed.'

'Yes, Mr Brett. I'm sure it won't happen again. Things have not been easy for Alex at home recently. I should have called. His father and I –' she choked.

'Oh… I'm sorry about that, Miss Dormandy, but it

is important that Alex follows the rules whatever difficulties he may be going through.'

Poor Alex. He'd lost two fountain pens this term. She just couldn't keep buying him new ones. Most of the time he was writing in pencil like the boys in the year below. She could imagine him, seeing the gilded pen catching the light in some unpromising corner, picking up the forgotten treasure and writing at last in flowing blue cursive.

Of course he needed to be punished. The headmaster was right. But Alex also needed to feel loved. She and he were both walking wounded and they needed a break.

On the train back to London she called the clerks. She got John, cheerful nineteen-year-old John.

'Hi, John. Miss Dormandy here. I'm all done in St Albans for now. Sentence is deferred till the first of October.'

'Right, I'll put that in your diary.'

She could hear the tapping of his keys down the phone. This was the easy part. Nothing for him to bridle at there. So far everything conformed to the model: clerk faithfully fills barrister's diary with the best-paid work he thinks the barrister is fit for and the barrister faithfully attends, performs, phones up after to report success and adjourned hearing dates. The more dates and successes, the more the barrister proves his worth and the more the clerk recommends him for better-paid work. Everyone gets richer and busier. It was a virtuous circle that Ophelia was just about to break.

There was no good way to say what she had to say. It would be unacceptable both to her clerk and to her head of chambers, and as a matter of courtesy and status, she ought to tell her head of chambers first. He was expecting to have her as his junior all week, expecting her to sit beside him in court and feed him page references for the points he made, to take a note of everything that happened and tell him what he'd missed – not to mention complimenting him on his closing speech. But she was going to do none of this.

'Um, John. Could I speak to Mr Dorchester, please?' she said.

'I'm afraid not this week. He's sorting out a right of way issue on his estate. He doesn't like to be bothered when he's in Shropshire.'

'I see.' She paused. 'I can't do the case next week, John. I have to take a break. I've... I've got trouble at home, and I can't go on right now. I know this is last minute and not what a barrister is meant to do but the circumstances are out of my control.' Well, she was out of control, at any rate.

'But your presence is required at Southwark Crown Court.' His voice was firm. It was not for her to cancel a case.

'I'm very sorry, John. I just can't do it. If I did the trial I'd mess it up. I'll come back in September.'

'Is that right, Miss Dormandy?' His voice was full of irony.

'I'm sorry, I really am. This is an exceptional event. I'll see you after the summer. Thank you.'

He didn't even reply.

She'd write to the head of chambers. She'd grovel, she'd explain, but would that be enough? She thought about what had happened to her colleague Mary Dannatt when she had taken off two years with twins. Mary had returned to work to find herself banished to Uxbridge Magistrates' Court. For three years she'd to defend young men who'd stolen t-shirts in foil-lined bags. Before this her clients were more likely to have packed bags with Semtex and her trials had been at Southwark and the Bailey. And Mary had had a better excuse. Ophelia knew she was destroying her career.

She dialled Samuel's mobile. He was probably in chambers, but she didn't want to call the switchboard and risk having to speak to John again.

'What's this, Ophelia? Ringing my mobile! Have you been arrested or something?'

She could imagine him jumping to his feet and pushing his flop of grey hair away from his face ready to meet whatever challenge she threw at him. He was what her father would call a 'good sport'. She almost wished she had been arrested. That would have been the sort of problem they were used to tackling together.

'Oh Samuel, just as bad. I've split up with my husband, my son is going off the rails and I nearly broke into tears in court. I am an utter wreck. I just can't do the fraud trial that you put me up for, you know, the one with Monty.'

Silence. Yes, an arrest would have been much better. At last, she heard him clear his throat, like a doctor preparing to break bad news. 'I see. Difficult times. I'm sorry, Ophelia. Monty won't be pleased, but I'll do my best to calm him down. You know his temper, though.'

She did. He'd been known, during particularly frustrating cases, to throw the file across the room.

'Thanks, Samuel.' She waited, hoping he'd say something encouraging, something about wanting her back soon, but she could just hear his breathing and the sound of objects being shifted around on his desk. Good sports were not necessarily good at emotional scenes.

'Pleasure, my dear. Good luck,' he said finally, and hung up.

She stayed on the train as far as Elephant and Castle and then got off. The stalls around the station were dense with tat, but her eye lit on a rainbow-coloured beach ball. It seemed a fitting emblem for her hopes and at four ninety-nine it was within her price bracket.

She bought the ball. It swung from her wrist in a thin plastic bag.

When she got home, Alex was in his room, packing his case for the holidays. His au pair was downstairs in hers, packing too. It was the end of the year for both of them, but for Ophelia, usually, summer wasn't a break. Alex would go to his grandmother's in Suffolk and she would carry on going to court but in a lighter suit. When she was feeling daring, she even wore sandals. She used to miss having Alex at home in the evenings, but she would go to Suffolk for weekends and she and Patrick used to while away the long week-day evenings in aimless chat, flirtation and speculation, like a couple before they had children. This year it would all be different.

She dropped her court bag where the umbrella stand had once lived and ran upstairs into Alex's room.

'Hi, darling!' she said.

His face was slack and sad and his shoulders hunched. He was waiting to be told off about that pen. She was sorry to do this, but it had to be done.

'I heard you got a detention for taking a boy's pen.'

He didn't look up. 'Yeah, Mum, I'm really sorry. It was on the floor by the sports hall. It was so nice. It was black with rings of gold around it and it was really smooth to write with. I should have handed it in. I'm sorry.'

She hugged him. 'Yes. You have to think how upset the other boy would have been to lose it.'

He sniffed. 'Well, he had another nice pen too.'

She squeezed him tight and the plastic bag with the beach ball banged against his back.

'Still, you know it's wrong, don't you?'

He nodded and she let him go.

'I got you something,' she said, holding out the bag.

He looked nonplussed.

She sat next to his case on the bed. 'This year I'm coming on holiday with you. I'll drive us to Granny's and this time I'll stay. I'll take you to the beach every day and help you build sandcastles and we can go to tea shops for scones and jam.' He looked at her with puzzled detachment. She pressed on, 'We can go bird spotting in the estuary and crabbing on the Deben. I'll take you to all the places I loved, when I was your age. I've told the clerks I'm not working all summer.' He nodded slowly, taking it in.

She kissed him on the forehead and he gave her a hug.

'Cool, Mum.'

———

But the holiday was scarcely better than work. Ophelia couldn't feel her old joy in the places she'd loved as a child. She didn't want to look for birds or shells or Roman remains. She didn't want to do anything. She and Alex stared at the sea and grew freckles together. Alex had bouts of furious digging in the sand and started to talk in random accents and odd voices, but mainly he sat slumped in morose silence.

Ophelia thought about how things had all gone wrong. When had the trouble really begun? She rooted around in her memory for the signs of her husband's betrayal.

There was the bottle of Paul Smith aftershave that had arrived in their bathroom around the time of the haircut. Patrick never used aftershave.

'Did you buy this?' she'd asked, putting toothpaste on the brush and looking at the new purchase.

'Umm, yes…' he'd replied hesitantly.

She'd jabbed the inside of her mouth so hard it bled but she hadn't pressed her questions. They'd slept, that night, with a gap like a river between them in bed.

The next day she'd brooded on that exchange, Patrick's awkwardness, and before she knew it, she was going through his pockets looking for a receipt. She'd wondered if it was a present or if he really had spent money on the thing. She wasn't sure which was worse but she wanted to know, whichever.

Like Alex, Patrick kept the detritus of his days in his pockets, on his bedside table, on the corner of the dressing table, in the bottom of his canvas bag. She found Twix wrappers; business cards from Bromley Council and Credit Suisse; pen lids; a torn sheet from Alex's homework; a receipt from a restaurant near Waterloo for fifty-nine pounds thirty and another in Deptford for sixty pounds ninety-five; half a mint; a pack of Post-it stickers; a receipt from a deli for two brownies and two lattes. She felt like an archaeologist studying a lost civilisation, not finding what she was looking for, but sifting the available remains. She didn't have all the data. Patrick would have been depositing things in his desk at work. He'd have left a trail of clues all the way there, in the bin at the green, on the bus to Greenwich…

Her fingers felt itchy from the dust under her nails and her mind dirty, as if she'd been watching pornography. She put everything in the rubbish and told herself she was being stupid.

On the beach in Suffolk she filled her hands with grey sand and let it run through the tiny gaps between her fingers. Patrick had never told her his lover's name and she had never asked it. She didn't need to; she already knew. She'd met her at that Christmas party. It was the way that Patrick hardly spoke to either of them that had seemed oddest. But then everything about Patrick had been strange then. All his gestures were exaggerated. He threw his head back too far to laugh. He repeated himself too emphatically. He told risqué jokes. He made a bet for real money about motor racing. He boasted about his tidy desk. And all the time the new temp Caroline had watched him in wonder, flicked her curtain of hair to and fro, and shifted her weight between impossibly long, honey-coloured, bare legs.

Ophelia stayed on the beach, feeling her hair turn brittle as straw and her skin toughen in the sun and wind. When her self-disgust grew great enough, she would cast herself into the long, cold breakers of the North Sea. Afterwards, she'd take Alex back to the house she'd grown up in, and they'd have tea with her mother and Wilf and go to bed early. The house, once so strikingly painted in strong, dark colours, had been repapered in tasteful Victorian damasks. Wilf's family collection of bird pictures and his anecdotes of book-club rows were all agreeable enough, and her mother took pleasure in all the same old rituals – dog walking, fish pie on Fridays, gardening – but the ghost of her father seemed to hover in the beeswax smell on the stairs, seemed to cast a tall ,thin shadow over the rug he'd brought back from India, seemed to lurk, neglected, in the unopened drinks cabinet and the dusty rolled-up projector screen in the cloakroom. Her mother told her she looked well, better every day, but she felt extinguished, broken. Her mother kept saying she ought to get back to work, that Alex would be fine here with her and Wilf, that her career needed her and she was a rising star; but Ophelia couldn't bear to leave Alex, who was all she had left. She was a fallen star with no more light in her than the rocks by the beach.

———

The summer passed. They returned for the beginning of Alex's school term.

On the first weekend in September they drove out to Stansted to collect the new German au pair who'd make it possible for Ophelia to go back to work.

Although she'd done this every year for the last five years, it felt quite different now. She felt anxious and exposed even before Freia emerged from the arrivals hall with four huge suitcases and a stranger's stare. She found herself talking too fast as she described their area and the language school Freia would probably want to go to in the mornings, and Freia just said 'yes' in answer to all questions. She felt, as she talked to her about their routines, that they had become an equation, not a family. Their lives seemed to reduce down to a series of transactions. And no sooner had Freia moved into the front room than she started to go out. In some ways this was a relief, but Ophelia couldn't help thinking that the true reason was that, even to this newcomer, their home felt hollow and wrecked.

Patrick came as soon as they were back and took Alex to a football game. In the week before, Alex had kept repeating, 'I can't wait till Saturday.' In the week after, he regularly burst into reminiscence, 'Henry was magic', and 'That should never have been a free kick!'

She and Patrick agreed Alex could go out with him every weekend 'for a fun day', as though that was his only chance of such a thing. Ophelia didn't ask for details. She didn't want to hear about them hanging out together at Caroline's house.

Ophelia still didn't call work, though one day she walked close by it to meet her friend Flora for lunch. She and Flora had been at school together. As twelve-year-olds they used to get into a frenzy about all the destruction caused by the Industrial Revolution. Ophelia's preoccupations had changed, but Flora had stayed true to their zeal, and seeing her always made Ophelia feel both nostalgic and worldly. Today she looked forward to a bit of polemic to distract her from everything else.

Flora stood in the door of the café, exotic in a red dress and strings of blue beads, on a street where even the buildings looked pin-striped. Tall, willowy and beaming a big smile, the sight of her was a tonic.

She kissed Ophelia on both cheeks and said, 'How wonderful to see you, fresh from our old haunts. Come, let's go in. I like this place because the owner is nice and they recycle everything.' Flora ushered Ophelia to a table by the window.

'Not the leftovers, I hope,' Ophelia retorted, and Flora let out one of her hooting, good-natured laughs. A couple of men at the next table looked up at the sound and smiled.

'Leftovers are recycled into the cat, not the customers,' Flora said, smiling back at the men.

Ophelia watched a tabby twitch its tail as it passed between the tables, indifferent and proprietorial. The room was dim, lit only by natural light through the shop front and a strip light above the counter, but you could see that the lino floor was worn and a little dirty. A smell of stale coffee wafted from the percolator and there was a friendly hum of conversation from the other tables. Flora looked around approvingly. Then she ran her hand over the table and asked, 'How was the holiday with Alex?'

'We used very little petrol going to the beach, ate vegetables grown by my mother and rabbits shot by my stepfather. Ecologically speaking, it was top-notch, but I'm afraid we were miserable.'

'I'm so sorry. It sounded so good for you and for him. Remember the fun we had at Alex's age, repelling Napoleon from our sandcastles?'

Ophelia remembered the digging, the building and smoothing, how they'd decorated their battlements with shells and sticks, and elaborated stories about the glamorous French sailors that were washed ashore after their boats were blown apart by the cannons. There was always a very injured aristocrat with a name starting 'de' whom Ophelia would nurse and then marry. Flora took more pleasure in getting the troops to surrender in large numbers.

'You captured a frigate of Burgundians and made them plant vines!' Ophelia said.

Flora laughed long and high, setting off an echo of laughter from the other table, which made her laugh again. Ophelia felt embarrassed for a moment and then she relaxed into the fun, joining in, remembering how they used to laugh so much together that their stomachs ached.

Flora got to her feet. 'Let's order some lunch. It's all organic.'

'Good idea. What actually tastes nice?' Ophelia asked.

'The wholewheat fusilli with tomato sauce is nice. Would you like that?'

Ophelia looked up at the board. It was edged in peace signs and none of the dishes were free from unnecessary elaboration.

'That would be fine,' she replied. She watched her friend go to the counter and fall into a conversation that looked far too animated to be about pasta.

'Sorry,' Flora said, when she came back, 'Marco was telling me how he always stirs the sauce in the same direction, like his grandmother.'

'Right,' said Ophelia, wondering what had happened to their conversation.

Perhaps Flora had the same thought. She leaned closer over the table and said, with urgent sympathy, 'How have you left things with Patrick? I bet he didn't expect you to make him go.' She paused and added quickly, 'Not that I'm saying you did the wrong thing. I'd have thrown him out years ago.'

Ophelia shrank back. Had she been too soft on him, or was Flora too emphatic? She felt too confused to say.

'We split so suddenly. It was like a stone that's been cracked in the frost but held together with some earth. You disturb the ground a bit, by doing something odd like buying a nice dinner, and the whole structure falls clean apart.'

'He never looked after you.'

'Well, he might say I didn't look after him. I was so busy all the time. But I was just trying to pay the bills. I wasn't sleeping with my colleagues.'

'Did he sleep with lots of them?' Flora's eyes flashed. She looked as though she might slice him up.

'Well, actually it was just a temp at his office. She was young and impressed and had long legs and a trust fund. Caroline. I suppose it was all too much for Patrick to resist.' She sighed.

'My point exactly.' Flora looked militant and folded her arms.

For all that her friend was trying to help, Ophelia wanted to resist so simple a conclusion. 'You've never been a believer in the long-haul relationship. I seem to remember you dumped your last man because he liked Westerns.'

Flora smiled. 'Well, maybe I was being a bit hard on him, but the gun culture was too much.'

A waitress came over with two steaming plates of soggy pasta. Ophelia guessed it had been cooked some time ago. 'Mmm,' she said, taking a few bites of the soft brown and red mush. 'I'm not sure I can taste whether he stirred to the left or right. Can you?'

Flora laughed quietly. Ophelia had got the right level of levity this time. Flora tucked hungrily into the pasta.

'Still, I miss Patrick horribly. I walk around London and I think I see him, all the time. It's because he's in my thoughts, I guess. Any lanky frame and square-cut chin and I'm running to catch up with his doppelganger.'

'But just think how many other attractive men you could find!' Flora's eyes twinkled encouragingly. Certainly, Flora never seemed to have any trouble finding admirers. Flirting came as naturally to her as freckles. But then she never knew what to do with a boyfriend when she had one.

'I'm worried Alex is missing Patrick a lot too. He only sees him on Saturdays. Patrick isn't even coming to his birthday party. I'll be doing tea for twenty boys on my own.'

'No, you won't,' Flora said, putting her fork down and looking defiant and excited. 'I'm going to help. I love parties, the decorating, setting the scene, and all the fun!' Ophelia thought of Flora's parties. They were long, rather dreamy affairs with no adrenaline-fuelled schoolboys.

'Thank you, but are you sure? Nine-year-old boys aren't very keen on joss sticks and candlelight. They're noisy and savage.'

'I know. I work with them all the time,' Flora said, abruptly.

Every now and then this dynamic came up. Flora would indicate that, as a social worker, she had a wider, deeper knowledge of children than Ophelia, or any mother, could have. When Alex was a baby, she'd been most insistent that Ophelia should have a feeding timetable and clear bedtimes, something that seemed impossible to Ophelia. She guessed that Flora would have liked children, but didn't want all the commitments that came with them, so she convinced herself she had the best of them anyway.

'Are you enjoying work at the moment?' Ophelia asked, to change the subject.

'It's very stressful. I've had to call the police in on a case.' Flora looked upset and stopped eating. 'One of my clients told me her stepfather hit the baby, his own kid, to stop it crying. He'd punch it in the ribs and after that the baby would be quiet. Poor thing. It worked because, with broken ribs, crying is too sore. The girl told me all this and then wanted me to promise not to do anything as she was scared they'd know it was her who'd told.'

'That's awful. Wh at did you do?'

Flora smiled, already cheerful again. 'I told her it would be OK and we'd send a health visitor for a "routine check". The health visitor found broken ribs and got the police. They never guessed.'

'That's good,' Ophelia said, enjoying her friend's pleasure in her work. 'God knows what I am doing… I am so broke; I ought to go to work too but my nerves feel too close to the surface. I'm worried they wont want me back in chambers. And even if I can go back, I'm afraid I'll be no good.'

'Don't worry. You're very bright and tougher than you think.'

'I hope so,' Ophelia said, wondering if she was right.

'And you mustn't worry about the party. It's going to be a hit. It's your birthday on the same day as Alex's, isn't it?'

Ophelia nodded. She'd been trying to forget that aspect of the day. She told Flora about the arrangements and began to feel better. It was beginning to sound like a manageable party.

Flora nodded and looked at her watch. 'Got to dash, but lunch is on me.'

She blew Ophelia a kiss and took the chit over to the counter. Even now, when she said she was in a hurry, Flora seemed to take a long time over paying the man at the till. Her compulsion to flirt was as strong as her good humour.

Ophelia stayed in her place, staring at passers-by through the window. Everyone seemed to be in a rush. She realised she felt a little left out. Maybe going back to chambers would be a good thing.

———

'I'm going back to work tomorrow,' she announced to Alex on Sunday night, as he was eating sausages and beans.

'Oh.' He was concentrating on an over-full fork. Once the last bean had made it, he said, 'Mum, I'm meant to bring a big box into school tomorrow. There was a sheet last week. We're making robots in DT.'

'If I get a wine delivery tomorrow evening, you could take the box in on Tuesday.'

'No, Mum. It can't wait. I'll lose house points if I don't have it tomorrow.' His voice was quivery.

She could think of only two boxes in the house: one was small and contained her father's treasure; the other was a good-sized cardboard box full of another sort of treasure – but then maybe those contents weren't precious any more.

She held the dusty paper in the flat of her palm, as though it might bruise in her fingertips. It was twenty years old, a museum piece.

My Dearest Ophelia,

The letters were big, brown, illuminated. The 'D' swept ecstatically up and then curved round into itself, blooming with flowers. The 'O' contained her portrait, smiling. The 'P' had a mermaid's tail.

How dare you run off like this, leaving me with only your library card photo? Don't you feel how I suffer? I'm supposed to be filing redundant plans for an architect whose 'meetings' are all in the pub. Mostly I file them in the bin and then retire to the photocopying cupboard for a nap and dream about you. My feelings about this work experience opportunity are like Voltaire's take on the Holy Roman Empire: neither work, nor experience nor an opportunity. Except of course that I have access to this lovely stationery and time to write to you. Which is a whole lot less satisfactory than having you in my arms.

What are you actually doing in Suffolk? Are you reading those books on Roman law or are you taking dogs for wet walks, eating coffee cake and drinking sherry with your mother, Wilf and whatever locals didn't fall out with your father? Are you thinking of me, as I think of you, continually?

Tell them you have a dangerous insect bite which has to be investigated urgently by a London specialist, or just tell the truth, as you always do. Say that we love each other and can't be parted. Because that is the truth, Ophelia. Our love is stronger than the sun.
Patrick

Xs for kisses filled all the rest of the space. They were so graceful, his Xs, long and slightly curling at the ends, like his lips, like his hair. Intense, persistent Xs, like those kisses on the platform at Liverpool Street until the guard's final whistle. Xs that were confident of being well received; exuberant, conspicuous, celebratory Xs. The Xs of a young man.

'Mu-um. Can I have the box yet?' Alex stood above her, tall for his nearly nine years – almost as tall as her – with a healthy frame but an uncertain presence. Maybe it was that he didn't stand still. He jiggled about, shifting his weight, impatient. He was so different from Patrick. Patrick, though he fidgeted, was sure of himself in space, slouchy but graceful, reckless. He used to ride around London on a bike with no brakes, and he preferred to climb through windows rather than bothering with keys and doors.

She looked down into the mess of letters and mementos from their lost years, the train tickets, beer mats, the postcards from America, Turkey, Egypt, the estate agents' particulars of their house... These had been the good times – although, when they bought the house, Patrick's lack of ambition was already complicating their choices. The fragments in the box seemed to breathe warm snatches of memory at her: of swimming side by side in the Mediterranean, almost too far out to sea; of sketching ancient ruins (Patrick catching the spirit of the structure, she struggling with the light and shade on two or three stones); of long conversations on Turkish buses showered with cheap eau de cologne; of him carrying her over the threshold of the house on their wedding night, getting stuck, losing her shoes, giggling, everything somehow new again. The heap of memories seemed fresher than the present, and she was drawn to it, as though it were a living creature she could caress and talk to.

Alex's chewed fingernails came between her and the box. They gripped its edge. She touched the back of his hand, restraining him, feeling the softness of his skin and the roughness of a hangnail.

'Just a minute. I want one last look at the stuff inside. Why don't you get the other things ready? You could find some buttons for his eyes and mouth and maybe your old hairbrush could stick out of his head.'

'But he needs to be *high tech*.' There was a hint of a whine lurking there and she nearly snapped at him, but an idea floated into her head.

'Hunt about in my court bag. I think there's an old dictaphone in there. We could record something, hide it in his head, make him speak.'

Alex rallied now and stuck his arms out straight in front of him, saying mechanically, 'I will exterminate, I will exterminate.' He shuffled forwards towards the stairs, looked down at them and continued in machine speak: 'Oh, no, stairs. I am going to fall down, I am going to fall down…' Then he threw himself backwards, so hard that Ophelia thought it must hurt. He kept his arms sticking out in front of him, pointing at the ceiling. 'I need an engineer, I need an engineer.' Ophelia laughed and he sat up and slid down the stairs on his bottom, dragging the carpet out of its nail grips with a tearing sound like a hairbrush pulling through tangles.

'Careful of the carpet!' she called. It wasn't much of a carpet now, but it had to last.

She looked back at the letter, crisp and yellow, its edges slightly curled, the ink fading. It belonged to another age. Not one of the thoughts which flowed over the page was still there. It was a relic, not something living after all.

She was not the same Ophelia either. All the cells in her body were different to the cells he had written to. In those twenty intervening years, every part of her would have decayed, dead cells shuffled off into her sheets, her clothes, her carpet, new cells grown in their place. She crushed the letter like a dry leaf in her hands and threw it into a black binbag she had ready beside the box.

She put her hand back among the mementos in the box.

She grabbed the cards and tickets and keyrings and threw them into the bag. The box felt like that place of lost things and failed purposes poets used to call the moon.

She jumped. Alex was beside her, staring at the box and holding two hairbrushes – *her* hairbrushes – in his left hand. In his other hand was the button jar, open. Behind him, down the stairs, lay a trail of buttons, like Hansel's path home. He hadn't seen them. He didn't see lots of things, and he was talking to her less and less. Only at night, when she tucked him up in bed, did he sometimes speak to her from the heart.

She pointed at the stairs. 'Look, Alex. You've dropped... And did you forget the machine? You could get it when you go down to pick up the buttons.'

'OK.' He handed her the jar and started to go back.

'No, take the jar to put them in.' She rattled it like a coin-collector. He blushed and took it back. She was sorry. She hadn't meant to hurt his feelings. 'You want to use my hair-brushes?'

'Yeah. I thought we needed a matching pair, for arms… if you can take all your yucky hair out.'

She raised her eyebrows. 'What will I brush my yucky hair with then?'

'Have it like mine. No brushing needed.'

'Your dad used to call my hair "the golden threads that bound his heart".'

'They didn't work so well in the end, did they?'

Her turn to blush, to feel her internal lift in freefall. People still sometimes told her she was beautiful, but she knew she'd aged in the last year.

She tipped the remnants of the letters and mementos into the black bag and tied it quickly shut, as though something hazardous might escape. She took it straight to the bin.

When the green lid swung down on it she was glad.

She came back into the house. Alex was just halfway down the stairs picking up buttons, dropping them again. She took the dictaphone out of her bag. She'd better make sure it had nothing she needed on it. She switched it to play, and her voice crackled out of the plastic pinholes: 'Advice on appeal...'

She shivered and pressed rewind so that a new recording would wipe it out. This had been her last piece of work, the case that had taken so much time it had ruined her marriage. At least she'd had Samuel next to her, but then Samuel had insisted they had to work every weekend for the six long months it had lasted. And she still couldn't get over the snigger in her client's voice on that last day, the day of his sentence, the day she'd gone and bought skate for dinner. He'd said to her, as his parting shot, 'Venus isn't in the ascendant for you.' He'd told her, apropos of nothing, to avoid all romantic gestures, and then he'd turned out to be horribly right. It was the prospect of dealing with people like him that made her dread going back to work. She handed the machine to Alex.

'Press record and exterminate as much as you like,' she said.

'Thanks, Mum. I should get some house points for this!' He looked pleased.

She smiled. 'I'm sure you will, if you cover him nicely. Better get rid of the Carlsberg logo. Do you want me to help?'

'I don't want to cover it. I'm going to make the beer thing important. "I will exterminate. But I am running out of fuel. More Carlsberg please. Then I can exterminate, exterminate."'

'You should make it Coke. Your teacher will think

you're a bit young for beer jokes.'

'Mu-um.'

He was always most childish when protesting how adult he'd become. Maybe it was her fault. When she treated him as a child, he became one.

She watched him holding hairbrushes up to the box, the empty treasure chest of her memories. She tried to see it as something of his, but she couldn't dislodge the suspicion that there was something of hers still left in there; some small evil or hope. A gnawing anxiety settled in her stomach, eating away at her. Maybe she'd feel better when the box wasn't in the house and she got back to work. Or maybe she'd feel worse.

She turned, as usual, to the fridge. A glass of pale white wine, cool enough to cloud the glass balloon as soon as it went in, held out a promise of muffled comfort, of a muzzier pain at the back of her brain. No wonder the robot needed beer. Alex probably thought all adults ran on alcohol.

Chapter Four

It was Monday morning and, like everyone else on the bus, she was struggling into work. Except that she didn't actually have any work waiting for her or anyone paying her to arrive. She might not even be welcome there at all. Still, she wanted to get to chambers early enough to look keen. She had to persuade the clerks that she was once again competent, marketable and available for anything – that is, if her head of chambers hadn't already told them that she wasn't worth the risk.

Her bus was turning and she was holding tight to the handrail to prevent herself toppling down the stairs in her high heels when her mobile rang. She let go so she could hunt in her bag, and managed a 'Hello?' before the bus lurched to a halt, sending her crashing into the curved wall at the bottom. It was a call from chambers.

'Oh, Miss Dormandy, we need you to help us out.' It was John, cheerful and uncontradictable as ever. Her heart beat faster. 'Helping out' always meant doing something unpleasant. 'We've got something for you at the Bailey. Got your court robes with you, I assume?'

'I'm just round the corner. I'll be with you in two minutes. What have you got for me?' She was off the bus now, half-running through the cobbled entrance to the Inn of Court, squeezing her small – robeless – bag into her side.

'Case of Gerald Barnard's. He has signal failure on his line.' John made it sound like a chronic condition, as though Mr Barnard's services were often interrupted on a Monday morning. 'Just a man charged with raping his stepdaughter who needs you to get him bail.'

She felt a twinge at that. She'd always hated child sex cases but of course she was in no position to quibble. John wouldn't even understand her queasiness. Sex cases were just part of the business. Like all the clerks, he'd left school at sixteen, but now he was so familiar with dealing with the law that he spoke like a professional. In some ways, Ophelia reflected, clerks were more professional than barristers. They went about their jobs more single-mindedly and they often made, in the end, more money. The head clerk, on ten per cent of everyone's earnings, was probably the richest man in chambers, and he certainly looked down on the over-educated, over-stressed barristers he called 'Sir' and 'Miss'. John, she guessed, would be just like that one day.

John pressed on, 'Barnard says you won't need any papers and it's bound to fail.'

So this was why the case had come to her. Barnard didn't want to do it. It would be legal aid, so practically no money, and it was hopeless, so absolutely no glory; no easing back into the profession for her. But then maybe Barnard had said it was hopeless because he didn't want it to matter that he was letting his client down, or because he hadn't thought about the case. Whichever, she had to take it on. And, as always, taking it on meant taking it all on, finding out everything she could and guessing at what she couldn't, internalising the client's dilemmas. Taking it on meant taking it in.

'Is Barnard on the phone? Can I speak to him?' she said.

'I'll put you through. See you in a minute, Miss Dormandy. You'll need to put your skates on. The case is listed with a few others at nine thirty.'

Her heart raced. She had very little time and she wasn't even sure where she'd find her robes. Maybe in a bottom drawer of her desk, if it was still there?

One more click of the phone and she heard the smooth, too smooth voice of Gerald Barnard:

'Hi, Ophelia, thanks for doing this. My train's cancelled as the driver didn't turn up *and* there are signalling problems at St Albans. Not that any of this will stop the rail bosses taking fat bonuses at the end of the year.' Excuses and blame; not a very impressive approach, but he was a colleague not a hostile witness, so she listened quietly to his account.

'Mr Godwin is an unemployed Romany with convictions for violence. I've represented him a few times after he's got in pub fights, broken a glass in someone's face, you know the sort of thing. This time he's charged with raping his fifteen-year-old stepdaughter. There's no chance of getting him bail. I told him he was on a hiding to nothing but he insisted. Good luck with him. I hope you don't waste all morning waiting for the case to be called on, like I did last time I was down there.'

'Where are the papers, Gerald?'

'Oh, if you want them you'll see they're on the top shelf behind my desk.'

So he hadn't even got the papers with him. Either he'd never intended to do the case, or he'd never intended to do it properly.

'I'll let you know what happens,' she said and hung up.

Her chambers occupied three floors of No. 1, Tullykettle Buildings, a plain Georgian terrace with chambers' names and the roll call of their members painted on the wooden reveal of each door frame. Ophelia checked superstitiously. She was still there, halfway up. Inside, the building had been stripped of its lath and plaster, creaky stairs, Dickensian ghosts. Shiny brass lights illuminated thick-pile carpets and cream plasterboard walls.

The reception was particularly dazzling, mainly because of Lisa, the receptionist, who had a big glossy smile, large gold earrings and jewelled glasses and sat behind a highly polished curving desk. If you were a client, she would offer you a seat on a Chinese Chippendale chair and a copy of *Country Life* or *Auto Mart* magazine. If you were one of the barristers, she would run her eyes over you in quick assessment, like a teacher checking your uniform, and then she'd wave you through to the clerks' room with a friendly greeting. Very little escaped Lisa.

Ophelia stepped in and saw Lisa raise her eyebrows. She faltered, wondering whether her mascara had run down her cheeks, or her stocking tops were showing under her skirt.

'Welcome back, Miss Dormandy. Long time no see.'

'Yes. Nice to be back. You well, Lisa?'

'Getting better. It takes a while, you know…' Oh dear. She'd completely missed some illness of Lisa's and failed to sympathise at the right time, or at all. So much could happen so fast…

'Look after yourself. Got to dash…'

Ophelia put her head quickly into the clerks' room. Mornings were always the quietest time here; the barristers were out at court and solicitors hadn't started to phone in new work. And so the clerks – who bullied the courts to squeeze in their barristers' cases, who bullied the barristers to take them all on, who coaxed the solicitors to send down the papers and who decided which of their barristers to recommend, who chased the fees and chose the biscuits, who later in the day had a phone at each ear and scrolled the court lists like traders poring over their stocks – now seemed almost pastoral as they chewed through their toast and letters. Their eyes grazed their screens and looked up at her without reflection. It was John, clean-cut, up-and-coming John, who spoke.

'OK, Miss Dormandy. All set?' Her eyes fell on a blue robes bag on the floor by his desk and he seemed to see her look. 'You want to take Miss Browne-Taylor's robes, to save time? She's doing licensing today, so she won't need them.'

She nodded gratefully. 'Thanks. I'll grab them now, dig out the papers and run over to the Bailey.'

'That's the style,' he said, like a personal trainer.

———

Miss Browne-Taylor's lace collarette was impossibly white and very large and the gown too made her disappear, as if she were a child dressing up as a barrister. Still, at least she'd had a good look at the papers. At least she knew what the case was about.

She rang and waited at the heavy metal door to the cells, hoping that the tannoy wouldn't call her into court before she'd had time to see Mr Godwin. She studied the new door – grey metal with a small square of glass and a shutter on the other side – and the old door, now just an exhibit next to it – four times as big, wooden, with big black nails and a metal grill – for six long minutes. In her hands she held her wig and a blue notebook with a small bundle of papers. She rang the bell again and began to turn over the allegation in her mind. The girl's interview with the police was very short and stilted but she alleged that he had made her watch porn in the afternoon while her mum was out at work and then had had sex with her. She said she was fifteen at the time. The mother's statement was very long and very detailed. Robert

Godwin's statement was one line: *I didn't do it.* In his police interview he lost his temper and refused to give details, but there too he insisted he was innocent.

The door opened and barristers and solicitors filed out slowly, talking to each other, ignoring the jailer and Ophelia. Once they'd gone, the grey-suited, grey-faced jailer said sharply, 'No point in ringing and ringing. We know you're there but we can't do anything with all the others in the way.'

She nodded and hurried along the narrow corridor, surrendered her phone and signed in.

'Godwin's in room two.'

Robert Godwin didn't even look at her as she came into the interview room. He stared angrily at his callused hands and his right bicep twitched. His huge arms were thickly covered in tattoos of snakes, daggers and roses.

'Robert Godwin? I'm Miss Dormandy. I've come to try to get you bail.'

He turned his head quickly, sceptically, towards her.

'You really gonna try? Not like that Barnard bastard?'

She looked him in the eye. 'Yes. I'm really going to try. But you have to help me do it.'

He nodded and she sat. Then he started to speak, like a man who has been thinking for a long time and has had no one to speak to, a man with a lot to say and no clear idea how to say it.

'It's all her mother Betsy's fault, the forgery, the lies. She made Trish a cripple when she was twelve, can you get that? She got her to wear a shoe with one heel higher than the other. And now she's faked this whole thing. She's forged Trish's birth certificate to make her fifteen last year. She was sixteen! I bet you didn't spot that. Barnard wouldn't even look at it. Bloody Barnard. He said I had to face facts. Facts!

You call these lies *facts*! I mean, I don't know where to begin.'

Ophelia smoothed the papers in front of her with the palm of her hand. She tried to sound calm, firm, confidence-inspiring.

'No. I see that. Shall we start with the question of bail, which is what we're here for today? You'll have to forgive me being brisk but we have very little time.'

'OK.' He was watching her attentively. Maybe she'd gone too far.

'They say you can't have bail because you'll go round and threaten them. Do you have anyone you could go to, a long, long way away? Someone respectable, maybe someone with their own business, or a teacher or something? Someone with no convictions?'

A smile crept over his face and then he broke into a broad grin. His eyes sparkled with glee.

As he stayed silent, she prompted him, 'You do?'

'My aunt married a judge up north. She always liked me but hated Betsy. Still, she sends us a card at Christmas.'

'Do you think she'd have you to stay? We're talking months...'

'Yeah, if you tell her Betsy's cooked this whole thing up. I mean, just let me show you – gimme the birth certificate...' He seemed to be going off track again, but she leafed through her papers and drew it out.

He jabbed at one of the pages with his finger. 'Look. The date of birth has been changed. See, it's all smudged.'

'Well, I don't think –'

'No, wait. Now, gimme the unused.'

Ophelia could tell this wasn't the first case he'd faced. She pulled out the small bundle of copies of other documents the police had seized, documents they weren't relying on.

He turned the pages and pointed. 'Look, here's her passport. Look at the date of birth. You see, they changed the birth certificate to make her younger.'

'Yes. This is very strange. It throws doubt on her credibility, but it isn't actually a defence, unless you're saying she was old enough and consented.'

He stared at her, exasperated. 'My defence is that I didn't do it, OK?'

She stared back. 'OK. So, you want me to call your aunt, tell her that your wife has been forging documents and getting her daughter to make a false allegation against you and you need her to give you a place to stay while you sort everything out?'

He nodded.

'Would she offer a surety too? Or would anyone else you know?'

'Try her. The judge is loaded.'

'What kind of a judge is he?'

'I dunno, but I don't think he wears all the clothes.'

'Probably a district judge, doing small civil cases. Give me the name, address and number and I'll ask if they can stand surety for, say, ten grand, OK?'

A new gentleness came into his eyes, as though he felt supported and understood at last.

'Yes. Tell her I'll do their windows, all the externals. Tell her that I will make myself useful.'

Ophelia gave him her pen and he wrote a name, address and number down on the front of her notebook.

'I'll see what I can do,' she said and got up to go. She had to hammer on the cell door to be released. She looked at her watch. The case was due on ten minutes before.

'Do you know what case they're up to in court three?'

she asked the jailer as he let her out.

'One before yours,' he said, pleased to show that he was on top of everything.

'Thanks. Sorry for ringing the bell so much earlier.'

The jailer almost smiled.

————

This was always the hardest bit, worse than appearing in court with a bad case. At least then you knew the ground rules and, often, the people you had to deal with. Ophelia had no idea who would answer the phone or what they would think. She went out of the basement to get a signal, up to the concourse outside court three. Another barrister was coming up to her hurriedly. He was probably the prosecutor, and she didn't have time for him now. She ducked into a window alcove and dialled the number Robert Godwin had written in big, round numbers at the corner of her book.

'Hello, Mrs Peake? It's Ophelia Dormandy here. I'm a barrister representing your nephew, Robert Godwin. I'm ringing you from the Old Bailey.'

A little frail voice just said 'yes' as though none of this surprised her. 'What is it, this time?'

'I'm sorry to spring this on you suddenly, but I wondered if you could help. Your nephew is in bad trouble and it may be that Betsy is behind it. You know Betsy, his wife?' Ophelia paused.

'Betsy's always up to something,' Mrs Peake said. So far Godwin's steer had been a good one. She'd work on the Betsy angle.

'Yes, looking at the papers, it seems pretty clear Betsy has committed a forgery, and lied, to make things bad for your nephew.' She paused again. This was the easy bit, but she'd need to tell Mrs Peake what the allegation was.

'Yes,' Mrs Peake said.

'Robert is adamant that he is innocent of the charge. Betsy has got her daughter Trish to say he raped her. There's no forensic evidence. It's just their word against his. Today, right now, I am applying for his bail. It's going to be difficult. The prosecution say he is likely to try to interfere with the witnesses. He needs somewhere respectable to stay, a long way away from here.' She hoped Mrs Peake would make the offer without being pressed.

'Yes,' she said.

'Is there any chance he could stay with you and the your husband? He says he'd be delighted to redo your external paintwork, if you like. Otherwise he'll be in Wandsworth Prison for months.'

'Will you tell him he can't smoke? The judge can't stand smoke. Or tattoos. He's got armfuls of them, I remember.'

'Yes. He could wear a long-sleeved shirt, I'm sure.'

'And he'll be needing us to stand surety too?' Mrs Peake had obviously done all this before.

'Yes, Mrs Peake. That would be very good of you, if you were able to go to your local police station with some documents. If you could make it ten thousand, that would be great.'

'Right you are, Miss Domby. You can say we're good for ten thousand, and you tell Robert he'd better not let us down.'

Ophelia imagined her, a small, dark, elderly woman in a twinset living in a mock Tudor house with a drive (it was called 'The Oaks'), telling her husband the district judge that one of her nephews needed to come and stay but not to worry, he'd do a good job on the windows, and he'd be good as gold.

The usher had come out of court three and was calling them: 'All parties in the case of Godwin.'

The prosecutor she'd seen flapping towards her earlier came up quickly behind and whispered angrily, 'I've been looking for you. This is the most hopeless application. Your solicitors didn't even –'

'I'm Miss Dormandy,' she said swiftly and went straight into court. This was all the communication that was necessary between them. He just had to introduce her. Everything else was a matter for the judge. And as things turned out, the judge was in a good mood. He was patient enough to let her show him the discrepancy in the dates on the documents. It made him beetle his eyebrows at the prosecutor.

'This raises some very serious questions, Mr Tring. I want this matter properly investigated, and an explanation as to why this wasn't picked up.' He was tickled by the thought of Mr Godwin travelling up to Berwick-upon-Tweed to live with District Judge Peake and his wife. 'Well, I'm sure that will be very improving. Mr Godwin will learn all about easements of light. Justin Peake has written a very good book on the subject. Do you know it, Miss Dormandy?'

She confessed she didn't. She was tempted to mention the long-sleeved shirt for dinner, but that would be telling too much. Still, she got Godwin bail.

Godwin called out from the dock, 'Thank you, Miss Dormandy', every syllable right. She began to feel quite hopeful for the day and that she might even do Godwin some good.

She went to see him once more in the cells. He was smiley and polite.

'Thank you so much, Miss Dormandy. It's a relief when you find someone who believes in you. I'm very unhappy with that Barnard guy.'

'Well, Mr Godwin, you could ask your solicitor to apply for your legal aid to be extended to cover a QC – that's a more senior barrister than either me or Mr Barnard, someone with lots of experience and clever ways around problems. If I were you, I certainly would do that. The offences you're charged with are serious enough to warrant this.'

Godwin put his head on one side, as if considering this. 'Maybe I've been unlucky, Miss Dormandy, but when I've had a QC representing me I've always gone down. I've not been that impressed with "Her Majesty's Queen's Counsel".' He said this last phrase in a mock-posh accent. He was clearly more than familiar with the legal world.

'Well, it depends on many things. There are good and bad silks, certainly. There is a specific person who, if I were you, I would want to represent me. Samuel Slidders is one of the leading silks of his generation. I've done many cases with him over the years and he's had some outstanding results. He's not young, but I'd say he's still at the top of his game.'

'OK, Miss Dormandy. If you say so.'

She felt he was studying her now, wondering what her real agenda was. She wanted to say: 'That's it. I just say what I truly think. No varnish. No hooks. There's nothing in this for me.' But she knew you couldn't make people believe you just by asking. She had to work at conquering his trust. Why was it that she seemed to have this instinct at work, but outside work she did it less and less?

Ophelia smiled and tilted her head inquisitively, as if they'd just met and she was going to draw him out. 'So you don't mind a little advice, every now and then?'

He laughed and the rumble seemed to start in his stomach. 'I hate it. The only woman I ever listened to was my grandmother. She was special.'

'In what way?' Ophelia kept her face open and eager.

'She could take the pain out of your stomach and stick it in someone else's. She made you feel like dancing. It was like she had music inside her all the time, the way she skipped about, even when she was old, and the way she hummed to herself. She'd swing me left and right, even though she was little and I was big, and we never crashed into anything. But if she didn't like a person, ooff.' He rolled his eyes. 'The farmer with the land next to us told her off for dumping rubbish and she gave him the eye. He got his hand caught in the thresher that afternoon. The wound went green and he died two weeks later. We didn't have trouble from no one after that.'

'Did you spend a lot of time with your grandma?'

'Yeah. Me mum was always off, somewhere...' Godwin looked away. It reminded her of the way Alex sat waiting for her on the stairs sometimes, with his toes pointing in.

'Yes. I wonder if I leave my son too much too,' she said, more to herself than to him.

Chapter Five

She enjoyed the walk back to chambers, the sun playing on the yellowing willow leaves as they swayed outside the handsome stone church at Holborn Circus, the efficiency and pace of the other walkers. But the warm floaty feeling of success did not last for long. When she got back to the clerks' room, she remembered what bigger battles she had yet before her. The clerks stared at her vacantly when she came in, as though unsure quite what she was doing there. Now that the crisis of getting rid of the Godwin brief was over, they'd lost interest in it. She stood her ground and they looked at her appraisingly, as though asking themselves: was Ophelia Dormandy someone they could sell? Her emotional walk-out in July would take a lot of living down. The wrath of her head of chambers could have black-balled her prospects. She daren't think what he had said about her. He hadn't replied to her letter.

As the eyes of the three clerks flicked over her, she realised that her skirt was too tight. It was the drinking, thickening her thighs. The problem with dressing glamorously was that if anything went wrong – if your clothes stopped fitting, if your darker roots started to show – it was more jarring and unpleasant than if you hadn't tried so hard in the first place. But being naturally short and pale browny, if she didn't make the effort she feared she'd be invisible. She checked her image in the mirror over the chimney. Her hair was bright and neat, the shadows under her eyes well concealed, her beauty spot evident. Still, she needed more than this to convince the clerks she was still good, personable, marketable.

'So, I got Godwin bail,' she said simply.

John met her eye quickly, surprised, pleased even. 'That's great. A good start.' Then he paused, as though his earlier train of thought was surfacing again. 'So, what are your plans, next?'

'I'm back.' She was defiant. He cocked his head sideways, waiting for more. 'I mean I'm back properly. Back for the long haul.'

That made him smile, with a flash of white teeth and a dimple. 'Are you going to work till you're older than Mr Slidders then?'

'He's an inspiration to us all.'

John nodded and waggled his head as if to say, 'Maybe for you, but I'm going to make my pile and retire at fifty. The long haul is for mugs.' He smiled and added, 'He'll be pleased to see you back. He's in his room.'

Ophelia was relieved. John wasn't making her feel unwelcome after all. 'Thanks. I'll go and see him. But, um, have you got any other cases for me, John? I mean, I realise I let you all down over the summer, but then splitting up with one's husband is a pretty exceptional event. I'm keen to put it all behind me now and get on with work.'

'Good.' John's eyes went back to his screen, indicating that the conversation was over.

'So you'll bear me in mind... for other people's returns?'

John turned to face her. 'Of course, Miss Dormandy.' He sounded overly formal. Errant barristers had to be punished, even while apparently being respected.

Then John's face softened and he raised his eyebrows. 'You

might want to ask Mr Slidders if he needs any help. I think he's a bit snowed under.'

'OK. Thanks. I'll be in my room or Mr Slidders' if you want me.'

She went to the cheque drawer. There had to be a chance of some money for her, after three whole months not collecting a thing. She pulled the metal handle and the drawer of the filing cabinet slid open easily. She ran her fingers over the names on the folders until she got to her own and then pulled it wide apart, to find nothing. She pushed the drawer shut with a firm shove, but it had filled with air and it closed slowly, with a sigh.

She went quietly through to the post room. One wall was taken up with rows of cubby holes, one per barrister, but they were not equally filled. Hers was half full of junky envelopes, not bulging like the others with files and champagne bottles.

She went to her room. The chair she sat on had once belonged to someone else. She'd appropriated it a few years before from the corridor, dusty and missing a caster on one leg. It was not comfortable, but she was pleased to find it was still there, tucked under the desk she'd bought with her first earnings, sixteen years previously. The desk was like a well-kept grave, clean and bare, with one photograph in a silver frame in the corner. She dropped her correspondence on the smooth wood and picked up the picture: Alex on his first bike, hardly able to reach the ground but grinning with delight. She hadn't seen that look on his face for a very long time.

The letters reminded her who she was supposed to be: Ophelia Dormandy, Barrister, marketing target for Hong Kong tailoring services, chartered accountants, professional portraitists, the *New York Review of Books*... They all assumed her wealth, all except for the one from someone who actually knew her. She wanted to bin this last letter unopened. She could see from the envelope it was from the bursar at Alex's school and she started preparing her response as she tore it open: 'It's just a cash flow problem. It happens all the time in my work. I should be paid soon for a case I did last year. I've been unwell recently, and I haven't been able to keep up the little work which pays more quickly...'

Dear Miss Dormandy,
It is with regret that we write to you again and this time at your work address. Our letters to your home have gone unanswered and the situation is now critical. Unless we are placed in funds within the next three weeks we will have to suspend your son from school. We draw your attention to Clause 4.1 of our terms and conditions...

But when would she get paid for the horrible case that had taken all last year and ruined her marriage? Maybe another year. She'd have to ask John for a summary of all she was owed, money she might be paid this year, next year, sometime, never, and then go back, again, to the bank. She threw the letter in the bin and got up, pulling her skirt down, covering that low-slung stocking top. She'd go to see Samuel. He was the one hope she had, and her only true friend in chambers.

As she walked past the window on the stairs, she saw how the day had changed. A blanket of cloud now blocked out the sun.

It took Samuel a moment to respond to Ophelia's sudden arrival in his doorway, but then his angular lined face softened and his eyes filled with jollity.

'Ha, Ha! You're back!' He pushed himself up from the

eighteenth-century bergère he'd bought from Sotheby's for twice its estimate with a little stagger she hadn't seen before. His complexion seemed as grey as the hooded sky in spite of the warm blush of his dusty-pink shirt. His braces at least were vigorous, embroidered with cheerful hunting scenes. His figure was still trim for all his sixty-five years, and there was something commanding in his manner in spite of his wild gesturing hands and a roguish smile. Samuel Slidders, Queen's Counsel – a 'silk', permitted to wear a silk gown, to get a junior barrister to do his work and to talk down to Crown Court judges – was just where she'd left him and was gratifyingly delighted to see her.

He gestured to one of the Regency dining chairs drawn up around the green-baize-covered table next to his desk. There were some more robust armchairs by the fire but he despised them, and only offered them to solicitors and the clerks.

'My dear girl, come and sit down. I'll get Betty to bring us some tea.' She wasn't really called Betty, she was Ruth, but then Samuel had his own names for everyone, and it was somehow impossible to object. Ruth had brought him a sandwich soon after she'd started as the chambers tea lady and when he complained it tasted off, she'd gone and fetched him a fresh one. He'd recited 'Betty Botter bought a pack of bitter butter' to her and she'd been 'Betty' ever after. Ophelia loved the way he got away with this, and everything else.

'How good to see you, Samuel. I was afraid you'd be cross with me.' She sat down with the sides of her feet pressed together and her hands folded in her lap, like an old-fashioned schoolgirl. He had that effect on her.

He looked a little embarrassed. 'Oh no, just glad to see you recovered. I tell you what. It's already twelve o'clock. Let's go over to the sandwich place and get a 'Samuel's

Special'. It's my new invention. You'll absolutely love it.' He flapped his hand around his desk until he located his keys underneath the Goodwood race calendar and then he gave her a quick sidelong look. 'You do remember Bellamy's, don't you?'

'Of course, Samuel. It's only been three months.'

''You sure?' For a moment he stalled. He seemed preoccupied, as though he was slowly verifying what she said against some internal diary. Then he sped on again, cheerful as ever, 'Of course, when we were doing our last case we hardly got out for lunch.'

'Nor home for dinner.'

Samuel seemed to pick up her regret and to want to magic it away. 'But we did such a good job, Ophelia. Remember how Crocodile Face crumpled when we challenged him with those figures you got? I don't think I've had so much fun in years... Come, let me give you an arm.' But when he walked her out of chambers, it was she who was supporting him.

All the way to the sandwich shop Samuel talked, telling her about his cases, about chambers politics, never once asking her anything. She started to wonder whether it was a professional habit not to risk asking things when he couldn't control the answer, and whether that might happen to her...

He stopped with dramatic suddenness in front of Bellamy's. 'Here we are, my girl, at the best sandwich place in London. Now, watch carefully and you'll see how it is done.'

He ushered her into the shop. Every surface shone – tiled walls and glass units displaying salads, sausages, cakes – all except for the huge blackboard where the menu was chalked up in capitals, with exuberant names, prices and exclamation marks. Among the options, she noticed the 'John Street Chambers Sandwich'. John Street Chambers were their keenest rivals and their choice of aubergine and gorgonzola was, Ophelia thought, typically over-complicated.

Samuel seemed pointedly not to mention their presence on the board. Instead, pressing her into the queue of suited men in front of them, he said in a conspicuously loud stage whisper, 'Now all the ingredients are good here. The trick is getting the right mix. I've tried almost everything and the best thing to have, the absolutely most delicious and satisfying sandwich, is the "Samuel's Special". It's smoked mackerel pâté, artichoke hearts and a squeeze of lemon on black rye, with a grind or two of pepper – heaven.'

The man in front of them asked for a 'Lazy Daisy with extra mayo' and Samuel shook his head resignedly. But when it came to their turn he was energetic again. He looked at the sandwich man's label and then at his face, which was young and unfocused, and he leaned over the glass to address him. If it hadn't been for the depth of the cabinet, he might have grabbed his shirt collar.

'Giovannino. Make me a "Samuel's Special", please, like I always have.' He paused and, seeing that Giovanni didn't respond, he hastily gave the ingredients, as though he'd only stopped for breath. Then he said, 'Ophelia, will you have the "Samuel's Special" too?'

'Oh yes. Can you make that two, please?'

Giovanni sliced and spread, squeezed and ground, but he seemed not to understand the most important part of the order. Maybe next time, she hoped, they'd have the manager and a better chance of getting Samuel's sandwich chalked up on the board.

The sandwich man handed them the wrapped parcels in a crisp green bag with a flourish, as though it were a present. 'That'll be eleven pounds ninety. Would you like anything to drink?'

Samuel patted his pink jacket in what Ophelia recognised as a mere gesture at looking for a wallet. 'Sorry, Ophelia, I seem to have forgotten my money. Can you pay for me today?'

She reached into her bag and drew out the solitary twenty from her purse. She'd have to start taking out more cash at a time, but she wondered when she'd have more to put in. She handed over the money, smiled at Samuel and said, simply, 'Betty will bring us drinks, won't she?'

Back in his room, they ate their overstuffed sandwiches over the paper wrappings. It took considerable concentration not to drop globules of pâté out of the end you weren't eating and they did not talk much. Ruth came in with glasses of water and tea and, rather too late, plates. 'Earl Grey with a drop of cold water so as not to burn your mouth,' she whispered to Samuel as she put the cup in front of him, turning it so the handle was perfectly placed for his right hand. Perhaps she was as attached to this ritual as he was.

'Betty, you're a treasure,' he replied, as he always did.

Ophelia wriggled her toes with pleasure in the easy sameness of things, and the sweet bergamot steam decongested her thoughts. She thought how little she needed Patrick now. Here, with Samuel, her world seemed comfortable and complete. But then her mind turned to Alex and his robot. She imagined Alex making it demand beer and his teacher frowning, uncertain whether this was imaginative or inappropriate.

Samuel finished his sandwich with gusto, licked his fingers, balled the paper bag in his hand and threw it, on target, straight into the black lacquered bin in the corner. 'Ha! So, pretty perfect sandwich, wouldn't you say, Ophelia?'

'I would indeed.' She didn't want to spoil the simplicity of the moment by asking him for work and she wasn't going to risk throwing her paper bag. She was bound to miss. She just sat smelling the tea in the stillness, trying not to hurry anything, but to live in the moment. As Patrick did.

After a minute, Samuel said gently, 'So, my dear, are you frightfully busy?'

'In fact, I'm not busy enough. I've got time to do anything you can recommend me for. I'm actually quite desperate.'

Samuel peered at her, as though getting a good clear look at her for the first time that day. 'Oh well, let me sort this out. I've got just the case for you. I was going to do it myself but I think you'd be much better at it than me. The client is a rich businessman, so it's private.' His eyes twinkled.

A private case: the Holy Grail for criminal barristers and clerks – no horrible legal aid forms. The clerks came alive at the sniff of a private case. Like truffle pigs, they could detect all relevant information about a privately paying client without seeing him, without speaking to him. You could see their eyes brighten and their sixth sense quiver as they edged towards agreeing a brief fee. They always knew precisely who could be worth what to whom. She wouldn't command anything like the fees Samuel would get, but this was bound to be a hundred times more than she'd earn doing anything else. Maybe Alex could stay at that school after all.

Samuel grinned at her, enjoying himself. 'It will be a fun case too. Challenging. I think the client may even be innocent.'

'Oh no,' she said, only half-joking. An innocent client was rare and stressful. Most cases were something like a sporting event: you won or lost but it didn't really matter. With an innocent client it mattered a lot. Was this, she wondered, partly why Samuel was passing the case on? Perhaps he didn't fancy the risk.

Samuel ran his hands over a small white file on his desk.

He always put his defence papers in white files. 'White for innocence,' he always said, though mostly the files contained the most palpable lies.

'These are the papers. Mr Mars is a banker, and he has a wealthy wife, and a family, and this case could break him. I mean, it may seem pretty trivial to you or me – only a bit of secretary fondling – but the consequences for him are huge. His boss is his father-in-law. If he's convicted he'll lose everything. And I just don't think it was an assault. I think she was probably willing. Even I can see he's a very attractive man.'

'But he's saying it didn't happen? He's running the wrong defence?'

'You got it. I knew this was the case for you.'

He picked up the file and held it out. Ophelia got to her feet and took it, trembling. She felt brittle as thin ice; a jabbing finger could break her. Samuel used to enjoy this level of risk. He'd always been tough, but now maybe his nerves were worsening. Or maybe he was just trying to help her. Whichever it was, she had to embrace this, the make-or-break case. Without taking risks she'd have no career.

'The solicitor is Jeremy Schwartz. I'll give him a call and square this with him now.'

She watched him punch numbers on his phone, wiggle his eyebrows as if limbering them up for a performance and then wink at her. He was a bit like this before going into court, except that then he needed the loo as well.

'Hi, Jeremy Schwartz, please. It's Samuel Slidders QC… Yes… Hi, Jeremy old fruit, how the devil are you? …Serves you right for marrying such a young woman… Of course I'm jealous! Now I wanted to let you know you've got a chance, a rare and lucky chance, to brief Miss Dormandy. She's just back from doing a case in the European Court of Justice which went short so she's got a teeny gap in her diary. I think she'd be perfect for the Mars case. Much better than me. Women always go down better with the jury, on a sex case. It'll make the defendant look gentler and more innocent if he has an attractive woman on his side rather than a battered old pugilist like me. And she's top-notch… Yes, you could probably save Mr Mars a little in fees… Absolutely your type. She can cope with anything… OK, great. I'll give her the papers now so she'll be ready for the conference… You're a lucky man… Yes, purple… OK, Jeremy, so long. Yup, always a pleasure.' He hung up and looked at her proudly. She blushed.

'Thanks very much, but what was all that about the ECJ? Their hearings never last longer than a day!'

'Poetic licence. Don't worry, my dear. He knows less about what happens there than I do. He won't ask you a thing. It sounded good though, didn't it?'

Well, she was stuck with that, so nothing to be said. It was an occupational hazard of doing business with Samuel that you got into these difficulties. She'd long ago learned there was no way of reining in the vividness of his imagination. It irked her though; she was painfully honest herself.

'So what was purple?' she asked, to change the topic.

'My tie. Do you like it?' It was a bow tie, black with purple spots. Classic Slidders.

'I love it. What kind of tie is Jeremy wearing?'

'Yellow, with green spots.'

'Wow.'

Chapter Six

She had just got back to her room with the Mars papers in her hands when her phone rang.

'Hi, Miss Dormandy. John here. I'm confirming the time of your con in your new case for Jeremy Schwartz. It's five thirty tomorrow, in chambers.'

The exact time of Alex's concert and she'd promised, very solemnly, that this time she would definitely come.

'Oh, John, thanks, but do you think you could shift it earlier in the day, or something. I promised my son –'

He cut her short. 'Can't be moved. Sorry.' He didn't sound sorry. He sounded annoyed. And immovable.

'OK,' she said weakly and hung up. She couldn't bear to think how upset Alex would be about this.

She opened the file to read the Mars case that was causing so much trouble, but instead her mind turned to home. It was five o'clock on a Thursday. Freia would be collecting Alex from after-school orchestra. He'd be hungry, snappy, oppressed by the hour of homework ahead of him. He'd slump in silence in the car and ask why there weren't any chocolate biscuits, and maybe have an argument with Freia about what music they listened to. He liked the Irish folk tape Patrick had made him; she liked Kiss FM. When they got home he would hunch silently over his exercise books while Freia made mysterious German salads with sugar in them. Alex had told Ophelia it was pointless asking Freia for help. He'd done that in her first week, and she'd got very agitated. She'd said of course she knew the answer, contradicted herself twice, and stamped off saying she'd only just arrived and her English was not so good, 'which was a bit irrelevant as the problem was maths'. Alex had taken to teasing Freia. Ophelia told him to show more respect but he never did. Still, she got the impression that both Alex and Freia were oddly comfortable with their bickering. She had even let him try on her cowboy boots.

Ophelia knew that if she went home now Alex would stop trying to do his homework himself. He'd throw a fit if she mentioned clarinet practice and there'd be an argument about pocket money. And that was before she even mentioned the concert. She'd be safer staying here a little longer, getting to the bottom of her new case. She untied the bow on the pink tape that held the white file closed and pulled it free. She began to read the witness statements for the prosecution.

Yelena Karpovska had come to London to work as a secretary. In Poland she was a radiologist but here you were paid four times as much just to type ninety words a minute and to book airline tickets. First she'd worked for the boss of ABM, Alan, who was a good man and believed in God. Then she'd become secretary to Matthew Mars.

She was glad at first. He was so kind and so charming, so charismatic. But soon he showed his true self. He was devious, selfish and a goat. He made her do everything, even collect his dry cleaning and buy his children's birthday presents – with her qualifications! And he always forgot her birthday and bought her the same perfume – Joy – every year for Christmas. And the way he forced himself on her was so callous and stupid! He had told her to come to the basement so he could show her some storage space for files – there was no space in the office – and he had taken her to the bike park, handcuffed her to the racks and put his hand up her skirt…

Ophelia got up and walked to the window. In the street below, barristers and clerks were filing out of the doors, shrugging their shoulders deeper into the coats, setting off for home. She went back to her desk and skimmed Yelena's statement to the end.

What a strange allegation, she thought. According to Yelena, on one occasion only, Mars had suddenly, with no context, no flirtation, fondled and pressed himself against her in the bike room while she squirmed and looked the other way. It was too detailed to be completely made up but too random to be true. And the gift of perfume was odd – too expensive and intimate if she was just his secretary, and she was too angry about it. No wonder Samuel said he might be innocent. He should certainly be acquitted, unless, of course, the jury liked her and hated him. There was always that risk, especially if someone on the jury had lost their own husband in some 'secretary fondling' incident. Ophelia winced and wondered where in his office Patrick had taken Caroline: the room in the basement where the coffee bags and the projector were kept, or the copying cupboard?

Thinking of Patrick, she remembered she had to speak to him. She dialled his work number twice before she actually completed it. She hated to disturb him, especially as a supplicant, but today there was no alternative.

It was the same receptionist as always who answered perkily, 'Arbuthnot Architects.' Nina.

Ophelia had met her a few times at parties. They shared a passion for shoes and this had become a trope of their bantering exchanges. But Ophelia felt they hadn't had this sort of chat for so long that she'd lost the tone. Also, she was too anxious about what Patrick might have said about her, and about what Nina knew about Patrick that Ophelia didn't. She wanted the conversation over before it began.

'Hi, Nina. Can I speak to Patrick, please?'

'Ophelia! How are you doing? Comfy in platforms?' Nina sounded exactly the same.

'Fine, thanks. Is Patrick still around?'

'Oh yes. Actually, he stays much later than he used to these days.' She didn't want to know. She heard a few clicks and then she heard Patrick's voice.

He sounded tired, even more tired than she was. This did not bode well. 'Hi, Ophelia. What is it?'

'I wondered if you were going to Alex's concert tomorrow night. I can't make it and he'll be miserable if neither of us is there.'

'You call me now to ask me to go to something tomorrow night?' He was indignant as well as tired.

'I think it was on the calendar I gave you, but please, can't you make time, for him?' It would have been better to assert that the concert *was* on the calendar, but she couldn't be sure. She'd have to rely on a residual sense of paternal duty, something of a weak force.

'Sorry, Feely. I can't this time. Things are going badly here. We're working on pitches and we keep coming second. We're demoralised and desperate. You wouldn't know how it feels.'

He'd taken to saying this stuff in their last few years – that she was the successful one in the relationship, the winner, the one who didn't need anything, all that rubbish. Of course it was difficult for him being an equity partner in a practice that made no money, where the rent was paid by an overdraft and he hadn't drawn a penny for a year. Of course he'd felt anxious and even a little eclipsed by her. He used to take cuttings whenever her picture appeared in the newspaper. Whereas she had stopped asking him what he was doing; but then she'd been so tired…

His voice seemed to be right inside her as he spoke, almost in a whisper, 'I'm really sorry. I've got these meetings in Hackney. Well, I know you don't want to know about all that, but I just wanted to say I am really sorry…'

She felt herself tremble as she realised that he was answering what had lurked unsaid in her mind. Their old closeness quickened in her, but this only made the conversation more painful.

'Goodbye,' she said, but she didn't hang up.

She listened to his breathing, to his whispered 'yes', and the soft click as he ended the call.

Chapter Seven

The prospect of telling Alex that it would be Freia, not her or Patrick, who came to his concert filled her with gloom. The music hall at his school held about two hundred people but it was always full for these things. It wasn't just mothers; siblings came, even fathers, slipping in at the last moment straight off the five thirty-five from London Bridge. There'd be printed programmes, a rousing introductory speech from the director of music, audience participation in the choral sections and resounding applause, especially for the better performances. It was a big deal. And all she had for him was an old excuse and some football cards.

She looked mournfully out of the window of her bus at a glass and stone office block. How stupid those arches were, floating above their pillars and supporting nothing at all. That's what Patrick would have said.

Once she'd have asked him question after question about architecture, but gradually she'd stopped. She'd stopped encouraging him too. She thought back to the last time they'd talked about what he did.

It had been in May. Alex was already in bed and the light evening made Ophelia want to sit outside and soak up the last of the day with Patrick. But Patrick had been bent over sheets of drawings at the dining-room table and he hadn't looked up as she came close beside him.

After a minute she'd said, 'What are you working on?'

He'd continued to draw as he spoke intensely, into his paper. 'It's my stadium. I want it to dominate its context like a cruise-liner seen past the little houses in a port, or like Wells Cathedral rising out of the plain. I want it like an alien space-ship in a sixties film. But how to get that retro-future look?' He'd looked up at her then, his eyes bright.

'Is that really what the client wants, something out of place?'

'I don't have a client. That's the beauty of it. I can design exactly what I want and sell it to anyone.' He'd given her a stupid grin.

'Or no one,' she'd said.

His face had closed down then and he'd drawn his head back into rounding shoulders, like a tortoise receding into its shell.

It was all so different from how it had been when Alex was a toddler, and they had given so much to each other unthinkingly. She remembered a Christmas Eve when she'd gone to bed early, tired after chasing pigeons with Alex in the park and all those endless bathtime games...

The bed had been cold without Patrick and she'd tucked her hands under her thigh to keep them warm. She must have slept then, till a crash at the window had made her sit up and see a strange dark shape behind the curtains. And then a red trouser leg beneath them.

'Ho, ho... *fuck*...' Patrick: as Santa.

She'd pulled him in, wrapped him in her duvet and they'd made love on the floor. He was everywhere, all over her. Her head, she later found, was among her shoes under the bed. They'd eventually climbed into bed and drifted into sleep.

Getting off the bus, she went into the greengrocer's, ripped a paper bag from the hook and filled it with apples.

The bag could take four without collapsing. She carried them carefully into the shop.

'Are these from Kent?' she asked, as she handed over the money. She'd got one of the 'boys', as the proprietor jovially called them, elderly Greeks who helped out but didn't understand very well.

'Very fresh, madam. You like some peaches too? They are *very good.*'

She shivered, thinking how they would be both unripe and rotten, and how Patrick had started to touch her without looking at her, and she replied, too vehemently, 'No, No thanks.'

When she got to her door she saw that Freia must have put a forty-watt bulb in the hall, the light was so dim through the fanlight. She could hear Freia talking animatedly in German on the other side of her bedroom window an arm's length away and she reflected that the girl had never displayed that much animation when talking to her. She wondered whether perhaps she should have tried harder to draw her out, but then she opened the door and saw something more important to worry about. Alex was not in bed. He was sitting, hunched up on the worn stair carpet in the gloom, his book perched on his knees, his eyes on the door, waiting for her.

'Hello, darling. Still up?' She kissed him tenderly on the forehead. He moved along on the step so she could sit next to him.

'What have you got there?' he said hopefully, as though she might have something magical in her bag, something that would make everything better.

'Coxes,' she said, sitting down next to him. She reached inside the bag and drew out the biggest apple. She held it out to him. Its skin was taut and red on top and flecked with green further down.

He took it distractedly and bit into it with a crisp crack. He ate it all, even the core. It was the only tidy impulse he had.

'I got you some football cards.' She fished about in her handbag and drew out a small stack of footballers. He took them without a word and flipped through them.

'Oh good. Gallas. I had him but I lost him at school.' He seemed very flat. He was always losing things. She wondered whether he was being picked on or whether he was disorganised; or playing out deeper feelings of loss with all his possessions. She should probably speak to his teachers, but that needed time, and nerve. Just at the moment, with the bursar's threat hanging over her, she didn't feel good about striding through those big wooden doors to ask for help and guidance.

As he studied the cards, she ran her fingers through his thick, curly hair. It needed a cut, but he hated the fuss. The springy mass of it, together with his slightly pointy ears, made him look different and a little wild. He could so nearly have fitted in. He was good at football, but he was always on the subs bench. He was gentle and polite (except at times, to her) but it was the wrong sort of gentleness. He didn't seem to make friends at school. Maybe he needed more encouragement to bring out his natural grace. Grace had been Patrick's thing: physical grace, strong opinions, and a desire to do nothing – apart from the occasional grand gesture.

She felt Alex look at her with a sharp curiosity and she shook herself into the present, though part of her was still thinking of Patrick, and the letters and cards from him that she'd thrown away.

'Did they like the beer-fuelled robot?' she asked.

He seemed to sink a little further into himself and he

mumbled into his knees. 'It was OK but the dictaphone got lost, so it wasn't funny.'

She ran a hand over his shoulders, trying to smooth out the knots of pain, but he turned to her quickly, as if this consoling gesture made him suspicious. 'You know it's my concert tomorrow, don't you?'

'I do, my love. But I'm not going to be able to be there. I'm sorry.'

'Mum!' Outrage transfixed his face. She tried to be soothing and calm.

'I know I said I'd be there, but a new case just came in. I spent all summer with you on the beach and I have to get back into work now. I need to earn some money for us to survive.'

His outrage gave way to watchful anxiety. She shouldn't have said 'survive'.

'Is it that bad, Mum?' He spoke quietly and seriously, like a confidant.

'It's just an expression, darling. But it is important that I do some work, obviously. I'd far rather be with you but I just couldn't say no to the case and the clerks couldn't, wouldn't move the meeting.'

'Which was it? I bet you didn't even ask.'

'Of course I did.' She was angry now. She paused. 'I said it was an impossible time but the clerks just ignored me. Even Samuel Slidders can't get them to do what he wants.'

'Yeah, but he's got *you* for that.' His cheeks had little red spots in them. This happened a lot, but the theme was new. He'd never attacked Samuel before. He'd always listened with patient amusement to her tales of their adventures in court. Maybe he blamed Samuel for all her late nights in that last long case, even for the breakdown in family life. It wasn't fair, but perhaps, for a boy without many options, it was more comfortable for him to blame Samuel than to blame her.

'It's the nature of the job, Alex, that makes us work so much. It's not Samuel's fault if I'm late. It's just the way cases unfold, the unpredictable things that crop up, the sense that you're the last thing between your client and an abyss… It's all this that makes you stay late in a crisis, and in one case there can be a lot of crises. Come, let's think about something else. Shall I read you some Huckleberry Finn?' He nodded, resigned, quiescent, and wiped his nose on the sleeve of his pyjamas. She put her arm around him and squeezed. 'Come,' she said and led him to his room.

She sat on the edge of his bed, beside a table covered in the flotsam and jetsam of his daily life: notes on scraps of paper, cereal bar wrappers, football cards. Thierry Henry was running, ball at his feet, at full tilt towards her from the wall opposite, and above her the planets were bright, orderly and labelled. She started to read. This was where she liked to be with Alex, on Huck's raft, floating down the Mississippi River, having a smoke and avoiding detection.

'Mum, look at the time!' he exclaimed suddenly. The hour hand was pointing at nine: bedtime, according to his school. 'Lights out, Mum.' He was right, of course, but she didn't want to stop. She wanted to float on with the adventure. Perhaps he was more grown up than her. He knew what he would have to face tomorrow and wanted to be ready. She just didn't want to think about it.

She put the book down and turned off the light. She went to kiss him and he had already turned away, curled up and facing the wall. He didn't respond when she dropped a light kiss on his cheek, but as she straightened herself he said, softly, 'Mum?'

'Yes?' she whispered back.

'Do dead bodies turn to stone?'

'No, darling.'

'But if they are caught in a volcano? Like at Pompeii?'

'Well, that's a bit different. We'll talk about it another time.' She kissed him again and he drew his knees up closer under his chin and tucked his elbows tight against his chest.

As she went downstairs, she could hear Freia on the phone again, shrieking at a joke or a coincidence, and she felt how long it had been since she had had one of those conversations. Now she was, not too busy exactly, but too preoccupied and lost.

Once she'd had lots of friends. At university she and Patrick had settled into a group with some of the actors she'd met doing a play in her first term. The play had been portentous rubbish but the shared pain of performing it became a bond and a source of hilarity for years afterwards. There'd been some funny architects from Patrick's tutor group too, and for years they all went on holiday together. They'd tried camping but a storm hit just as they were pitching their tent and the great white dome they'd planned to sleep in had risen like an angry ghost over the campsite until the wind dropped it over a cliff into the Normandy sea. They'd stayed up all that night drinking and switched to hotels after that. Most of them had children now and they'd given up the joint holidays but they still met, usually for dinner, and mostly still in the same group. They'd felt closer than family. Patrick had been very high status with them all and he'd helped give the group its character: teasing but good-natured, a bunch you could speak your mind to. How she missed them! They hadn't met for months – or was it longer than that? – and now she felt she couldn't bear to see them again.

Work, if she could get enough of it, would be a

consolation. Alex and Flora and work. Tomorrow she was meeting Mars. Perhaps his case would come to her rescue.

Chapter Eight

Lisa's glasses sparkled and her eyes were friendly as she greeted Ophelia.

'Good morning, Miss Dormandy – again.'

'Good morning. And yes, Lisa. I'm back now.'

'We're glad to have you,' Lisa said, and Ophelia felt her heart swell a little at this pleasantry, though she knew it wasn't an expression of any great emotion, or even of a groundswell of support for her here and in the clerks' room. Still, a benevolent gatekeeper made you feel warmly disposed towards the institution and made the day seem more likely to go well. She smiled back and continued into the clerks' room with a general wave of greeting that wouldn't require any response. She didn't look in the cheque drawer. She didn't want to look needy, though she was. The cashpoint had refused to give her more than a hundred pounds. If she didn't get an overdraft or a cheque, she wouldn't be able to pay Freia *and* buy food. Best to avoid Samuel this lunchtime. She wondered if she could risk asking the clerks what she'd be paid for representing Mars and when it would come.

She checked her pigeon-hole for any new briefs or notes. The only letter was from a legal publisher advertising a book on hearsay –'indispensable to the criminal practitioner' – for two hundred pounds.

She went to her room and opened the Mars papers again.

Just thinking about Mars and his secretary made her miserable. She hated to think how much fornication went on in offices all over town. They should put bromide in the water dispensers and spikes like pigeon deterrents in all the cupboards.

She called her bank but her manager was far too busy to talk. His assistant left her in no doubt that it was most unlikely that Mr Smith would find a moment to call her between the series of very important meetings which were detaining him all day. She was still sitting, quivering with impotent anger and anxiety, when she got a call from Samuel Slidders.

'Ophelia, my dear, it's lunchtime. I sent Betty out for one of my sandwiches for each of us. Can you come down for yours now?'

Samuel was grinning at her when she came in but she noticed that his face was the colour, almost the consistency, of the grey clay Alex used to use for making animals. 'Have a seat, my dear, and let me tell you about another new case I've got for you. And have a nibble of your delicious sandwich.'

Ophelia wondered if this new brief was the case of Godwin. She hoped so. It would make her feel better to know she was bringing work to Samuel, not just the other way round. She eyed the sandwiches. They looked very difficult to eat without disaster.

'Thank you, Samuel. You really are looking after me!' she said and sat down.

'Let me tell you about the case. It's legal aid, I'm afraid, but we do need to do these cases to remind us how bad things are out there. Our guy lives in that trailer park you pass by on the way to Kingston Crown Court. You know, the one separated from Surbiton by the *cordon sanitaire* of the A3?'

She nodded. Surely this was her case.

'He's accused of raping his stepdaughter, a fifteen-year-old with learning difficulties and one leg shorter than the other…' Samuel's eyes drifted out of the window as though seeking refuge from the squalor of this allegation in the well-kept garden beyond.

Ophelia's jubilation ebbed. Maybe she hadn't done the right thing in recommending Samuel for this case after all. He seemed weary and sad.

'If this is the case of Godwin, I just got him bail. He showed me how you can prove forgery on the part of the complainant's mother.' She hoped to rally him with this promise of excellent cross-examination, and it worked. He sat up straighter and his eyes seemed to crackle with new life.

'Show me!' he said, pushing the brief towards her. Ophelia's writing was all over the front of it, giving the terms of Godwin's bail, and yet Samuel seemed not to have noticed her involvement. Maybe he kept his scrutiny for more important parts of the papers.

She turned to the exhibits and showed him the birth certificate and then the passport in the unused section, and he got very excited.

'Oh good! We'll have some fun with this, won't we, Ophelia? I'm so glad to have you as my junior again so soon. We'll mash the mother. Mash her! She won't stay upright in her white stilettos when we hit her with this!'

Ophelia wondered if his enthusiasm wasn't perhaps a touch excessive. After all, they hadn't any material on the girl.

'Thank you for the sandwich,' she said, and took a squashy bite.

They ate in silence for a few minutes.

'Oh, um, Samuel,' she said, her latent concern surfacing

in the calm, 'you don't know a good solicitor who does family work, do you?' She'd been turning the question of divorce over in her mind for weeks, reluctant to do anything definitive.

Samuel shook his head. 'I'm afraid my divorce was so long ago that my solicitor is probably dead. Luckily, I haven't needed one since and as you know, I've never done that sort of work. I'd ask Jeremy for a recommendation, if I were you. He'd have a very shrewd idea who'd be the best value.'

She was touched by Samuel's low-key sympathy and constructive help. She felt a tear grow in the corner of her eye. Please, no tears, she said to herself, taking another bite of sandwich and tasting mackerel mingled with nasal secretion.

The phone rang and Ophelia picked it up. 'Mr Slidders' phone,' she said, like an old-fashioned secretary. It was John, sounding conciliatory.

'Ah, Miss Dormandy, I thought I'd find you here. Your con will be in room three. I'm sorry, but all the other rooms were booked.'

'OK, thanks. What's wrong with room three anyway?' She had always been given room three.

'Oh nothing. Nothing at all. It's just most people seem to prefer the others. But as you don't mind, that's great.'

She hadn't, of course, but now she sort of did. Status was like that, better not looked into. The more you looked, the more subtle gradations you found. For some people, she guessed, it was a life's study and a great source of pleasure and frustration.

As she walked back to her room from Samuel's, she realised she hadn't asked him anything about Mars. She ought to have checked if Samuel had given him any advice already, but she didn't want to go back and ask now. It was the sort of thing you had to do off the cuff, while you were on the topic already. She didn't want Samuel to think she was nervous and to start regretting that he'd given her the case at all. With her history, this case felt like it could be a last chance.

Chapter Nine

Ophelia stared at her photograph of Alex on his bike, remembering those bent-over runs as she had held his waist and propelled him along the straightest path in the churchyard and how he had wobbled and pedalled and toppled over.

The phone on her desk exploded into her thoughts. It was set too loud for this small room.

'Yes?' she said.

'Oh, Miss Dormandy, we've managed to switch things round for you. Your con is in room four now.' John sounded as though he was telling her that she was being very spoiled.

'Wonderful, John. Thank you so much. I'm sure Jeremy and Mr Mars will be pleased too.' She guessed the upgrade was for them, not her, after all.

'They're there already,' he said, meaning: hurry up and get down there.

She picked up the white file and a pen and a counsel's notebook and skipped down the stairs, determined to put on the best show she could. As she let herself into the basement floor where all the conference rooms were, she bumped into Ruth, whom even she had come to think of as Betty. Her eyes twinkled.

'Your con's already got tea. That's a very nice suit you're wearing,' she said.

Ophelia felt curiously touched. It was a nice suit, rather forties, figure-hugging, buttoned to her neck with velvet buttons and collar. Did she imagine it or did Ruth actually wink at her?

Mars had the most arresting face that she had ever seen. His eyes were a bright, Nordic blue with large pupils which seemed to suck in information like hungry pits. His lips were full and mobile. His clothes were soft and yet sharply tailored, hanging easily from a slender but active body as though he had never worn anything but handmade suits and shoes of soft pointy-toed leather. She felt that, even as a child, he would have been impeccably turned out, and would never have let himself get dirty. It was five thirty but there was no shadow of a beard on his high cheekbones.

Ophelia extended her hand. 'Good afternoon Mr Mars. Do have a seat in one of these rather floral chairs.' She felt embarrassed by her elaboration, but the chairs had struck her, just then, as having far too many roses woven into their covers for a serious barristers' chambers.

He took the chair at the head of the table. 'I'd say they were a mix of Mortimer Sackler and Tess of the d'Urbervilles.'

Ophelia wondered if his expertise was genuine. He was scrutinising her now, waiting perhaps to have his attribution acknowledged. She felt herself blush. 'So long as they don't make you uncomfortable,' she said, turning to the easier presence of Jeremy Schwartz.

He was shorter than she'd imagined, shorter than her, but he made up for this with the amused authority in his face, lined by sixty-five years of wry smiles, with a mass of frizzy grey hair that bushed out of the sides of his head, and with his choice of bow tie: pink with green spots. Samuel would have been impressed.

'Good to meet you,' she said, shaking his surprisingly cold hand.

'Likewise. Samuel's been talking about you for years. Now we know why.'

She wasn't sure she liked that. It made her sound merely decorative. 'He always wants me to do his schedules...' she replied.

'Not many of those in this case.' The solicitor wrinkled up his forehead as though to emphasise his puzzlement at her irrelevant riposte.

She took a seat and indicated to Jeremy to make himself comfortable and then offered them tea from the pot Ruth had provided earlier. There was a bit of fuss over cups and saucers and milk and sugar for Jeremy. He liked three spoon-fuls, 'One of my foibles,' he said cheerfully, and Ophelia guessed he enjoyed his eccentricities.

Once everyone was furnished with their tea, she started, 'So, we need to think carefully about our approach in this case. It seems to me, reading Yelena Karpovska's statement, that she is very upset with you, Mr Mars. The jury will need a coherent explanation as to why she is so upset, or they may conclude it is because of what you have done to her.'

Mars looked at her notebook, as though dictating what she should write in it. 'All I can think is that it might be some kind of revenge.'

She frowned. Perhaps this calm was all he needed in the face of difficulties at the bank, but it wasn't good enough for a jury. 'Revenge... for what?'

'I didn't give her a raise this year and she was definitely not happy about that.' His mouth answered her questions with a calm fluency, but his eyes seemed to float away from the proceedings, resting now like a butterfly on the rose-covered back of an unoccupied chair. He'd need to engage a lot more with the issues if he wanted to persuade a jury.

'Why didn't you give her a raise?'

He looked out of the window towards the garden. Jeremy watched silently.

'Well, we'd had trouble with her for a while. She'd been turning up late, leaving early and spending too much time on eBay. I didn't have much of a choice when it came to the raise, and when I called her into my office and explained the position she collapsed onto a chair. She started shouting at me, threatening to ruin my life. I assumed she'd get over it but I guess I was wrong. I guess this is exactly what she meant.'

Ophelia could see the scene. He was telling some of the truth, except that it wasn't the money that had made her so unhappy.

'Why would the lack of a raise make her *so* angry? I know yousay in your statement that everyone else got one and she needed money to send to Poland, but that isn't enough to make her want to ruin your life. Not unless she's a nutcase, and if she was a nutcase you wouldn't have employed her for five years…'

'I don't know if you picked this up but she has…' He hesitated as if looking for a way to put this nicely, 'quite a strong sense of her own worth. I mean, she was a fantastic secretary. She was very intelligent. I was lucky to have her. But she had a terrible temper.'

'She says you gave her perfume every year at Christmas…' Ophelia let the sentence hover, not quite formulating the question, suggesting it. She felt Jeremy's eyes fix on her and she knew she was onto something.

But Mars was cool. She suspected he could take much more pressure than this. 'I give all the staff something at Christmas. Everyone likes to feel appreciated and a happy office is an efficient one.' Mars put a thin brown briefcase on the table and got out some sheets with clocking-in times.

She could see where he was going with this, but she wasn't ready to leave her point yet. 'The perfume didn't make Yelena happy, did it? She was annoyed at always getting the same thing.'

An exhalation escaped Mars's lips. 'I'm afraid there were a lot of things that annoyed her.'

'Was she angry with you for some other reason… as well? I mean, this is quite extreme revenge she is taking on you. She will have to go into the witness box and say lots of very embarrassing things. If she was making this up because of some deep, frustrated passion; if there'd been something more between you, and you broke it off, then all of this might make more sense.'

There was a silence which no one appeared willing to break. Mars looked down at his hands and Ophelia followed his eyes over the long, neatly trimmed fingernails and the platinum wedding ring. Jeremy tapped his pen on the table, as though to bring them out of their reverie, and Mars looked up at him, talking to Jeremy, not her.

'No, nothing like that.'

Ophelia realised she felt sorry for him, sorry to see how trapped and uncomfortable he was with the lie he was telling. She wondered if he understood the risk he was running.

'But you see, the jury might like her. They might not think she'd be that spiteful for a relatively small amount of money, and then you'd be in an even worse position. The sentence for this offence, after a trial, would be a year in prison, even for a man of good character.'

He turned and stared at her as though she'd said something shocking and out of turn. '*What?!* This isn't what the QC said.' He looked to Jeremy now, as though demanding an explanation from him.

Ophelia swallowed. She should have asked Samuel what he'd said. She should have prepared the ground better. What she said was right, but was that enough?

'That's what the guideline cases say, Mr Mars,' she cut in. 'On a guilty plea you get a reduction of up to a third, depending on how quickly you enter your plea.'

His eyes drilled into her, connected at last with what came from his mouth: 'I am not pleading guilty to this. Do you understand?'

'Yes, Mr Mars. Of course I do. Could you tell me something more about yourself, about your work, your home life?' she asked gently.

As he answered, she looked at her notebook and wrote quickly. She felt he was leaning very close to her now, that their confrontation had somehow made them more intimate.

'After university, I joined a bank because my tutor suggested it. It was easy for me but I didn't like the company very much. A man I did respect, Alan Bove, told me he was setting up his own private bank and would I join him, so I did. And then I met his daughter and I married her. Alan runs everything at ABM. It does well and I have my own clients. I can't complain. When I married Angelica, Alan gave us the dower house on the estate and we had the children, David, Jonathan and Hugh. They love the estate more than anything. I've built a tree house in the big chestnut and sometimes the oldest two sleep out all night. They pretend to be hiding out in hostile territory and make raids on the vegetable patch.' His eyes took on an amused, affectionate glow and he stared out of the window. Ophelia felt a tightening in her chest. He was a loving dad at least.

'Does Alan know about this allegation?'

'No. That's been my only piece of luck in this whole thing. He was on a business trip to the States when it all blew up. He wouldn't forgive the smallest indiscretion.'

So, an affair was an indiscretion. Ophelia tried not to scowl. She was amazed at how calm Mars was, in the circumstances. He'd been running a big risk for a long time, she guessed, having an affair with his secretary right under his father-in-law's nose. He must have a very cool head, cool enough to run a hopeless defence rather than a good one.

'Would your wife come and give evidence?' She felt like Samuel now. Samuel loved calling his clients' wives.

'Of course. She's very supportive.' Supportive sounded dull. To win this case, Mars would need her to be charismatic,committed and appealing. He needed the jury to feel his glamour, and the strength of his marriage. The wife would be important.

As Samuel might, she folded her hands over her notebook and looked at her client. If he had something good to say, she'd remember it. 'Tell me about the bike storage place.'

'What can I say?' He ran his tongue over his lips as if to savour the various possibilities before he chose one. 'I went there once, when we took on the building.'

'Is there a security man near there? Is it by a car park?'

'No, there's no one,' and then he added, after a teasing pause, 'unfortunately.' Ophelia wondered if Mars was almost enjoying his lie now; at least he seemed to enjoy showing that *he* knew *she* knew all about it.

He turned to Jeremy with a more combative tone. 'Why would I ask her to come to the bike park in the first place? How could the bike racks be an appropriate place to store files when people need to park their bikes there?'

Jeremy wrinkled his forehead. It was more a formal gesture at puzzlement than a genuine reaction. He seemed detached from the proceedings, unimpressed with Mars's answers. He was leaving the questioning up to her in any event.

Ophelia said, 'You can't think of anyone who kept their bike in there who could give evidence about it, about how often it was used, that sort of thing?'

Mars turned back to her. 'I'm sorry. I don't know.' He said this as though he were genuinely sorry not to be able to oblige her, as though he'd just missed finding the right man.

Jeremy cleared his throat, announcing his interruption: 'So, Mr Mars, any last questions for us?'

But Mars didn't look at him. He was watching Ophelia, seeming to seek some extra acknowledgment as he replied, 'Maybe if something occurs to me I could call you both?'

Ophelia stiffened. She *never* gave her number to clients. 'We can meet early before court to go through anything that occurs to you. I'll tannoy you if I don't see you.'

But Jeremy was already making her position untenable. He was writing his mobile number on a piece of paper and passing it to her so she could do the same. She made a last-ditch stand: 'You won't need my number.' But now Jeremy was looking at her with amusement, and a smile lurked in the corners of Mars's mouth too.

'Better safe than sorry,' Jeremy said encouragingly. Blushing and feeling she'd made something of a spectacle of herself, Ophelia scribbled her number on the paper.

Mars tore off the corner with the numbers on it and folded it up very small. 'Thank you. I'll keep this safe,' he said, tucking it into his wallet.

Mars turned to Jeremy. 'Can I give you a lift somewhere? I've got the car out the front.'

Jeremy wrinkled his nose. 'No, thanks. The Tube is quicker at this time of night.' He picked up his bulging file and bustled ahead. Mars got up quickly and went after him, and Ophelia followed behind. When he got to the door to the street, Jeremy stopped and turned to shake her hand.

'OK, Miss Dormandy. All set for Monday?' Jeremy was looking at her closely as though waiting for her to say something that would set the tone for the case, that would show she could lead as well as listen.

She gave his hand a brisk shake. 'All set. We'll bring some class to the Old Bailey yet.'

That seemed to work. Jeremy gave an approving nod and shook Mars's hand. Then he paused and nodded in the direction of a sports car, black and shiny as a stag beetle. He shook his head and said to Ophelia: 'He was offering me a ride in that!'

'Maybe it has hidden wings,' she said, casting a sideways look at Mars, who beamed back not at all put out that she was teasing him.

Jeremy nodded goodbye and hurried away with little steps and a big bundle. She wondered what could be in the file to make it so big: Mars's property portfolio? His divorce papers?

An expectant silence hovered between her and Mars. He seemed to be waiting for something from her. The light was changing from grey to violet and the drama of the shift seemed to hold them abstracted for the moment.

The door flapped behind Ophelia's back and Monty Dorchester, her head of chambers, stood behind her. They hadn't communicated since her letter in the summer. He blinked several times as if trying to take in who she was and what to do about it. She jumped sideways to let him pass.

'Sorry, Monty,' she said.

He blinked again and shot past her without looking up, as if he was as embarrassed as she was.

She turned back to Mars. 'I'd better go. I'll see you later.' Later? She should have said Monday. Mars held out his right hand and she shook it quickly. Then she turned inside without another word. She went back to the conference room for her papers and sat down. She finished all the chocolate biscuits on the plate.

She felt heavy and slow as she came back up the stairs to go home and she almost didn't say goodnight to the clerks, but then she reminded herself that she was relaunching her career and was still in debt and she made herself step into their room. It must have got late, she realised. Only John was still there, munching Bill's biscuits. He looked relaxed after his long day. Maybe he felt easier now he was alone, unsupervised.

'Hi, Miss Dormandy. You have a good weekend now.'

'You too. Good night, John.'

'Yup,' John said, preoccupied with his screen, which seemed to have something flashing on it. Was he gambling? she wondered.

She shivered when she got out onto the street. The temperature had fallen with sundown and her coat had no warmth in it. She felt as though everything important was over now: Alex's concert, the meeting...

But there was Mars's sports car still in the parking space in front of her, gleaming in the street light. As she stared at it, the driver's door opened. Mars got out and stood facing her, tense with purpose.

Did he want to tell her that he'd had the affair with Yelena and that he needed her help to keep this hidden or to bring it out in some way that would not harm him? Perhaps she should never have raised this. Now it would look as though she was coaching him. Jeremy wasn't there to protect her and bear witness that she didn't cross the line.

'Can we go somewhere, for a quick chat?' he said.

'It's difficult now.'

'Please. It won't be long.' he asked her, not begging, but letting her see how necessary he thought the meeting was.

'Just very quickly,' she said. She didn't want John to see her alone with Mars, so she walked smartly away, nodding to him to follow, leading him to the wine bar round the corner.

When they arrived in the familiar brown-panelled room, she checked to see if there was anyone she knew, but the place was almost deserted. Mars seemed at home there. Perhaps he was assured and loose in his movements wherever he went. He led her to the most hidden corner at the back of the room, behind a half-panelled screen. There was a big barrel for a table, two black painted chairs and a shelf above with an old pottery bed warmer. Mars pulled out a chair for her to sit down. 'I'll just get the drinks,' he said, as though they did this every night and he knew exactly what she wanted. She felt out manoeuvred but secretly pleased. No one had done this for her for a very long time.

He returned from the bar with a bottle of Chablis, two large glasses and bowls of olives and crisps. It was welcome. Too welcome.

'Cheers.' He lifted his glass and smiled at her. He was relaxed, but eager. She picked up her own glass jerkily.

'Yes,' she said and they touched glasses. She took a quick sip and pressed on, 'So, what is it you have to say?' She felt he was letting the agenda slip and she needed to haul it back.

He paused, as though he was about to say something difficult, and yet he seemed to glow. 'I feel bad about Yelena.' It was a short confession perhaps, but any more would have been too compromising.

She needed to know what he'd decided to tell the jury. 'Does it make any difference to anything?'

He shook his head and let out a long, low sigh, 'I just feel bad. That's all. It doesn't change a thing.'

She nodded and sipped again.

Mars leaned in closer. 'You must have to deal with a lot of very difficult and sometimes very bad people,' he said, almost apologetically.

'There's almost always something likeable about them,' she said and smiled. 'You think what a terrible life they have led when you see the long list of their previous convictions, but then you meet them and they usually have some sort of charm. It is my job to find the best in them, after all.'

'In me too?'

'For the purposes of presenting your case to the jury.'

He took an olive and rolled it in his mouth. A fragment of a poem Patrick had once read to her drifted into her mind:

He whose strenuous tongue can burst joy's grape

He flipped and rolled the olive and she could not take her eyes away. She took an olive too and bit into its hard and salty flesh. 'So do you want to tell me about your world, and your interests, out of the confines of the events on the indictment?'

'I collect flowers and butterflies and women with narrow ankles.'

'Tell me about the flowers and butterflies.' She sipped at the wine, tasting honeysuckle and thinking, My ankles are OK.

'I have a beautiful rose garden at home. Angelica loves that too. But I have other interests she appreciates less. I am a member of the Paphiopedilum Society.'

Ophelia took another big drink, fearing she'd gone too deep this time. 'What on earth is a paphiopedilum?' she asked, hoping she wouldn't regret it.

He touched her hand, lightly, as if to reassure her, or even suggest that she could have some affinity with this mysteri ous thing.

She repeated, 'What is it?'

He seemed to look inwards at some projection of his mind as he replied, 'It's a slipper orchid.' He reached for his brief-case. 'I have the magazine here. Let me show you. There's one of mine on page thirty-two…' He pulled out a magazine with a flower on the cover and flipped over the pages before handing it to her.

Ophelia looked at the page he offered. There was an article with pruning tips and beneath it a photograph of an extraordinary white and green flower. It was topped by a petal in the shape of an onion dome, white with green sweep-ing lines following the arabesque curve of the outside edge. The centre of the flower was a green cavity leading down into a bulbous vessel of petal, which was white with green veins, glistening and moist, more like an organ than part of a flower. He pointed at this and said, 'You see, that is the slip-per. I think you would love my orchids. They have such strong individual characters.'

'Where did you get that?'

Mars didn't move his eyes from the picture. 'The best of my collection were plucked from the leaf mould of the Kimbalu National Park. This isn't strictly legal, by the way.' He whispered the last phrase and she stiffened.

'I was hoping you'd make your position better not worse, Mr Mars.'

With supreme confidence, he reached over and squeezed

her hand. 'I was hoping that too,' he said. 'Your good opinion matters a lot to me, Miss Dormandy.' He let go before she could complain.

She blushed and sipped at her wine, feeling dizzy, but alive.

'So, if I may be so impertinent as to ask, what drew you to law in the first place?'

Mars had confessed to her, and she felt an answering urge to relax her guard and speak freely. 'I think it was seeing my father arrested. I wanted so much to be able to stop the police. I wanted the weapon of the law.' She ran her hands over her forearms, feeling a chill at the memory.

'So you help free those caught in the net,' he said, scrutinising her.

'Like butterflies…' she completed his image. She thought back to what he'd said earlier about collecting flowers and butterflies. 'You collect butterflies?' she asked. Then she remembered something she'd read in his case papers. Yelena had said he had a tattoo of a butterfly on his thigh. It had seemed a thing too intimate to ask.

'I've been a lepidopterist since I was ten. My favourite is a red admiral I caught by the Zambezi River. It's called the 'butterfly of doom' because it was abundant in Russia in 1881, when Tsar Alexander II was assassinated. The markings on its hind wings seem to say 1881.'

So that would be what he had on his thigh.

'I have to go. I'm neglecting my son. Thank you for the wine,' she said.

He held out a hand. 'You haven't told me about your son.'

'Well, I have one. He's nearly nine and I was meant to be at his concert tonight.'

'I'm sorry,' he said, 'I know how these things matter.'

She nodded and walked smartly out of the bar thinking, yes, defendants could be a lot more charming than you expected.

For most of the way to the Elephant, she felt almost cheerful, running through snippets of her conversation with Mars. But the closer she got to home, the more anxious she became. Alex would be waiting for her, full of hurt and anger and Patrick – would not.

Chapter Ten

As the bus took her down Camberwell Road, Ophelia's eye lit on a dirty plasticated banner announcing the new premises of an African church, 'The Rock of Redemption', inside a derelict shopping mall. Could anyone hope to find salvation there? Even the more modest claim of the next-door solicitors, 'Help with all your criminal, immigration, housing and divorce needs', seemed over-optimistic. She wouldn't risk taking her problems there. Her spirits lifted a little as she looked the other way, down into the green, with its teenagers on the baby swings and thin drunks lounging on the mound of grass by the rosebed, like poets or lovers. This was a kind of chaos that anyone could join, where your losses became general and irrelevant. And yet how the Victorians had once loved this place! They'd mounted terracotta balls on the corners of the surrounding buildings and, on top of the old bank, a lead temple.

The bus lurched to a halt and she tumbled down the stairs to the street. There were people everywhere on the gum-studded, uneven pavement, their faces tinted orange by illuminated kebab signs and sodium lights, all struggling to get somewhere; to the mobile top-up centre, to the late-night barber,s. And here was that outpatient from the mental hospital in his Prussian military uniform – again.

At last Ophelia reached the quiet of her own street, but

she still felt the pressure of other people's lives and ideas. This was a neighbourhood where residents organised meetings, published articles, made crab-apple jelly and loved Hogarth. Their energy and pride was manifest in the tidy Georgian facades, the freshly painted thirties terrace, the manured camellias, the well-spiked lawns.

When she'd first come here with Patrick, the area had delighted them. It had fitted their own eclectic energy. They'd even been to an occasional local dinner party and written letters to the council about tree planting. Now, alone, she felt unsettled and overwhelmed by it all. Maybe the long summer in Suffolk had been a bad idea. She was still, a month later, having re-entry problems. Her area gave her an itch in her scalp and a sense of foreboding.

Alex wasn't waiting for her when she opened the door, which was a blessing and a pity, she felt. It was better for him to be in his bed, not straining his eyes and making his bottom sore on the stairs, but she'd half-expected to see him there, just where he'd been last time, and his absence felt like a gap in space that everything else might topple into.

She found him in bed, reading in the small white cone of light. He did not turn his head to look at her, or to speak, but carried on reading. She sat down next to him on the bed and kissed his forehead.

'Hello, sweet pea.'

'Hello,' he said, flatly.

'You're reading Huck Finn?'

He nodded, but still without looking up.

'How was the concert?'

He shook his head, setting his mouth firmly against any words that might carelessly fly out.

She stroked his head in silence, waiting. 'So…?'

'I don't want to talk about it,' he said through scarcely parted lips.

'Please, darling, tell me something about it.'

Now he looked up at her at last and his eyes were blood-shot and wet. 'Why should I? You're always asking questions, like you haven't any other way of talking. And you never actually *do* anything. You never *come*. Everyone else's mother was there.'

He was right, oh dear, he was right. She didn't come to things, or not enough. And she did ask too many questions. It had become a habit of thought. Maybe her profession was to blame, or maybe that was just an excuse she was making for herself. Maybe she asked questions as a shortcut to intimacy, instead of looking for a more imaginative way to communicate. Still, now was not the time to worry about this.

'Sweetheart, I'm sorry. I would have loved to come. I just couldn't move the meeting. Like I said, I needed this case, this chance…'

'Yes, and it was my big chance to make a complete idiot of myself.' Tears sprang from his eyes and her stomach twist-ed with shared pain. She kissed him again on the forehead and they were peaceful together for a while.

'You played so well at the weekend. I was proud of you.'

But when she spoke he became angry. He gripped her wrist for greater emphasis. 'And what's the use of that if someone takes my music and I think I can remember and then I get muddled when I see all the other mums and dads staring at me and wanting me not to be as good as their boys and I muck the whole thing up? What's the point of being good at the weekend, huh? What's the point of you being proud of me if you are never bloody there when I actually *need* you?' He turned his face away from her and stuck it into his pillow. She could hear him struggling to catch his breath. She stroked his back, but it didn't seem to make things any better. He was rejecting her now. She was worse than a failure.

'Can I read to you?' she tried, quietly.

'No. It's time for lights out. Can't you ever get that straight?' He spoke with grim pleasure in being able to point out another of her failings.

'Chat in the dark, then?' This had always been one of their treats and, to her pleasure and surprise, Alex grunted in what could only count as assent. She switched off the light and addressed his silhouette, the still slightly upturned nose, the broadening shoulders, the chewed hands close to the mouth. 'I saw a man tonight who looked like he was born wearing tailored suits. If I get rich, maybe I should buy you one?'

'Would that make you want to spend more time with me?'

She gave him a hug. 'Your dad never wore a suit. He used to say he wasn't old enough yet. When I asked him how old he had to be he said "forty-eight".'

'What will you wear when you're forty-eight, Mummy?'

'What do you think? Glasses and furs? Nothing but Chanel? I'll certainly have to make some money for that.'

'What about Grandpa? Did he wear suits?'

'Yes. He always wore suits, but it was when he was forty-eight that he started to need them, when he really needed to look respectable.' She hadn't made the connection between Patrick's joke and her father's plight before. Her brain seemed to lose access to so much in it these days. Only Alex could sometimes randomly throw up the links between her conscious and her unconscious mind.

'Oh? Why?'

'Well, that was when he was arrested. He was suspected of cheating.'

Alex nodded, as though this made sense of lots of things that had puzzled him. Ophelia expected him to ask more, but instead he said, 'I thought he died when he was forty-eight?'

It was like a blow to her stomach, remembering that. 'Yes. It killed him, the stress of it. He died of a heart attack.'

'You won't get stressed about money, will you, Mum?'

She felt as if Alex had lit a flaming torch in front of her eyes. They burned and streamed with tears. Thank God for the dark.

'No, my darling. You mustn't worry. I'm completely different from him. I'm young and fit and in no danger of a heart attack. I've got a respectable, occasionally well-paid job and I'm definitely not about to be arrested by the police.'

'Was Grandpa guilty?'

It seemed a shame to spoil his standing in Alex's eyes, but she felt it was necessary now, to make Alex feel safe. 'Yes,' she said. They were both silent for a while as the revelation sank in. Then Ophelia leaned forwards and kissed him once more. 'Sleep tight. It's your birthday tomorrow.'

He whispered back: 'And yours, Mummy; your birthday too, remember?'

She shook her head. 'Not something I look forward to. When you get to my age the years just start to bring decay.'

He reached up and touched her face lightly on the cheeks and forehead. 'Still pretty solid,' he said with a smile.

She grimaced. 'Goodnight, sweet pea,' she whispered and went downstairs to tackle the most complicated cake-making she had ever attempted.

Chapter Eleven

The sun stretched its fingers through the gaps between the curtains and rings, reaching across the white artex swirls on her ceiling and making the silicate chips in it shine like crystals in fresh snow. The morning of her thirty-ninth birthday intruded so brightly that she felt it must already be eight o'clock. How odd that Alex hadn't yet burst into the room, bouncy and impatient to begin the celebrations. Still, it would be a tiring day, so if he could sleep in, so much the better. It was a Saturday, and there was no immediate hurry to be up. She shut her eyes and listened to a distant noise getting gradually louder, a rumble of small wheels on the pavement, clicking as they passed over the joins in the slabs, speeding up as they came downhill, eerily unaccompanied by any human voice or tread. Skateboard, not suitcase, she told herself as it passed beneath her window and began to fade.

Then she heard someone moving around in the kitchen, banging cupboard doors shut. It was too unlikely a time for a burglar or for Freia, so it had to be Alex. She wondered whether she should leap up and make him a full English breakfast as a birthday treat, but she didn't want to move. Her under sheet was soft and smooth (too soft: the cotton had worn to transparency in some places). The duvet rested on her with a comforting, but not oppressive weight, like a sleepy lover's hand. Now she could hear Alex clumping up the stairs and another sound too: the slip and chip of mugs and plates on a tilting tray. She feared for carpet and crockery, but held herself still, hoping for the best.

He appeared, exuberant, in the doorway. 'Happy birthday Mummy. I've brought you breakfast in bed.' His hair and ears seemed to stick up even more than usual, and glee shone out of his bright blue eyes, his dimpling grin, his Marmite-smeared mouth. He lurched towards her and got the tray down on the bed just before the coffee mug tipped past the point of no return with a cheerful 'Phew!'

She grinned back at him, pleased to see him so happy and determined to make things nice for her. In truth, she'd always disliked breakfast in bed; your knees were always in the way and your bed would be full of crumbs until you changed the sheets. 'Thank you and happy birthday to you too. This is very sweet of you, Alex. Next year it's my turn. I'll cook you an enormous fry-up. He nodded and she patted the bed, showing him where to sit. 'This looks delicious. Would you like one of my pieces of toast?'

'Mmm, please,' he said, reaching over. She picked up the mug of coffee and sipped it meditatively as he munched and sprinkled crumbs over his T-shirt and the duvet.

'So, how does it feel to be nine?'

'Cool.' He nodded enthusiastically and bounced over to the window to peer out. 'Great day for the party.'

Her eyes fell back on the tray and she saw that under the toast plate there was a card, or rather a folded-over piece of paper, with a drawing on it. She pulled it out and studied it. He'd drawn a football pitch with two teams, red and blue. The reds had the ball, or rather a red player with very sticky-up hair was kicking a dotted line with a ball at the end of it, just inside the goal posts. 'Good goal, Alex,' she called over. He bounded back and peered at his work appreciatively.

'Look inside,' he said, and she read in big capitals slipping sideways across the page: *'HAPPY UNBIRTHDAY MUMMY love Alex'.* She looked at him for an explanation. 'You aren't having birthdays any more,' he said staunchly.

'If it's an un-birthday, does that mean I am getting younger? Eventually we'll end up the same age.'

He giggled at that, but seemed to prefer his own logic. 'No, you just stay exactly the same. The 'un' bit just stops the day becoming a birthday, just cancels it out.'

'Good. Well, I'm glad we've got that straight.'

She jumped out of bed hastily and reached on top of her wardrobe for the ill-wrapped package she hoped would make him happy. 'Here, my darling. This is for you.'

His eyes lit up as he saw how bulky and irregular it was. 'Thanks!' He tore at the thin green tissue, leaving bits on the floor and gradually exposing the new Arsenal away strip. He hugged it and beamed, and she felt those were probably the best-spent fifty pounds that she could remember. He was already pulling off the old T-shirt he was wearing, turning a resplendent yellow and blue.

The phone rang. 'That'll be Granny,' she said, reaching for it. 'I'll pass you over to say thank you. There's a present downstairs from her…'

'Mum!' she said, thinking how she'd been missing her. She'd been so pleased to find her cards, one for herself, one for Alex, and so grateful for the thought ('this is to buy yourself something pretty and frivolous'), and for the two hundred pounds which would actually go on groceries and wages, that she was quite sure it had to be her mother, phoning while she got Wilf's breakfast ready, to wish her and Alex a happy birthday.

'No. Sorry to disappoint you, Feely. It's me.'

She had the churning feeling she got in her stomach when

she had waited all day at court for her case to be called on, when all her initiative was spent and five thin coffees were sloshing around in her gut, and suddenly the tannoy called her case in front of the judge.

'Oh.'

'Um. Sorry. Sorry...' Two sorrys were always worse than one. They made the apology absurd.

'Yup?'

'Oh err... I just wondered... could I come by and drop off a present for Al?' Since when was Alex, Al? Patrick was becoming sloppy and over-familiar. God, she shouldn't let this get to her.

'We've got a party later so you'd better get here either before eleven or after four.'

'I'll come now. If that's OK.'

'It's OK. That's what I just said.'

'OK, and um, happy birthday.' He sounded very tentative, as though he was afraid of offending her, and suddenly she felt a wave of tenderness towards him.

'Actually, I'm having un-birthdays from now on. Alex says that's better, at my age.'

He laughed. 'I can't afford to stay young. It's only my grey hairs that make people think I might know what I'm talking about.'

She found herself laughing too, head back, eyes to the ceiling, staring at the whorls that were like icing on a wedding cake.

'Alex is enjoying being nine. You'll see.'

'I'll be half an hour. Bye.' He was gone, but he was about to be back. Her cheeks felt itchy and hot and the bone behind her eyebrows ached. She'd paint herself a brave, pretty face today.

When the bell went, Alex ran to answer it. She watched

from the kitchen doorway as Patrick stepped over the threshold with a plastic Waterstone's bag dangling from his wrist and gave Alex a hug.

He bounced his hand on Alex's standing-up hair and said, 'You're looking even bigger than you were last weekend.'

Patrick was looking the same as ever, same black jeans and rumpled cord jacket, same black jumper, unshaven chin. Apart from the haircut, he hadn't changed his style since they'd first met. He used to say architects didn't need to be smart; not ones who practised from offices in Deptford, anyway. He was still wearing the watch she'd given him as a thirtieth birthday present: a 1930s design classic. He moved it to and fro on his wrist, as he always had. It was something to fiddle with, and he always fiddled with something; before the watch it had been his cigarette lighter. When he first started twisting the watch strap, he'd told her he was rubbing the kisses she'd had etched into the back of it right into his skin. It made her feel uncomfortable seeing him still doing that now.

Patrick handed Alex the Waterstone's bag with an apologetic shrug of the shoulders and Alex took it with good grace.

'Thanks, Dad.' He opened the bag. 'Oh yeah, *George's Marvellous Medicine.* That's a good story.'

It made Ophelia's heart swell to see him so considerate, to see he wasn't sulking and saying it was a baby book he'd already read five times when he was seven. Alex wouldn't have had the same restraint with her, but maybe that was proof of their intimacy. Still, watching Alex and Patrick together in the corridor, there could be no doubt that Alex was his father's son. They laughed at each other's silly faces with the same demented chuckle.

'I'd better go now.'

He patted Alex's head and darted a quick questioning look at Ophelia. She realised she'd been listening to the sound of an engine running throughout the whole exchange. Maybe there was someone with him, waiting at the wheel. She felt her arms prickle with gooseflesh. Maybe it was Caroline. Soon she might start to hoot. Or maybe she was too in love for that.

'Right,' she said, randomly.

When the door closed behind Patrick, she heard the car roar away and the hall seemed suddenly dark and full of shadows. Alex skipped back up to his room, but she stayed staring at the door until it seemed to warp. Then she turned and walked upstairs on the wood by the handrail, went to the bathroom and ran a deep, hot bath.

Chapter Twelve

She felt better as they entered Dulwich. It was so prosperous, well planted and well loved. The street signs were made of freshly painted timber: old-fashioned finger posts pointed you to friendly-sounding places: 'Herne Hill' and 'the library'. Broad brick houses were protected from the road by soft-shaped hedges; body boards and ski equipment were neatly stowed in their adjacent garages. The pavements were full of smiling people in flat shoes with children on wheeled devices. The adults would greet each other and fall into step as the groups of children and tricycles merged and accelerated towards the park.

Just beyond that paradise of strollers and ice-cream eaters, behind a duck pond overhung by willow trees and frequented by herons, near a boys' school larger and pointier than the Houses of Parliament, and just before the land rose up in a green hill – you might call it the first of the South Downs – the Dulwich Sports Club nestled between astroturf pitches. Here, in the breeze-block and rubber sports hall, Alex would celebrate his ninth birthday. It was an easy enough rite of passage, a game of football supervised by a cheerful competent man in a tracksuit – 'Just call me coach' – and then upstairs to the festivities room, with its lower ceiling and louder echo, for tea.

Ophelia and Alex stood in the entrance foyer watching he

guests arrive. Alex could tell who was drawing up without even being able to see into the vehicles. He knew which cars were associated with which boys and, most weirdly of all to Ophelia (who'd been driving the same old Citroen for the last ten years), he had strong ideas about which ones were best.

'Here comes Rory. His dad just bought this. It's the new Audi SR3 series... Oh, and that's Jake... cool Merc.' If cars were necessary to make you cool, Alex would have to suffer being uncool for a very long time.

The boys were gathering fast, milling and joshing, bouncing around each other like a swarm of midges, and by the time there were fifteen of them, Ophelia called over to reception for the coach to carry them away. She'd wait here for the stragglers, she said.

Then a new Bentley drew up. Even Ophelia knew this was smart. She watched Elvira, the ex-model now fashion journalist from her street, stepping out with boots as soft and tight as gloves. Her brown silk dress matched the crisped beech hedge behind her and floated out from her elfin frame as she moved. Her son Edward seemed to shrug himself out of the car. His head was hidden under his hood but a diamond flashed in his ear and he moved smoothly, as if on hidden tracks, towards the club house. He was thirteen but he looked about forty, older than his mother, older than Ophelia; self-contained, worldly, sure. It seemed impossible that he and Alex had once shared a nanny. Elvira wafted up to Ophelia, enfolded her in a cloud of sandalwood and musk, and touched her cheek with a gracious kiss.

'Darling, this is marvellous of you. I've never been here in my life. How clever of you to find it. I'm sure they'll have a fantastic time. Fatima, my housekeeper, will pick Edward up at the end.'

Ophelia nodded but Elvira had already turned away.

Edward did not look up. He was complete and gloomy in his grey sports clothes, like a cumulus. She didn't speak – it would have seemed foolish – but she walked to the sports hall and he followed her, making not the slightest sound.

Alex was running about with the rest, looking happy. That was the main thing. She walked back to the entrance with a spring in her step and saw Flora speeding towards the plate-glass doors on her red bicycle. Silk flowers were twisted around the handlebars and the wicker basket at the front. Patches of fabric were stuck to the frame and mudguards. This was not a bicycle you'd misplace in a bike rack. Smiling, Flora propped it against the glass, pulled a canvas bag from the basket and made her way into the centre.

'Happy birthday! Happy birthday!' she was saying before she'd even cleared the doors. She gave Ophelia a huge hug. 'Weird place this. Half the cars are four-wheel drive.'

'You see tractors too sometimes. It's practically Sussex.'

'The roads all seemed pretty well metalled to me.' Flora shook her head.

'Err, excuse me. Could you park your bike properly please? There's a bike area in the car park.' The irritable voice came from a weary twenty-year-old on reception.

Flora pulled a caught-out-by-teacher expression. 'OK. Sorry.' She handed Ophelia her bag and went back to the bike. Ophelia noticed she didn't lock it. She nearly called out and then she thought, among the various perils of this place, theft of your decorated bicycle wasn't one of them.

Flora seemed to guess at Ophelia's thoughts. As she came back she said, 'I never lock it. It's bad karma.'

'You're safe here, but in town? Wouldn't it be worse karma if you lost the bike?'

Flora shook her head and smiled patiently at her blinkered friend. 'If you lock it, that makes it more likely it will be stolen. It tells the world you have no faith in it.'

Ophelia nodded. That did just about sum up her feelings.

Flora reached into her bag. 'I didn't have time to wrap it, but I thought this might help you – it helped me. I hope you like it.' She was holding out a book with the title *What Colour is My Balloon: or how to discover your true self* in large cursive writing above a sea of smiling faces.

'Thanks. I am feeling a bit confused at the moment.' It was the sort of book that until recently Ophelia would have scorned. Now it seemed palatable, almost appealing.

'And there's this too.' Flora produced a bottle of champagne. Dear Flora, this was much too generous, and it was just what she felt she could do with *right now.*

'Shall we go and drink it upstairs in the party room, before the boys come out of their football game? I've got to blow up lots of balloons and I'm sure this will help. You'll have to advise me on the colours as I haven't yet read the book…'

Flora grinned. 'Happy to help.' It was one of her good qualities. She didn't mind being teased.

The room looked even more chipped and dismal than she remembered. The walls, once sky blue, were yellowed. The tables were long and thin with nicks here and there in the vinyl tops, and the chairs had pockmarked the floor with their innumerable positions. A decade of 'festivities' must have happened here, a hundredweight of crisps, sausages, Hula Hoops and Twiglets been eaten and thrown around.

Ophelia looked mournfully into the bag of decorations she'd brought with her. 'Oh God, do you think we can rescue this place? I'm sure you have a better eye than I do.'

And so she did. Flora could even get the antennae on the

caterpillar balloons to stand up. Ophelia's attempts looked like hydrocephalitic worms. Best of all, Flora actually enjoyed it. She was rather as Ophelia remembered herself at Christmas time as a child, happily pulling out angels and streamers from the decorations box with little clucking noises and the occassional '*oh yes!*' and finding just the right spot for them on the tree, while her father decked the room in gaudy lights likely to fuse the whole system. She made the room a cheerful sight, with all the semblance of a proper little boy's party.

Ophelia sat down on one of the chairs. 'I think we've earned the champagne, wouldn't you say?'

'Do we use these?' Flora was holding up a stack of plastic pirate cups.

'Aye, aye, me hearty.'

Flora eased the cork out and the pop made something relax in the back of Ophelia's head. Maybe that was what some people got out of acupuncture, she thought, watching Flora as she tipped the cups and poured.

It seemed to fizz behind her eyes and tickle her brain. Flora started to giggle as she passed over a cup.

'Let the landlubbers lie down below…'

'Bottoms up!'

Flora poured another cup for each of them and put her feet up on a plastic chair. 'So how was it, going back to work?'

'Not too bad. Maybe, like you said, I am tougher than I thought! I was very pleased to see my old colleague Samuel. He didn't tell me off for dropping everything before the summer. He gave me a case and I got one for him too. The clerks are a bit circumspect, but if I do everything right I hope they will come round. Anyway, I should be busy enough to stop myself getting maudlin.'

'How's Alex reacting, after having you to himself all summer?'

'Well, he's at school now...' She wouldn't mention her anxiety about fees. Flora disapproved of private schools anyway. 'But he was very annoyed when I missed a concert of his.'

'This will be a hard time for him. I've seen lots of kids, when their parents split, becoming very cut loose. Often the parents over-compensate, give the child too much...'

Ophelia bridled. 'Well, at least I'm not guilty of that. I'm too broke to spoil the boy.'

'Of course, I didn't mean you would.'

Ophelia drank. The champagne tasted flatter now, and too sweet, and she was full of regret.

Flora leaned forwards confidingly and asked, 'Are you still feeling wretched about Patrick?'

She nodded vigorously before trying to explain. 'I didn't know how much it would hurt... us all... when I chucked him out. I feel I've brought a terrible misfortune on us.'

Flora looked almost fierce. 'But that's ridiculous. It wasn't your fault that he started shagging that temp in the office.'

Ophelia felt wounded by this attack, even if it was meant for Patrick, not her. She wished Flora would be a little less emphatic.

'Patrick likes posh girls,' Ophelia said. 'He has a thing about escaping his famine-racked Irish ancestry, even though his dad was a dentist in Surbiton. Caroline was tall and leggy with a flat on the King's Road. How could he help himself?'

Flora rolled her eyes.

Ophelia warmed to her subject. 'I was never quite posh enough. His mother used to tell me his first girlfriend stood to inherit most of Sussex. Still, she was a nice woman, and didn't treat me any worse when she found I'd never inherit more than half a Suffolk vicarage. Of course, Patrick hates the country, so the whole land thing was especially bizarre. But Patrick used to enjoy tales of eccentric aristocracy.'

Flora shook her head and frowned and Ophelia felt hollow again. She'd thought it might have made her feel better, disparaging Patrick, but she felt as though by belittling him she'd belittled herself.

Flora slapped her hand firmly on the plastic arm of her chair. 'Ophelia, you're far too ready to take the blame for everything. Maybe that's OK at work, maybe that's what you're paid to do, I don't know. But it's not OK in everything else. Give yourself a break. And have a refill.' She poured her a cupful and carried on.

Flora had a theme to develop and she wouldn't let go. Sometimes Flora could be very insistent. All that doing good made her so sure she was right. She never backed down in an argument and she always took the woman's side. Ophelia wondered if she hadn't picked too reinforcing a confidante. Perhaps, because she was a barrister, she often found she drifted away from a point of view when it was too trenchantly and one-sidedly expressed.

'I think you take on too much at work as well. I worry about you, Ophelia.' Flora was in full flow now. 'Sometimes you talk as though your client's guilt is your responsibility. You let yourself get too close. That's how nasty people can get to you. One of these days, it'll lead to disaster. Will you promise to be careful, my sweet?'

Ophelia shook her head and smiled. Flora did exaggerate sometimes.

But there was no more time to argue this one out. The boys were approaching like driving rain, pounding along the corridor to the party room. Ophelia drained the last of the champagne from her pirate cup and stood up. The boys nearly flattened her as they swelled in through the double doors, bright-faced and high-spirited.

'That was *such* a good save, Archie.'

'Hey, man, let's get a *drink*.'

Used to each other's jostle, they organised themselves quickly around the long tables, squeaking back their chairs, tipping them, clutching handfuls of Hula Hoops. But they were clumsy with the drinks. A bottle of Fanta was already emptying itself with a low sobbing sound over the edge of one table. Ophelia picked up the bottle and offered it around. Flora grabbed another and in about four and a half minutes five litres of fizzy drinks had disappeared into the effervescent boys. The sausage rolls and crisps and Twiglets went too. Only the neat white Marmite sandwich squares she'd made, like her mother used to, remained in a neat pile, along with the napkins. She passed the plate around and some boys took them, some shook their heads or ignored her. They were in their own world of jokes and silly faces.

'What colour is a burp?'

'Oh, I know that one!'

'Don't tell. What colour is it, everyone else?'

The boys laughed in anticipation. 'What?'

'Burple!' They swung back on their chairs and laughed at themselves laughing.

'In which country do people's tummies rumble most?'

'Which?' three voices chorused, eagerly.

'Hungary!' More cheering and laughing. Some boys even fell off their chairs in their exaggerated hilarity.

'What did the traffic light say to the car?'

'Oh, that's a good one!'

'What is it, Nick? What did it say?'

'Don't look, I'm changing!' Now the falling about had become the real game, and most of them catapulted themselves off their chairs onto the floor, and each other, in a convulsion of laughter.

Ophelia could see that Alex was painfully pleased, eager to join in. She watched him struggle with his shyness and launch in, too early, while the boys were still reacting to the last joke: 'What happens in the middle of nowhere?'

The boys looked puzzled. This didn't sound like a proper joke. Ophelia felt her heart constrict and watched the colour rise under Alex's freckles.

'What?' someone asked, impatiently.

'An H!' Alex announced triumphantly, and some of the boys laughed politely.

'Maybe it's time to do the cake,' Ophelia said. As she went to the counter she heard another boy's voice. It was slow and distinct and made everybody sit quietly, tensely listening.

'What goes ha, ha, ha... clunk?'

There was an absolute silence for a few seconds and then lots of boys called out: 'What?'

The joker paused and the tension mounted.

'What?' one of them repeated.

His face was expressionless as he delivered the punchline: 'Someone laughing his head off.'

A collective intake of breath, a thrill of shock, and then they exploded in loud laughter, not falling about this time, but each individually declaring how impressed he was in his fervent response, like an oath of allegiance.

Flora whispered to Ophelia, 'Who's that?'

'Edward. He's four years above Alex but he lives in the street and they had the same nanny for a short time. He's the son of the model Elvira Bessant. She used to be on the cover of magazines and now runs them.' Flora wrinkled her nose and said nothing.

'Cake time!' Ophelia announced. She carried it very

slowly and carefully to the table. The cake was in the shape of a football and she'd balanced it on an old egg stand from a chocolate Easter egg. It had taken her hours to make and ice. Nine candles burned like a halo around the top.

'Happy birthday to you...' she started and they all joined in, apart from Edward, who was watching her carry the cake with a superior smile, as though he was waiting for it to fall, for a chance to snigger. She tightened her grip and took even smaller steps, remembering Alex with her breakfast tray that morning.

'Phew,' she whispered in his ear as she put it in front of him. He looked from her to the cake with obvious surprise and delight. He blew out the candles in one long breath. She handed him the knife. 'Cut slowly,' she whispered, 'and I'll hold the stand still.' Alex bit his lower lip as he brought the knife smoothly down through the cake towards his mother's hands, and then stopped. He passed the knife back to her with a grin and an exhalation, pleased with this first trial of his nine-year-old prowess. She completed the cutting, making segments of orange sponge which rocked on their convex edges like so many pieces of unseasonal melon.

The cake went, some into tummies, some into small compacted balls which got thrown into cups as a trial of skill, or thrown at other boys in pure devilment. Just as Ophelia was beginning to wonder whether she should do something, and what that might be, Flora whispered, 'Look, parents to the rescue.' They were standing with wan smiles at the doorway, surveying the wreckage.

Ophelia walked over to them cheerfully. 'They all had a nice time,' she said. 'The football ended in a draw so honour was even. Don't let them forget their party bags.'

'Thank you so much,' they chimed, making a grab for their sons, and repeating their thanks forcefully, to make up for their sons' reticence. Only Edward didn't have a parent ,but Ophelia recognised Fatima, the small housekeeper who polished Elvira's door knobs with a vengeance, half-hidden by the others.

'Hi, Fatima. Edward's ready to go.'

She watched Edward saunter slowly over to Alex, as though the room was quite empty and nothing was going on around them. He gave him a high five and said, 'Cool party.'

Alex blushed with pleasure. Then Edward turned away and came to where Ophelia stood with Fatima. Ignoring her, he said to Fatima, 'Let's get out of here.'

She watched them go, Edward first and Fatima trailing after him, like a younger sister.

————

It was Alex who saw it first. It looked like a tall, thin gnome, hunched incognito on their doorstep.

'Someone's left us something!' he called excitedly, pointing at it. He was flushed with the sense that everything was benign, because it was his birthday. Ophelia, because it was hers, was not.

'It's probably just an empty bottle left by a drunk. It's in a paper bag.' Nonetheless, Alex leapt out of the car and bounded up to check it out. He waved a piece of paper he'd taken from underneath.

'No, Mum. It's a present. It's for you.'

How strange. She didn't have any actual friends in the street, no one apart from Elvira that she'd exchange more than four words with, and if Elvira had wanted to give her something, she would have wafted over with it when she dropped off Edward. She locked the car and walked slowly up to the doorstep and immediately recognised the brown ink, the long, looping letters written on the outside of the paper bag:

Ophelia,
Sorry, forgot to give you this. Happy Birthday.
Love,
Patrick
PS I hope you don't mind me writing to you.

She opened the bag and looked inside. Australian Chardonnay. He'd probably got it from the Mini Market for five-ninety nine. She lifted the bottle out and stuffed the bag straight away in the green bin outside. She clutched the bottle to her chest and wondered whether he'd forgotten it earlier, or whether it had been an afterthought, something he'd brought back himself, on his own. She wondered whether he'd had to think of an elaborate excuse to go out and come round. She hoped so. She didn't like to think of him saying to Caroline as they left, 'Damn, I should have had something for her too. I'll nip round to the Mini Market.' She tried to tell herself she would put it on the side in the dining room and keep it until she had a friend over. But she knew she was gripping it too hard around the neck, almost strangling it, because an ache was rising up her spine and her feet were feeling swollen like those pink and blue caterpillar balloons, and what she needed, *needed*, was to put her feet up and let the golden liquid slip down her throat and the scent creep upwards to the back of her nose, making her scalp and eyebrows tingle as though she were sentiently alive.

Chapter Thirteen

'Hi,' said Ophelia brightly, walking in past the clerks to the cheque drawer.

'Good morning, Miss Dormandy,' John called back. 'There's nothing in there, but we do have something for you over here.' John was holding up a full, fresh-looking, big brown envelope and his eyes had that private-fee gleam. She hesitated. She didn't quite like the look of the envelope. She couldn't help feeling it held some extra challenge or forfeit.

'Take it,' John said with a hint of impatience. 'It's for the Godwin bail app. Turns out he didn't have legal aid so we got him to pay you privately. Quite a result.' John was looking very pleased with himself. 'The trial will be legal aid, though, I'm afraid.'

She felt her heels sink into the soft yellow carpet and she had the sensation that she was on quicksand. At any moment she, John, his desk and his envelope would all disappear silently into the ground. But the envelope was in her left hand now and her right hand was reaching in, feeling the smooth sides against the back of her hand, closing on a wad of paper held with a band. She drew out the bundle and looked at it: six fifty-pound notes. A lot more than the fifty-four pounds she'd have got on legal aid for that work. She'd hardly ever seen fifty-pound notes, although she imagined her father must have had them. One day he'd come into her school with the whole year's fees in cash in his briefcase. She'd told him the school wouldn't take the notes, they'd only take a cheque, but he'd ignored her. He'd walked her briskly to the door of her classroom and said, 'I'm going to go and brighten up the bursar's day', and he'd left her there, embarrassed, sure he wouldn't pull it off. Now she was the one with the large bundle of cash. Maybe tomorrow she'd carry it to Alex's school, to the author of that threatening letter.

She peered at the notes more closely. That line through the middle was a bit thin. A forger she'd once represented had told her to watch out for that. She felt John looking at her, waiting for her to say thank you or goodbye.

'Um, John. I'm not sure about this...'

It wasn't just John who stared at her now. Even Bill was glaring at her. She hurried over her words, tripped herself up. 'They look a bit funny, these lines in the middle. I think we should have the notes checked. I mean, I don't want to cast aspersions on Mr Godwin, but the provenance is potentially suspect.'

John raised his eyebrows without replying. His look said, 'It isn't a matter for barristers, what their notes look like. This is a matter for us and you'd be well advised to drop the point now.' When he actually spoke, his voice was mild and reasonable: 'Leave it with me, Miss Dormandy. I'll take them to the bank for you.' He held out his hand, open but commanding like a parent, and she had no choice but to give it back and hope that he would do the right thing.

'Is Mr Slidders in yet?' She wanted to check in with Samuel before Godwin arrived for his conference. She wouldn't say anything to Samuel about the forged notes. His reaction would be the same as John's.

'Yes. He's upstairs.'

She nodded but instead of going up, she went out of

chambers again. She'd decided to do at least one good deed that day, to make up for everything else.

A van was parked outside Bellamy's with its back doors open and crates of aubergines, lettuces and carrots lay fresh and bright on the grey pavement beside it. It was the same man who'd served her when she'd come last time with Samuel, Giovanni. He was carrying crates into the shop and nodded at Ophelia. 'Sorry to keep you waiting,' he said.

'Not at all… busy time,' she replied and waited in the shop until the last crate had come in and the supply van had disappeared to wherever white vans went. White vans were one of the mysteries of London, she thought. They were everywhere, dirty and incognito, carrying everything you could think of: plumbing parts, plasterers, roof slates, bay trees. They were like white blood cells rushing about, repairing the city under stress.

The sandwich man was behind the counter now. 'Could I have two croissants, please, in separate bags, and two cappuccinos?' He nodded and turned away to make the coffees. He put the two paper cups on the counter and the warm smell of coffee hovered about them. 'Thank you, Giovanni,' she said gently, as if they'd known each other a long time. 'I wanted to ask you something. You know the gentleman I usually come here with, with the bright ties?'

Giovanni nodded.

'He always has the same sandwich. You know, smoked mackerel pâté on black rye with artichoke hearts, lemon and rocket. He calls it a Samuel's Special. I wondered if you'd consider putting it up on the board, like the John Street Sandwich. I think people would like it very much – more than that one…'

At the mention of the John Street Sandwich, Giovanni's mouth curled. Maybe he didn't like the sound of it any more than she did. Maybe John Street had paid to get their name on the board. Giovanni smiled.

'Is a good idea. I'll ask my manager.'

'Thank you.'

'Seven pounds forty, please.'

She baulked at the price, but she had her mother's two hundred pounds and the thought of Samuel's pleasure ('best croissants this side of Paris!') and his delight if he found his genius for sandwiches celebrated on Bellamy's blackboard, to justify the expense.

Samuel grinned when she came in with the bulging bags, but she noticed that he didn't attack his croissant with his usual gusto. He picked the flakes meditatively from its shiny surface as he spoke.

'It's a depressing case, this Godwin affair,' he said. She didn't remember him ever being as gloomy as this, however sordid or doomed their case had been. He seemed to try to cheer himself up: 'But at least Jane Gilhooly is our solicitor. Do you know her? She's very bright. Does lots of civil work.' It was an article of faith in the criminal field that everyone who did civil work was bright.

'No, I don't know her. I liked Jeremy Schwartz, by the way. He seemed to know a lot more than he said.'

'Oh yes. He's a real pro. Not like the new guys. Running a defence is a matter of pure instinct for him.'

'I'm hoping our case will all come together on the day. I'm no more persuaded of Mr Mars's defence after meeting him than I was when I read the papers. But he's an interesting, even appealing, man.'

Samuel gave her an old-fashioned look and then coughed with a nasty choking sound. He drank some water and waved his hand as if to say, 'Pay no attention.' Then he cleared his throat and said, 'But what about Godwin – are you going to tell me he is charming too? It seems unlikely.'

'He's fond of his grandmother.'

Samuel raised his eyebrows. 'Oh well, in that case...'

The clerks called to say the con had arrived before Samuel had finished his croissant.

'Ophelia, my dear,' he said, 'would you go down first? I just need to freshen up.'

'Of course.'

It was Jane Gilhooly's jacket which she saw first, post-box red with shiny buttons, bold but soberly cut. Her face too had a flush of cherry on her sensible, friendly features. Miss Gilhooly got up without seeming to move at all. She offered Ophelia a well-kept hand: French-polished nails, small emerald ring, skin lined but soft.

'Glad to meet you at last,' Jane Gilhooly said, and her delivery implied higher status than her words.

Robert Godwin had made an effort too. He was wearing a long-sleeved shirt. He seemed embarrassed at seeing Ophelia, as if he was a little ashamed of something in their previous conversation.

Jane Gilhooly sat and folded her hands on top of her file. It was much thicker than Ophelia's and had different coloured papers in it. Ophelia knew some of the codes: pink for attendance notes, blue for faxes, green for copies of correspondence. Perhaps a red jacket indicated female solicitor who does civil cases.

'Mr Slidders will be here in just a moment. Mr Godwin, are things working out well with your aunt?'

He drummed his nails on the table, annoyed perhaps by this small talk. 'Mmm. She gets me to do gardening.'

'And you've had no news from her about your ex-wife, or Trish?'

He shook his head, drumming his fingers a little harder,

like water gathering speed on the boil.

The door opened with a crash and Samuel Slidders stood in the frame, stooped but immaculate in his dusty-pink suit and purple spotted bow tie and handkerchief. He waved a delighted greeting at Jane Gilhooly as though it was the greatest luck that he should have found her there.

'Jane, my dear! Has my junior been looking after you? No tea yet? Hang on, I'll call for Betty.'

Jane smiled, charmed by Samuel's camp, stagey gallantry. Ophelia had seen before how solicitors cherished his odd-ness, felt it was somehow essential to his genius.

A new rich note sounded in Jane's voice as she replied, 'Thank you, Mr Slidders. I'm sure Mr Godwin would like some tea. He's been travelling a long time.'

Samuel nodded to Ophelia, who knew this was a cue to sort out the tea. Betty wasn't in yet, so she needed to do it herself.

When she came back with the tea things, she was struck by what a team Samuel had created in the room. Robert Godwin wasn't drumming his fingers; he was flipping through the papers and saying, 'You see! You see!' There was a flush in his cheek and she could see he was on his favourite topic.

Samuel cut in, 'Yes, Mr Godwin, that's an excellent point you've made. We have got Betsy banged to rights on the forgery. There's no answer to it!'

Godwin thumped his hands on the table triumphantly. 'Yes!'

Samuel was leaning forward and jabbing at the papers with his index finger, animated with Godwin's passion. 'We say Betsy is a practised liar. We say she made up a false compensation claim for Trish three years ago, getting ten grand from the Criminal Injuries Compensation Board for an assault that didn't happen – Jane, we need some more detail here, if you can get onto the CICB, please? We say she's such a monstrous mother she made Trish wear shoes that crippled her so she'd get this money, and then she took the money herself. Correct so far, Mr Godwin?'

'Yes.' Godwin spoke more quietly and intently now. He flashed a look at Ophelia as if to say, 'you were right, this QC is dynamite.'

Samuel pressed on, enjoying the excitement, 'And then she finds you are having an affair with a friend of Trish's on the trailer park and she is very angry and wants to get rid of you, but she also wants more compensation so she makes Trish say she was raped by you instead. Betsy alters the birth certificate so Trish is under sixteen and she makes sure the complaint is about stuff last year so there could be no forensic evidence to prove you innocent. She thinks she can get Trish to do whatever she says and if you're convicted the CICB are bound to pay up again. Yes?'

Godwin nodded, content that he had been so perfectly understood. Samuel went over the details a few more times and Jane also chimed in with comments in a similar vein, but Ophelia began to feel more and more uncomfortable with what was going on. Obviously it was good to make Godwin feel they'd cracked his case, but there were many unpalatable things that they simply weren't dealing with. She sat silently listening and drawing tessellations in her notebook until at last Samuel, sensing some reservation in her, turned and said, 'Ophelia. Let's hear from you about this case.'

'Well,' she hesitated. She didn't want to spoil the good mood, but sometimes truths had to be confronted.

'I've been thinking about Trish. I've been wondering how we call her a liar. What do we say is her motive for trying to get you convicted of rape? It's one thing for Betsy to want to harm you, Mr Godwin, but how does she persuade Trish to play along?'

Everyone in the room stared at her as if she'd said something unsayable. Then Jane Gilhooly answered coolly, as if she considered this an unnecessary question. 'It's clear from the papers that Trish was having an affair with another man, Ron. It wouldn't be hard for her to say that whatever she did with Ron was something she did with Mr Godwin. Betsy would have known about Ron and she was very good at getting her daughter to do whatever she wanted.'

Ophelia completed the logic of this, looking at Samuel as she did so. 'So we say Trish lies about Mr Godwin, using the knowledge she's picked up from Ron, in order to please her mother?'

Godwin exploded, 'I'm not having you call Trish a liar. She's a poor girl who never had any kindness from anyone but me. I'm not having my lawyers call her that.'

Samuel was silent and Ophelia felt a little let down. Still, she wouldn't back down. 'But Mr Godwin, we do have to put your case to the complainant. We can do it gently, and you need to give us hints about how to do that, but it has to be done.'

Mr Godwin slapped his hands down on the table. 'I'm not having it. You aren't doing that to my Trish.' He stood up and paced the room. 'You are my lawyers. You have to do what I say.'

'Yes, Mr Godwin, but what I'm saying is just what follows from your account. You say you are innocent, that there was nothing improper between you and Trish. She says there was. So we have to say she is lying, for various reasons, all Betsy's fault and all that, but still, it is our case that she is saying something untrue.'

Godwin stared at her as if she had betrayed him. Then he

walked to the door and threw it open. He stepped out, tugging at the door to slam it behind him, but the brass self-closing mechanism slowed its movement to a steady purr. In the corridor beyond they could hear him letting himself out of the basement and running up the stairs.

'Oh dear,' she said.

'Yes,' said Samuel. 'He's not coming back today.'

Jane pursed her lips and gathered up her files. 'Well, that was a short con.'

Ophelia felt they expected her to say sorry, but she didn't feel sorry. She looked down at her notebook and waited.

Jane got up. 'I'm going to head back to the office. Nice to see you again, Samuel.'

Samuel got to his feet and gave her a gallant bow. 'A pleasure as always. Let's just hope our hot-headed client doesn't do his case any more damage tonight.'

Yes, Ophelia thought. Samuel understands people like this. He knows Godwin's desperate, and could do anything.

After they'd shown Jane to the door and got back to his room, Samuel said, 'You know, Ophelia, in one way you were right, in there, but in another you were quite wrong. You have to give a man hope, you see. You were giving it to him a little too straight and he couldn't take it. You have to treat your clients a bit like children.'

Ophelia felt her pulse race so fast she found it hard to think. She knew she was under attack now – here, where she'd always felt safest, in Samuel's room. She couldn't tell if he was right or she was. 'Is that why you didn't tell Mars he would go to prison?'

'Absolutely. What good does it do? He wouldn't change his plea because of that and he didn't ask. It seemed a kind of violence to foist the information on him, unbidden.'

She put her head in her hands. Samuel was right. She was

always doing this. She remembered how she used to nag Patrick with damning questions: 'But will it ever make any money?' or 'Who would want to pay an architect for a stadium design drawn without any team in mind?' She hadn't let him hope – and look what had happened to them.

'Now, my dear, don't fret. It's just a small thing. I know you say things straight because that's how you think, which is, in itself, an extremely useful asset.' He spoke gently to her, and she was grateful. He was giving her hope too.

His telephone started to ring and he gestured for her to answer it.

'Hello?' she said.

'Oh hello, Miss Dormandy. Just calling to say I paid that money into your bank. No worries.' It was John.

'The notes were OK then?'

'No worries, I said.' He hung up. Well, that was that. Best not press the issue.

'Samuel, have you ever had any trouble with payment from a client?' she asked.

Samuel shook his head. 'Once I had trouble being paid. Now I ask Bill to make sure that my solicitors always have money up front, on account, before I do any work. Oh, and of course I'm ex-directory. I wouldn't want anyone knowing where I lived or anything.' Ophelia thought of her name in the phone book, just after Dorkmann.

Samuel looked at her under hooded brows. 'I mean, take a man like Godwin. He's fine in chambers. He gets a little heated and jabs the pages. He might even swear a bit. But he's contained. He knows the form. But in another context he could turn nasty, you know.'

Ophelia nodded, thinking how much Samuel still had to teach her.

Chapter Fourteen

Ophelia walked back to her room feeling at such a low ebb she wasn't sure she'd make it up the last steps when her mobile beeped with a text. She sat on the window seat on the stairs and hunted for the phone, hoping this would rescue her from herself.

It was a number she didn't recognise. She opened the message:

Do come and meet me at the orchid house. It is very close by and won't take you long. I want to show you a Paphiopedilum rothschildianum. 19 Doughty Mews, WC1. Matthew Mars

She felt a shiver of exhilaration. Doughty Mews was only five minutes' walk away. She knew it was wrong even to consider going to meet him. It was a no-no for professional reasons as well as personal and moral ones. But she'd never received an invitation quite like this. And just now her life felt like a prison from which she longed to escape. For once she wanted to let go of everything, to run from her involuted thoughts and tedious duties, and have an adventure. She felt a flare of contrariness, and daring. She was always using her intelligence to protect her clients from their own wrong-doing; surely this time she could use it for herself?

The street was quiet, and her high heels sounded like a pick chipping at its cobbles. Number nineteen had a wide sheet of frosted glass on the ground floor, stretching along where once a stable door would have been. Next to it was a small solid door with a combination lock. It was open. She peered in.

Looking in the doorway, she could see a jungle of turgid leaves, voluptuous petals and long white roots reaching out of the earth like adventurous worms. She could smell bark and moss and greenness, like celery, and soft notes of – was it vanilla? She stepped inside.

The atmosphere was damp and warm, like a tepid Turkish bath. There were flowers everywhere, spilling out of baskets on the walls, tumbling off the branches which criss-crossed the space, clambering up heaps of rocks and hanging from nets in the ceiling. They were so bright and various they seemed like young people at a fancy-dress party: improbably shaped, highly coloured, coquettish and vying for attention. There were bright pinks and greens and purples and oranges and whites. There were black nodes and blue points and white puffs, frills and looping curls and tufty whiskers. Some had slippers like distended bladders, some like babies' ears or ballet shoes. Ophelia turned left and right, marvelling, taking it in.

'Hello.' Mars stepped out from behind an island of flowers. Surrounded by his orchids, he too seemed exotic. His lips were coral pink and his skin translucent like the petals. He looked down into her eyes as if considering whether she was a fertile growing medium.

She stepped back. 'So which is the *Paphiopedilum rothschildianum?*'

He put his hand between her shoulder blades to guide her ,and she liked the pressure. 'This one,' he said, stopping in front of a delicate purple orchid with long, thin petals which stretched out horizontally, like a hummingbird's wings. 'This is my favourite. It's very rare. Touch its slipper. It may move.'

He picked up her hand with his and directed her finger to the purple lips. The feeling of his hand around hers seemed innocent, brotherly, and very intimate. She felt herself tremble. The tiny purple pouch quivered under her finger. It was sticky. He was very close to her, close enough to hear her pumping heart and feel her pulse race under his tightening grip. She thought how the flower seemed to glory in its conspicuous finery.

'I call it the Emperor, because it wears Tyrian purple,' he said, catching her thoughts.

She felt his eyes shift from the flower to her, studying her as if she were one of his collection, with an intense, proprietorial gleam. 'You belong here,' he said solemnly, as though she'd passed some mysterious test. In spite of thinking this sounded a little silly, Ophelia couldn't help but be pleased. She loved passing tests.

'Do you spend a lot of time here?' she asked, watching as he ran his finger along the granite edge of the border.

'No. Not nearly enough. I can't get away. Ava, my orchid assistant, comes on Tuesday mornings to clean and tend the flowers but the rest of the time it's empty.' There was a sadness in him that made her feel almost tender.

He sat down on the ledge and she joined him. They stared in front of them at a tangle of yellow orchids tumbling over a branch.

He spoke quietly to her now, as if he were confessing his most private secrets. 'I harvested most of my original specimens on trips to Malaysia and Borneo. Ava smuggled them back in muddy bags of boots so they looked like forest debris picked up on a hike. I've bred and crossed these orchids so many times that they now have a new identity. In fact, almost all the flowers you see have been created here, so they aren't banned on the CITES list.' He looked at her with a trace of nervousness, as though he regretted that he'd ever frightened her with the knowledge that his flowers had the taint of illegality.

'They live better here than in any tropical rainforest. Humidifiers thicken the air and once a week sprinklers open and drench the room with ionised water. You see how the roots hang and reach out? They suck up moisture from the atmosphere. That's why we keep it so thick with steam. I love the way it makes your eyes feel soft and the dripping sounds you get as the moisture falls off the leaves. I've been wondering whether I should keep some birds here too, to complete the tropical theme. I want this to be a little paradise. I want it to be perfect.'

Ophelia was moved. It was beautiful. Everything was artfully arranged to convey natural abundance, and Mars's intense desire to remake Eden had something heroic, if doomed, about it.

'What about your butterflies?' Ophelia asked. 'Wouldn't it be lovely to have them flying around here too?'

He caught her hand in his and his eyes shone. 'I can think of nothing more lovely in the world. But of course that's quite impossible. They hardly live longer than a day.' He squeezed her hand as if to say, 'our time together is precious and evanescent too.'

'So where are the butterflies?'

'I keep them in my study in sliding drawers. You'd love their iridescent wings and delicacy. My wife doesn't like to see them. This summer we were having breakfast on a houseboat in France and a Camberwell Beauty landed on my plate, drawn by the jam. I turned my glass over and caught it, but in the time I was gone to fetch some formaldehyde Angelica let it go. Do you have any idea how rare it is to find one of those butterflies?'

'I live in Camberwell,' she said, struck by the coincidence.

'I knew you were a rare specimen.' He laughed with a fresh openness she hadn't seen in him before. 'And you look especially beautiful when you are puzzled by something.'

His laugh was catching and she joined in, though she knew this meant she didn't mind him flattering her.

'My ex-husband used to tease me just to get me to frown.' It was the first time she'd ever used the term 'ex-husband'. It made her feel a little cold inside.

Matthew Mars bent over her. His lips were soft as they touched her cheeks, her eyelids, her lips, the tip of her nose. At first his kisses were light as a butterfly landing, but then he pressed down on her mouth, teasing, exploring. Ophelia's body tingled but her mind held back, sceptical and at bay.

'I think you look most beautiful of all when startled by a kiss,' he whispered, and she began to thaw.

She returned the kiss.

A familiar beep sounded from her handbag: only a text from Patrick made that sound on her phone. She felt found out in a shameful act. Then again, would Patrick care? The problem was: *she* cared. If he were here, Patrick would make her laugh and see the place in an interesting light. He would bring it alive, something this fancified, smooth-talking lepidopterist would never do. Mars took himself too seriously for that.

'Sorry,' she said and stepped away from him. 'I shouldn't do this.'

He looked at her quizzically and then, to her relief, he

held out his hand in a business like way. 'No problem. I'm glad you liked the flowers. Come again.'

It almost made her regret refusing him, he was so gentlemanly about it. She shook his hand. He tightened his grasp, a last indicator that he was still interested in her, but she didn't return the pressure and he let her go.

'Thank you. I'll see you on Monday. Goodbye.'

He nodded, took a cigarette out of his pocket and placed it loosely in his mouth. She walked away, and as she wobbled back down the street, she fished in her bag for the phone with the text that had brought her to her senses, praying it would say more than:

I'll come by at 10 for Alex tomorrow.

But it said just that. She turned off her phone.

She knew she hadn't deserved any better. Why would Patrick, whom she'd thrown out for falling into intimacy with someone at work, run back to her now, just because she realised what an easy mistake it was, and how she missed him?

Chapter Fifteen

At least she still had Alex. She would surprise him by being early, and she'd help him with his homework. She'd core him an apple and run his bath. She'd just hang around, available for whatever conversation he wanted. She might even tell him about the orchids. Except that if she did he was bound to ask too many questions about the owner and she was bound to say more than she ought. She'd tell him everything else.

The front door opened before she turned the key. Freia was standing there, brimming with things to say. She must have been looking out of the window to see her come home.

Today her hair was in blond Heidi plaits on either side of her head and her make-up was almost invisible; a more old-fashioned model of German youth than usual. Even the nose ring had gone. Freia pressed her hands together as she spoke, as though she was trying to squeeze her sentences into a more manageable shape.

'Ophelia, my parents have been calling me so much. I need to ask you whether they should sue their neighbours in our home town because the neighbours' dog has been pushing at the fence until it is too weak and it fell down today and it smashed my mother's light which my brother gave her for her birthday.' Freia came closer and the smell of strawberry lip gloss made Ophelia feel a little queasy. 'My father tells them so often that they must chain the dog and he only painted the fence this year and now it is damaged too. So how should we take them to court?'

'Um, I'm not sure. Let's look at it later... Where's Alex?'

'He is at Edward's house. You once said to me that one should have a passion – did you have a passion for law? Is that what you always wanted? I am thinking maybe it would be useful if I became a lawyer.'

'It was what I wanted, yes. When did he go to Edward's?'

Freia wouldn't let her go. She was blocking her path in the narrow hall, biting the end of her Heidi plait. Ophelia's throat felt dry, her head heavy. She didn't like Alex going to Edward's house. Was there wine in the fridge? She tried to remember.

'Not long ago. So do you think my parents have a good case?'

Anxiety and irritation fizzed inside Ophelia's head. 'I don't know, Freia. I haven't the slightest idea. I'm a criminal lawyer in England. I can't advise your parents on their neighbours' dispute in Bavaria.' Freia made a hurt huffing sound and turned on a cowboy-boot heel into her room.

Quickly, Ophelia sank a glass of wine into her beating chest. It helped a little, though she felt ashamed to be drinking, precipitately, alone. She drank the second glass more slowly. Then she went to rescue Alex from Edward.

Fatima answered the door but said nothing. She just stood back out of the way so Ophelia could come in. The hall was wide, Georgian, but dazzlingly white and it led into a generous curving stairwell. She saw a small red-coated figure falling through the elliptical hole in the middle of the stairs and she heard Alex's voice, Americanised: 'Oh no, they killed Kenny!' followed by hysterical giggles and then pounding feet, and she saw Alex skipping down the stairs, missing alternate steps, oblivious to her. At the base of the stairs she saw the red shape, now identifiable as a teddy bear in a hooded red mac. Alex's eyes were big and staring, and his movements were clownish and noisy.

'Alex. Can you come home now, please?'

'Mu-um!' His eyes flashed at her and his voice was his own now, but full of resentment and disappointment.

For a moment she hesitated, doubting herself, and then she heard Edward upstairs, calling down to Alex, 'Come *on*, man. Tell your mum to go away.'

Alex turned away from her and started to walk up the stairs. Ophelia lunged forward and grabbed his wrist. She tried to do it authoritatively, not roughly, but he squealed in outrage, 'Mum!'

She didn't let go. Her hand seemed stuck to his wrist and her arm flowed with fear and love towards the child that pulled away from her. After what felt a long time, he softened under her grip, relaxing or giving up; she didn't know which. She let go.

'Hey man, come *up*!' Edward called but Alex shook his head.

She felt triumphant but embarrassed now. She almost said something to Edward, but as he hadn't yet acknowledged her existence, she decided against it. Instead, she said to Fatima, as she got to the door, 'Thank you. Maybe another time... '

Fatima just nodded. She and Alex walked out into their street in silence. Alex's feet fell heavily on the slithery wet leaves. When they got to the kerb he stayed half a pace behind her. A car swished towards them on the glistening road and she stepped back level with him to avoid the arc of spray from its wheels. Then she took his hand to cross the road and he did not resist.

When they got home, she could hear Freia talking excitedly in German, probably telling her parents what a disappointment Ophelia had been over the great fence question.

'Come,' she said gently to Alex and she led him upstairs to her room. She sat on the edge of her bed, patting the mattress next to her. He sat down, still mute but meek. 'I'm sorry if I embarrassed you back there.'

'It's like you won't give me my freedom. And you never give me any money either. You know how much pocket money Edward gets? Thirty pounds a week!'

Ophelia sighed. He needed more from her, but maybe it wasn't money, after all. She hoped not.

'Yes, but his mother runs a fashion magazine. Money isn't an issue for her, I guess. But I don't think she gets to spend any time with her son.'

Alex snorted. 'Edward doesn't care about that.'

'I hope that's another difference between you?' she hazarded, her voice trembling slightly.

'Yeah, Mum. It was good to have you with me this summer.'

It made her hands and arms tingle, like little electric shocks shooting upwards, as though the love that had flowed down them to Alex, as she held his wrist at Edward's, was flowing back up them now, to her.

'But Mum, now you are back at work, it's like you've been sucked away to another planet again.'

She wrapped her arms around him and squeezed. 'I'm so sorry, Alex. I do get caught up in things. But I've got something for you. Something just between you and me. A sort of heirloom.'

Alex looked up brightly now, the old fun and curiosity returning to his face with a flush. 'What's the secret?'

Ophelia smiled. 'Yes. I suppose there is a secret...' She

reached under her bed and drew out a small, oblong black box with a trapezoid lid which she put on her lap.

'This was my great-grandfather's despatch box, but the secret isn't about him, it's about my father, Orlando Dormandy.'

Alex wiggled himself deeper into her soft duvet, settling in with anticipation.

Ophelia began her tale: 'Orlando Dormandy was a very charming man. He made everything fun, everything special. He could make the sourest old bat giggle like a schoolgirl and the most pompous bigwig laugh at his oldest habits. He could sell anything. And he did. He sold shares and pictures, bronzes, and, in the later years, gems. It would be a big thing in our town, when he went on a gem-buying trip. He talked about it for months beforehand and when he came back he invited the key people to come over for a buffet supper and a slideshow. He'd show wonderful pictures of the places he'd been to, the mines, the rivers, the emeralds of Zambia, the sapphires of Madagascar, or best of all, Burma. It was partly a travel journal, a tourist's account, and partly a sales pitch. And people would come with their cheque books and leave with the stones, delighted and thousands of pounds poorer. He kept the stones wrapped in a little twist of paper, a *brifka*, and he took the utmost care opening it, as though a genie might emerge, full of curses and bad temper, if he didn't do things with the right care and ceremony. It was wonderful. Except that they were not really emeralds and sapphires at all.

'It was alexandrite that was his undoing. He was more excited about this stone than any other. He said that if you had seen a beautiful alexandrite you would never want another stone, because it was all the stones, simultaneously. Its colour changes depending on the light you hold it in. He said alexandrite was more valuable than diamonds. He had been to Alexandria, he said, and he had brought home the prize: three carats big, and worth a hundred thousand pounds. For this special event, he cast his net wider, he invited Ipswich's top businessman. But Ipswich's top businessman knew a thing or two about stones, and he had a friend in the police force.'

She opened the box and drew out a twist of paper. She put it carefully on the duvet between them and then very cautiously opened it. Deep green stones glittered there, staining the white beneath. Alex gasped, coming up close to look.

'These were supposed to be from Zambia, but really they were from Chatham, every last one.'

'Can I touch?'

'You should use tweezers to pick up gems. Here, these were your grandfather's.' She reached into the box and handed him a very ordinary-looking pair of tweezers. 'My father said you had to practise doing acrobatics with them, so you got used to holding a gem and not dropping it, so the tweezers became a part of your body. Do you want to try and pick one up?'

Alex nodded and bent over the paper with the tweezers wobbling in his hand. He got the pincers around a small stone and lifted it gingerly into the air. It sparkled in the lamplight, throwing a prism of colours on the white curves of the ceiling. He laughed with pleasure and his grip slipped slightly, and the emerald fell and disappeared into the thick-pile rug. Alex let out a desolate cry and went down on his knees. Ophelia dropped down too.

'Maybe it doesn't matter losing them,' Ophelia said. 'Mother always said they were bad luck.'

But already Alex was grinning. The little sharp shard of green was in his fingers again.

'Got it,' he said.

'Keep it, if you like.'

He beamed as broadly as if she'd just bought him a hot chocolate fudge sundae.

'Now, put that in a safe place in your room and let's get your homework and everything done. I promise I'll come home early tomorrow so we can talk some more about it all.'

She watched him go. His feet seemed to drag on the floor a little.

She poured herself another glass of wine and remembered she'd switched off her phone. Maybe Patrick would have sent her another text. She switched it on, hoping. Three new messages, two from chambers and one from an unknown number.

The first was from John: 'Miss Dormandy, can you please call chambers urgently? It's about the case of Godwin.'

The second was also from John: 'Miss Dormandy, you must phone Jane Gilhooly straight away if you get this message before six o'clock.' She checked her watch. It was nine.

The third message was: 'Miss Domby, it's Mrs Peake. You got me to stand bail for Mr Godwin. Well, Robert hasn't come back and we're very worried. Could you give him a ring and talk him round, please? His number is...' She gave the number.

Panicking, Ophelia rang it. In her hurry, she didn't think to withhold her own number. She listened as the phone rang and rang. She told herself she wouldn't have been able to talk Godwin into going back up north even if she had rung two hours ago. Still, she knew she'd messed things up. She knew exactly where Godwin would be now. He'd be in the trailer park, looking for Trish. He'd lose his bail at the very least.

Chapter Sixteen

All weekend the prospect of her 'make-or-break case' for Mars oppressed her and now it was about to begin. She was on her way to the Old Bailey to meet him when her phone went.

'Miss Dormandy, it's Jane Gilhooly here. I'm sorry we didn't speak on Friday. I'm afraid Mr Godwin was picked up by the police at the trailer park on Saturday morning. He was found drunk and unconscious. The good news is that they aren't saying that he contacted the prosecution witnesses.'

'Maybe he got drunk too quickly?' Ophelia said, swaying as her bus swerved.

'Yes. He doesn't strike one as a man of much self-restraint.' This shared criticism of their client seemed to bring them a little closer and Ophelia felt relieved. Miss Gilhooly went on:,'He's been in Wandsworth Prison for the weekend. They want to bring him up for his breach of bail in front of a Bailey judge today.'

'Well, I'm there anyway, doing a trial in court four,' Ophelia said quickly, struck by the coincidence and not thinking through the ramifications. 'If you can ask the Bailey listings officer to get Godwin's case called on in my court, I could deal with it first thing.'

'Good. I'll do that then. He's in the cells already if you want to take some instructions.'

After her last contact with Godwin she didn't want to talk to him at all, but she did need to check he didn't have some excellent excuse, so after she'd filed through the gun-detecting airlock at the door to the building, after she'd forgotten and then remembered to collect her keys, she walked down the steps to the grey door in the secure basement.

Her interview with Godwin was short. He wouldn't look at her and refused to answer any of her questions. His fists, face and shoulders seemed clenched tight. She left quickly.

She took the lift up to the top of the building where the ladies' robing room was. As always, there was a strong smell of gravy when she opened the door. It must share a ventilation shaft with the kitchen, she thought, but how zealous of them to be making the gravy at nine in the morning.

She, however, was not feeling very zealous at all. She punched her name into the computer ('or you won't get paid, my dear', as the ushers would cheerfully remind you.) She applied a thick coat of red to her lips. This was the only advice she remembered getting from her headmistress: red lips for public speaking to help your audience follow what you say. It had become her – only – pre-court ritual.

When she got to the concourse outside court four, she saw the well-cut shoulders and profile of Mars in front of the case lists. He spun round as she approached, as though they were playing grandma's footsteps, but there was something a little tentative in the way he said, 'Hi. Good weekend?'

'Fine, thanks. Is Jeremy not here yet?'

'Do you need him?'

She felt the tips of her ears glow and she shook her well-brushed hair forward, trying to cover her cheeks too. 'No. Shall we have coffee in the canteen? Jeremy will find us there.'

His lips twitched, as they had when they had held a

cigarette in the orchid house.

Mars took the best seat in the room, a table by the window with noone else sitting too close.

'How do you take your coffee?' he said. She felt she had never met anyone so assured as this in her whole life.

'White with no sugar, please.'

She watched him join the queue. The strange thing was that however expensive his clothes were, whatever the differences in wealth and expectations between him and the boys in hoodies in front of him and the lady solicitor in polyester behind, he looked perfectly at ease among them. He made the coffee lady positively glow as she served him the two cups. When he came back to their table, Ophelia nodded her thanks and kept her eyes fixed on her notebook. She needed to re-establish their professional relationship, and to go through the essentials of his case, as is doing last-minute revision for an exam.

'So you agree with Yelena that you had an argument on the second of June, but you disagree on what it was about. You say it was because you refused her a raise (and we can see from your work diary that that *was* the day for salary reviews) and she says this was the day of the assault?'

'That's right.'

She could feel his eyes on the top of her head, which was all she was presenting at the moment, and she wondered vainly whether darker roots were beginning to show through.

'And you agree she didn't come into work after that?'

'Correct.'

'Good morning.' She looked up and saw Jeremy standing next to their table. His tie was dark navy, with only the subtlest hint of pale spots within it.

He sat next to Ophelia and launched himself straight into

the conversation, but in a whisper. 'Now, Mr Mars, there's one point that's been bothering me. The complainant says you have a tattoo on your upper thigh. The jury may wonder how she knows that. We need to give them an explanation.'

Mars nodded, all attention. Ophelia held her breath. She should have asked this question herself. Barristers had no business being bashful.

Jeremy spoke very slowly and carefully, as if dictating. 'She sat in the same room as you for years, didn't she? She didn't have a separate room?'

Mars spoke softly. 'That's right.'

'So she would have heard all your phone conversations, for four years?'

'Yes.'

'So if you were asked, how did she know you had a tattoo, what would you say? Because you do have a tattoo, I assume?'

Mars kept his eyes on Jeremy as he replied, 'Yes... I think it was last year, a friend called me to ask if I'd come to the Turkish baths with him. We joked together that we would have to have the place to ourselves as, for gay men, my tattoo might be a come-on.'

Ophelia knew she wouldn't have led him so certainly, and corruptly, to the lie he'd have to tell. Jeremy looked quite pleased with himself. He studied his client in silence for a moment before saying: 'Of course there may be some gay men on the jury.'

Mars shrugged. 'I'll just take everything as it comes.'

Jeremy's face creased into a deep-set smile. 'That's the attitude.'

'Good. I'll get you a coffee. Back in a sec.' Mars walked briskly away, as though he wanted to distance himself from what had just happened, to change the tone.

Ophelia turned quickly to Jeremy and whispered, 'They had an affair, didn't they?'

Jeremy gave her a patronising smile. 'Of course, but he can't admit it. That would finish his marriage and maybe his job. He'd rather take the risk of telling only half the truth to the jury. He thinks, because he didn't commit the offence he's up in court for today, that he's safe. What do you think?'

'I think there's always a danger of being found out in a lie…' She stopped herself, too late. Jeremy was staring at her in consternation. She hurried on, trying to sound confident, 'But I think that the jury will think he needn't force himself on anyone. He is too handsome, charming, of good character…' Mars was coming towards them now with a cup of coffee and she lapsed into silence.

The case of Godwin was called into court and Ophelia excused herself. She realised, as she sat with her respectable private clients, that it would be most unfortunate if they saw anything of the Godwin case, so she didn't explain why she was going. 'I'll see you in court,' she said, jumping up ,and they looked bemused at her hurry.

Mr Godwin took a long time to come up from the cells, so the judge was annoyed even before the hearing started. The clerk and Securicor lady in the dock tutted and drummed their fingers, at least partly, Ophelia guessed, to indicate that the delay was not of their making.

'Miss Dormandy, where *is* your client?' the judge asked, as though perhaps it could be her fault he wasn't there.

'In the cells, My Lord,' she said, and steam seemed to come from the judge's ears.

When Godwin came in he didn't look up. He put his fists on the edge of the dock and rounded his shoulders. He was dressed just in a vest, showing greeny-blue snakes circling both arms. This was not how to impress His Honour Judge Rose.

The clerk asked him if he admitted failing to go to his bail address and being found drunk at the trailer park where the prosecution witnesses lived. He grunted.

'Is he pleading guilty to this?' the judge asked.

'It isn't disputed, My Lord,' Ophelia replied.

There was a rustling noise over by the door. Jeremy and Mars had come into court. The usher had sat them on the side, but they could see and hear everything.

'Does Mr Godwin have any explanation for his conduct, Miss Dormandy?'

Godwin exploded from behind her, 'My lawyers were driving me mad. They were calling my stepdaughter a liar. I had to find her, whatever you lot say.'

The judge's brows darkened. 'Miss Dormandy, can you control your client, please? If he tells the court about privileged conversations with his lawyers, his whole case will unravel.'

'But it already *has!*' Godwin groaned from the dock, and the despair in his voice was palpable. It made even His Honour Judge Rose blanch.

The judge swallowed and said, 'Mr Godwin, your bail is revoked. No penalty for the breach. Take him down.'

Mr Godwin called out from the dock, 'Don't bother to come and see me, Miss Dormandy.' He got her name right. This time she would have preferred if he hadn't.

Mars's case was called on straight away, but she still had time to see, as she turned to them at the side of the court, a look of consternation on both Jeremy's and Mars's faces. They must be thinking that when they hired her they'd been sold a pup.

The first part of the morning seemed to pass quickly. The

jurors, mainly female, were better dressed than most inner-city jurors and they sat up with great attention as the pop-eyed prosecutor outlined the facts of the case. This was exactly the sort of trial jurors wanted to try, and to tell their partners about. They seemed to look even-handedly at every-one in court, alert. But it was when Yelena walked into court that things became interesting.

She was tall and thin with a long-well-structured face, and quick, nervous energy. She twitched her nostrils and stalked up to the witness box on her magnificent, restless legs like a thoroughbred horse. Were long legs, Ophelia wondered, always a characteristic of the husband-alluring secretary? At least Yelena didn't have Caroline's curtain of hair. She had a black bob and she wore a red dress.

'Would you *please* sit down, Miss Karpovska,' the judge interposed. She'd banged her toes and heels into the witness box three times while taking the oath and giving her name. She obeyed the judge, but she paid no attention to the prosecutor's questions. She just said whatever she liked, ges-ticulating with her long arms and shouting angrily at Mars in the dock.

'He claims to be the perfect daddy but *I* bought all the children's presents and reminded him of their birthdays: David, twentieth of June, Jonathan, nineteenth of September, Hugh, third of January. He had no idea himself. *No idea.* The man is a total fraud.'

The prosecutor tried to get her back on track. 'Tell us what happened on the second of June.'

'You don't understand anything. He is a liar. He tells me to go home and then he says I am wrong to leave work early. It is ridiculous. He says he likes intelligent women but it is nonsense. He doesn't listen…'

The prosecutor tapped his biro on the lectern and spoke

more irritably. 'What happened on the second of June, Miss Karpovska?'

'He tricked me. Again he tricked me. You would think that by now I would have learned, but no. I do not know how I can have been so stupid. Except that he does this to everyone. He makes everyone stupid. He can draw you in, every time. So, he tells me to come with him to see where we could have a new storage. We have too many papers, I can hardly sit at my desk it is so full. So he says, "Yelena, come with me and I show you where to put all these things," and he takes me down in the lift.'

'Was there anyone else around in the office, when you went?'

'How do I know? I am too busy to look what everyone else is doing. He takes me down to the cellar. He says it is not convenient but it will do. He takes me to a room with metal loops in the floor. He says it is a bicycle park but no one uses it. And suddenly he handcuffs me to the bars and he starts to undress me. I cannot move. I shout at him but he does not stop and no one comes because we are away in the basement and no one can hear. And then he takes off his trousers and he shows me this butterfly tattoo on his thigh and his member, his ridiculous pointy member and he says, "This is for you", and he rubs it up against me. It is disgusting. Disgusting.'

Ophelia felt herself spinning. She could see the scene, but differently. Yelena was handcuffed, but willing, and she was advancing with her mouth…

'Afterwards he smoked a cigarette. He wouldn't release me until he had squashed the butt into the floor.'

The cigarette hadn't been in her statement but Ophelia remembered how he'd reached for a cigarette after their own unsatisfactory clinch, how it hung from his lips as she left.

'Miss Dormandy, have you any questions?'

The judge's voice made her start. She felt confused by the scene she'd been imagining, forgetful of what questions she was meant to put to the witness. Money, she told herself. Mars had said this case was all about money. Yelena Karpovska was lying because she didn't get a raise. No one would believe it, but that was his case. Ophelia just had to get on with it.

'You were very disappointed not to get a raise on the second of June, weren't you?'

'Disappointed not to get a raise!' Yelena Karpovska laughed long and hard. 'That was the least of my worries on the second of June. Did you not hear my evidence? He sexually assaulted me that day. He humiliated me. And you say I was disappointed about a raise!'

Ouch. Ophelia saw she had no control over this witness, that she was in danger of looking odder than the overwrought complainant. Still, she had to soldier on, though she felt she was wading in thick mud with over-large boots on.

'Your desk was next to Mr Mars's desk?'

'No, there was a bin between us.'

'But you could hear his telephone conversations easily?'

'I do not listen. I do not care to make my life any more difficult than it already is.'

'Surely there were times when a conversation jumped out at you, when its content was surprising, memorable?'

'No.'

'But there was a time, wasn't there, when he had a conversation about not being able to go to a Turkish bath because his tattoo attracted too much attention?'

'Never.'

Ophelia knew she was getting nowhere and she was exhausting herself and everyone else. Every question she asked elicited a more emphatic denial. Even when she pointed out that the cigarette had not been in the statement Yelena parried with an unassailable 'So?' and Ophelia felt herself sinking deeper, confusing her own memories of Mars with what she'd read of Yelena's, and what she'd guessed at. She had to stop. This was only going to get worse.

'No more questions, Miss Karpovska,' she said firmly, as though she had completed a successful cross-examination after all.

The judge looked at the clock. It was half an hour before the usual break but he told the jury to have an early lunch before they moved onto the rest of the prosecution case.

She darted straight for the ladies, so she could have a moment to think what to say to her client and solicitor. She would have liked to leave the building, to walk alone through the quiet backstreets and let the chill autumn air sweep into the dark corners of her mind and blow away her shame and the lurking fears that stopped her from thinking straight. But she knew that Mars and Jeremy would be waiting for her and she knew they would not be happy.

She was right. They were sitting together in the canteen. Anger and disappointment overhung Mars's face.

'I thought you would destroy her,' he said. 'but you just let her go. You didn't lay a finger on her.'

He seemed to be looking at her from a long way away and her chest ached to see this. Jeremy was staring at her too, mystified.

'Miss Dormandy must have a strategy. I'm just at a loss to know what it is. Enlighten us, won't you, Miss Dormandy? What are you up to here?'

Ophelia drew herself together. 'Well, she didn't break-down and admit she was lying, but that is very rare. I think she came across as a highly excitable, unreliable person. She couldn't even stay still and listen to the questions.'

Mars put his head in his hands and his voice seemed to come from somewhere deep in his chest as he said, 'I can suddenly see myself going down for this and I am very, very unhappy. You could have unpicked everything she said. She loves me. Women only wear red when they are in love. Or want to be in love.'

Ophelia gulped. Was that right about women and red? Perhaps *she* wore red when she wanted love. She'd planned to wear red the night of the skate dinner with Patrick. She'd wanted to regain their romance, but too late... Oh dear, this was all taking her a long way from her task. Perhaps she could have unpicked Yelena Karpovska's evidence, if only she'd been able to concentrate. This was the only way to run the case. An unreciprocated passion on the part of Yelena would explain the spite. It was a mean line to take, when they'd obviously had an affair, but it would work better than the money motive. She was losing the plot here. Still, whatever her doubts, she mustn't show them now. Jeremy would never brief her again and the message would get back to the clerks, who had their reservations already. She had no one on her side now.

She stood up, defiant. 'Well, I think it is very hard to judge at this stage, but when you give your evidence all the pieces of the jigsaw will suddenly fall into position. Now, if you'll excuse me...'

They didn't try to stop her. They were too fed up with her for that. She stepped out of the room and ran down the fire escape and out into the fresh air. The doorway was crowded with defendants smoking and studying their gold medallion rings, but at least here the air was cold in her lungs and she could hear the tannoy.

When she went back to court, everything seemed dreary. The prosecutor called the police officer who'd arrested Mars in the office car park 'next to a new black Lotus Elise'. The police officer then read out his repetitive questions from Mars's interview and the prosecutor took Mars's part, but he stumbled over the more complex sentences, emphasising irrelevant words, as if it were a foreign language. Behind her, Ophelia could feel Jeremy brooding and Mars despairing over the low calibre of people in the criminal justice system.

The usher stood. 'This court stands adjourned until ten thirty in the fore noon. God save the Queen.' She caught up with Mars and Jeremy in the waiting area and adopted a breezy tone, hoping to shift the ominous cloud in their faces.

'Tomorrow is your day, Mr Mars. It'll be your chance to tell them how it really was.'

He didn't reply or even look at her.

As she walked out of the building she checked for messages. There was just one, from Patrick:

I was back in college today (they are rebuilding the library) and I saw a girl who looked like you and I wanted our time again. Forgive me, Ophelia…

And this made everything even worse. It was typical of his ill-considered, feckless, flirtatious ways. He didn't even know what he was saying himself: did he want her, or a pretty undergraduate? Or was it just that he had liked having her back then, when she'd been as pretty as that? He was offering her nothing but wistful, pointless crap, and pain, a continuous, aching pain, like the feeling she'd read about in amputees, in the space where the lost limb had been.

Chapter Seventeen

She walked south, dragging her black wheelie bag like a reluctant pet. The bright autumn sun made her blink and she could hear her mother's voice, sensible and practical in the face of chaos and disgrace: 'Sometimes the best thing is just to go for a walk.' Her mother had green wellies and country lanes by her back door, but Ophelia had all London before her. Her towering heels made an echoing sound on the concrete slabs, telling her she was making progress.

The river drew her, big and brown and sure of its course eastwards through the city, pausing only to eddy at the stone pillars of the bridge. She walked along the South Bank, peering down at the water's edge, looking at the scraps of timber and brick and clay pipe that the water had deposited on its last trip up and down the riverbank and which the swelling tide was now about to reclaim. The mud gave way to sand as she came level with Gabriel's Wharf, clean, dry sand like the Suffolk beach Alex had spent the summer digging, and here someone had used the sand to build not a moat and a castle, but a smooth, fat elephant head with huge, wide ears and a trunk travelling up the centre of his face. The fresh breeze had blurred the edges of the elephant's eyes but he seemed happy and dreamy wallowing by the water as the river crept up to meet him. Ophelia stood and watched the wavelets flap at his huge strong neck, caressing him down into the water. She turned away while his eyes were still there, patiently, pleasantly awaiting their destruction. The sand gave way to mud again as she neared London Bridge and she saw a wine bottle sticking up proudly in the black ooze, gradually being refilled by the advancing tide. It seemed to remind her of some forgotten thing, some other bottle, a message in a bottle…what was it? There was something important she had missed, that she could almost remember… The bottle itself was disappearing now and she felt an instinct to turn for home, though the day was still relatively young.

Away from the river, everything seemed suddenly hard, chill and grey and a big red bus felt like a kind of deliverance. The great diesel engine and central heating system thrummed beneath her and she, and the other bodies, created such a fug that they might as well have been trapped in a cloud for all she could see out of the window. But still she puzzled over that feeling she'd had looking at the bottle. It had reminded her of another bottle propped upright where she hadn't expected it.

She gulped. It was Patrick's present, the wine bottle on her doorstep, the bottle she'd caught up so hastily, the wine she had so immoderately drunk all by herself. There was something still troubling her about it, something about the message. What had it been?

> *Ophelia*
> *Sorry, forgot to give you this. Happy Birthday.*
> *Love, Patrick*
> *PS I hope you don't mind me writing to you.*

Writing to you? What writing? There was this note – handwritten, certainly – but was it *writing*? She tried to remember exactly what she had found. The paper bag had been turned so she would see his message and it was held upright by the bottle just nestling in the reveal of the door. She'd picked it up and seen the metal bottle top and, in an instinct for tidiness, she'd taken the bottle out and put the bag straight into the bin. She hadn't peered inside the bag at all. Had there been a letter? He had a history of letters… *I hope you don't mind me writing to you.* What had he written?

The rubbish should have been collected that morning, but she ran home from the bus stop, in case. Sometimes there were delays, other contractors… Her heart crashed against her ribs and the wheels on her bag clipped the paving edges so fast it sounded like it was galloping. But when she got to the bin and flung open its lid there was nothing in the bottom except for a damp plastic bag that had got stuck. There was no way of knowing what Patrick had said, short of asking him, and she couldn't think how she could do that without giving away how much she cared.

She flopped down on her doorstep and got out her phone. Although she suspected Flora might not be the best person to ask about this, she was the best friend she had. A friend was what you needed at times like this. But then you never knew, when you made a call, what the other person was actually doing…

'Hello, darling. I'm just, sorry, running…'

Ophelia could hear an announcement in the background: 'Would passengers Flora McDonald and Brad Mitchell please proceed immediately to gate number seventeen…'

'Sorry, Flora, are you late for a flight?'

'Yes, I'm coming back from a Buddhist retreat. I know, I know, think of the carbon emissions. But it was a spiritual experience. So much so I didn't get to the airport on time… You OK?'

'I just realised Patrick sent me a letter which I've thrown away unopened.'

'Best thing to do with it, I'd say. Don't let him get to you, darling. If he has something important to say, he can say it face to face when he sees you one Saturday to take Alex out. If you want to tell him you lost it, tell him on Saturday. What ever you do, don't lose your cool, OK?'

And in the background, ever more urgent: 'Would Miss Flora McDonald *please* make her way...'

'Will you promise, Ophelia? I don't want to worry about you worrying about him.'

'OK. Thanks. I'll do what you say. Have a good flight, if you make it!'

'Right, I'm there now... Sorry, here's my passport... Bye, darling...'

Ophelia stared at the malevolently empty bin, wistfully composing Patrick's lost letter:

Dearest Ophelia,

My life is vapid and ridiculous without you. I can't draw buildings, only your face. I eat Caroline's slimmer's dinners and try not to listen to her half-witted anecdotes. I feel like a lost sock in an abandoned tumble-drier.

All of this is terrible but bearable until I see you and you behave as though I'm the postman with a package to sign for, and the package is OUR SON. Please, if you ever had any feeling for me, tell me you will meet me for a drink, just a drink, whenever, wherever.

I am drowning, Ophelia. I stare at the river from my office window and I imagine its currents pulling at my ankles, filling my shoes and my sleeves, drawing me down into the roil of it, turning me with the driftwood in that great London soup.

Or

Sorry not to have got you a more imaginative present. You deserve better, as you know. Which is why you got rid of me.

Or

You looked tired this morning. I hope you aren't working too hard.

Or

I'm so sorry not to have given you this before. Here is a cheque for all those electricity bills I said I'd pay, and didn't.

No. Not that. Maybe there had never been anything at all. Perhaps she'd find out on Saturday. Or perhaps she wouldn't even ask. Now, she decided, she was going to wash her hair.

First she had to see Alex. He was already in his room, although it was only seven o'clock and he didn't look particularly pleased to see her. His head seemed to fall heavily forward and his eyes didn't focus on her. She kissed him on the forehead and he gently shook her off.

'Hi, Mum.'

'Homework done?'

'Is that *all* you care about?' He still didn't look at her.

She felt annoyed and hurt. 'No, obviously not. It's just something I have to check.'

'It is... thank you.' He spoke in a rather final way, as though to indicate that now she was dismissed. She couldn't think how to turn the conversation without annoying him more. It seemed foolish to press him with stories of her disastrous clients, or his flawed grandfather, when he didn't want to know.

She went to the door, but then came back. It seemed too long since they'd had a 'chat in the dark'. She sat down on his bed without saying anything and after a while he said softly, 'Can we move to Suffolk?'

'Darling, that would change everything.'

'I know.'

'But you'd have to have a new school and friends and you'd hardly see Dad and I don't know what I'd do... Why do you want to be in Suffolk? Or is it that you don't want to be here?'

'It's nice there. We have time together and you don't mind me going off on my own. You're always so sad here and you spend all your time with criminals.'

She stroked his hair. She was glad of the dark so he wouldn't see the tears welling in the corners of her eyes. 'I'm sorry if I'm too stressy and absent... but I think you'll like London more, as you get older. Your dad and I do. We used to walk all over it together, not with any particular plan, just to see where we ended up. Your father hates the country. You should read what he wrote about it on the back of the sketch he did at Auntie Claire's house.'

Alex perked up a bit at this. 'You mean the picture on the stairs?'

Ophelia jumped up, glad to have found a diversion. She unhooked the picture and brought it to Alex, turning to the reverse side. When she'd had it framed, she'd had a window inserted into the back so Patrick's rant would be legible. That was ten years ago. 'Shall I read it to you?'

Alex snuggled deeper under his covers and wriggled in anticipation. Ophelia read:

While you are out 'getting some fresh air' – and chilblains and a streaming cold – I have been trying to see what you middle-class English people love about the country. I've been sitting with my watercolours staring out of the broken pane of your sister's kitchen window. So much for the little patio where I would be sunning myself if this was any decent kind of summer. Instead I'm painting the eighty-seven oaks which stretch away from here in ten straight lines, like a crop, or an army with just three casualties, and just as I begin to admire the structure and knobblyness of the trees I see a strange green man coming out between them – green wellies and Barbour and tweedy cap, country camouflage, and a great big GUN over his shoulder, walking right up to the cottage like he's going to shoot me. He's all ruddy and handsome, probably just your type, and I think in London this guy would be locked up but out here it's just fine to go round killing rabbits and birds and inconvenient husbands. And I have to go and hide in the loo until I'm sure he's gone away. The dark smudge on the left is him coming out from behind a tree.

Ophelia turned the picture over. When you knew what you were looking for you could see an ominous darkness beneath one of the canopies of loose green brushstrokes. It wasn't even a human form. It was a mess of shadow in an otherwise charming, evenly lit, sylvan scene. Alex peered intently at it.

'Who was the green man, Mum?'

'Some harmless local, I expect. I'm sure he wasn't going to shoot Dad.'

Alex leaned back against the bedhead, staring out in front of him, and she quietly got up and replaced the picture, thinking how surprising Patrick's odd flares of jealousy were, the way he often said someone was 'just her type', as if he'd seen her fall for lots of men. She'd given him no cause. Maybe his fear of her infidelity was born of a fear of his own. He had strong flirtatious impulses, but he'd been true to her, she was fairly sure, until Caroline. 'Our love is stronger than the sun,' he'd said to her once. And it had been. For a while.

When she came back, Alex seemed not to have moved.

'Mum, what happens when children do something bad?'

'Well, they get arrested. They go to the youth court. If they're between ten and thirteen, the prosecution has to show they knew they were doing a bad thing. Under the age of ten, children are said to be incapable of committing a crime. *Doli incapax*, they used to call it.'

'So I couldn't be a criminal, yet?'

She gave him a big hug, trying to squeeze these strange thoughts out of him.

'You, my darling, couldn't be a criminal, ever.'

Alex seemed satisfied by this and let her go, but she felt worried. He'd never expressed a view on their lives before. Perhaps something was troubling him here, perhaps Edward had been mean to him, or maybe he didn't like the criminal company she kept, especially now Patrick wasn't here to provide the ballast of normality.

But she didn't want to call Patrick, not now everything was so confused between them. Also, after her disastrous suggestion to have Godwin's case called into court when Mars was there, and the way she'd lost the plot when cross-examining Yelena, she felt everything she did that day was bound to go wrong. She couldn't risk speaking to anyone except her mother.

'Mum, it's Ophelia.'

'Well, of course it is. I've got this new phone that tells me. Is Alex enjoying the Just William books I sent?'

'Yes, thank you very much.'

'It's getting quite competitive here about who is doing the

flowers for the church this Christmas. Mrs Heaslip says my sprays were too weddingy last year.'

'Haven't they got other things to worry about?'

'Since your Dad died and I married Wilf there hasn't been nearly enough to gossip about. But tell me, how are you doing?'

Her mother was so sane and sensible, so rooted and knowledgeable in her little area, Ophelia found she just wanted to listen, to soak up the mother love without talking. Most of what she had to tell her mother would be too baffling and disturbing for her to follow, and what was the point of that?

'One thing you would be interested in. I was just invited to an orchid house, by a collector.'

'That's great! I knew you'd get a taste for horticulture in the end. You mustn't over-water orchids, you know.'

'They're beautiful.'

'Mmm. Your sister gave me one, but I can't say that orchids are my favourite flowers. A little too *exotic* for me. But you won't tell Claire, will you? Now we need to fix a weekend when you and Alex will come and see us.'

'Yes, please. But at the moment Patrick is taking Alex out on Saturdays...'

'Oh yes, Patrick...'

There was a pause and Ophelia knew exactly what her mother was thinking. She was missing her son-in-law, regretting the split. She'd never actually blamed Ophelia, not in so many words, but...

'How is the young Patrick?' her mother asked, finishing her sentence with playful emphasis on the epithet.

'He told me he needed to look old, or no one listened to him.'

Her mother chuckled. Everything about Patrick used to

tickle her. 'I *always* listened to him, but then no one listens to me. Your sister is planning to send Arthur to *boarding school.* Can you imagine, the poor little mite, just because his big gruff dad went there.'

'Claire's husband isn't a bear, Mum.'

'I'm not sure, darling. I'm not quite sure.' She spoke so earnestly that Ophelia laughed out loud.

'It's so good to talk to you, Mum.'

'Would you like any mittens? I'm just learning how to do thumbs.' Her mother didn't like conspicuous displays of affection, just the warm practical prattle of busy days.

'I bet that's hard.'

'Pretty tricky. But maybe they aren't your thing?'

'No, Mum, but thanks.'

'I know. You have to be so chic in London, so *manufactured.*'

'Actually, Mum, I think in London you can be *anything you like.*' As she said it, she remembered how she used to argue with her mother and sister about London, how a love of London was another thing that she and Patrick had shared, back when they also loved each other. Now that they weren't in love any more, the city too seemed more hostile.

'Well, your old room is waiting for you, whenever you want to escape,' her mother said, as though she understood this.

'Thanks, Mum. I'll call you soon. We'll fix a date.'

'Look after yourself, my dear.'

Her small, wrinkling, busy mother shooed away the shadow of Mars and Godwin that hung over her. She didn't even need a drink. Not until she began to think of Patrick, and Alex hanging out with that odd older boy, and Samuel... something was bothering her about Samuel... She went to the fridge and got out a bottle.

Chapter Eighteen

She did not realise who they were at first. They were so perfectly a unit it was impossible to imagine them as individuals and she admired the sheen on their coats and hair, the intimacy of their two close but not-quite-touching bodies, the polish and point of their shoes, their similar shapes: tall, sharp-shouldered, camel coated. She was just about to look away when a voice she knew came at her from the couple.

'Miss Dormandy, this is my wife, Angelica Mars-Bingham. Jeremy said she could give evidence today after me.'

Ophelia didn't miss the implication: Jeremy was running the case now, not her. She held out her hand.

'It's a pleasure,' she offered, amused at the embarrassment she saw in the wife's face as she tried to decide whether to greet Ophelia as a tradesperson or as someone she might meet at dinner. Mars answered her predicament by pressing on her arm, directing her away from Ophelia to inspect a large statue of Queen Victoria. Ophelia went into court, where the usher and the clerk were chatting about the lives of celebrities, and she was glad to be invisible. All parties were called into court and Mars sauntered in like a man who expects to be listened to.

When he stood in the witness box he instantly took over the proceedings with a natural, graceful command. He spoke easily and well, slowly enough for the judge to get a note, but without seeming to disturb his rhythm. His voice was rich and full, plain enough to sound normal, but it drew you with an unexpected emotional undertow. He described his family and his work proudly, but without boasting. He told them he was lucky to have found such good workers and that Yelena had been an excellent, intelligent and attentive secretary. She had had problems at home, in Poland, and he had tried to help. He knew about her mother's infirmities and she knew every detail of his life too, just as you'd expect after sharing a room for four years. Of course she knew his children's birthdays. She knew everything; she made it her business. He wasn't surprised she knew about the tattoo. He wasn't a man to keep anything secret.

But, he went on, Yelena's concentration had been slipping for some time. She'd started to have fits of temper when the least thing went wrong, like the photocopier – with which she was in a long drawn-out struggle. She'd become more and more distracted from the job. It was with great regret, he said with a convincing crack in his voice, that he had witnessed the decline. He'd tried to intervene, to offer more sympathy, but that only seemed to make things worse. Indeed, thinking back on it, the real problems started after she asked him to come and stay in her cottage in Poland and he'd said he'd need a villa to accommodate all his family, what with the three children. She'd been very angry after that, he said slowly, as though he was gradually understanding the significance of what he was saying as it came out of his mouth. 'Perhaps she hoped for more in our relationship. Perhaps she wanted me to be more than just her boss, and she was disappointed...'

The prosecutor bounced up like a jack-in-a-box at this and his eyes popped out even more as he puffed, 'This wasn't put to Miss Karpovska in cross-examination. Miss Dormandy cross examined at length and no such suggestion was ever made.'

The judge swivelled his glare in Ophelia's direction, but Mars was quick, disarming the criticism before it came.

'I'm so sorry, I just realised now. It's not, I hope, too late? You want, I am sure, to get at the truth?'

Ophelia marvelled at his sureness of touch. Yelena was probably right: he could draw you in, every time.

The judge raised his eyes, surprised, impressed at the witness's sang froid and his remarks were addressed more to Mars than the prosecutor. 'Miss Karpovska can be recalled. No harm done.'

The prosecutor turned to whisper urgently to a case worker behind him but Mars carried on with his account. He produced the attendance sheets which documented Yelena's early departures and the accounts that showed every member of staff in the office received a wage increase on the second of June, except for Yelena.

'She was so proud. First she was disappointed in her affections and then she felt humiliated over the money. I am sorry to say it but I think she wanted revenge...' He said this gently, full of understanding, even forgiveness.

The prosecutor stood and put the sordid details of the allegation to him and Mars batted it all back as easily as if he were an overexcited shareholder at an AGM.

Ophelia called Angelica Mars-Bingham to the stand. She took up her post with anger and alarm in her face and her hands seemed to flutter like a bird's wings in the cold. She stood stiffly and she did not look at the jury. Her eyes were fixed on her husband in the dock, staring at him as though she thought, if she looked away, that he might disappear. She spoke with a soft, slightly lisping voice, the voice of a girl, but her eyes were fierce.

They had the most marvellous marriage, she said. She was the envy of all her girlfriends. He would never debase himself, or another. He was not someone who could do these sordid things. They were in love. They had three beautiful boys. She bought all the boys' birthday presents. He never smoked. He never lied. She loved him more than everything in the world. No one could be a happier wife. The prosecutor did not ask her a single question and the judge thanked her warmly for coming. She took her seat in the public gallery and kept her eyes glued to Mars all of the time.

Ophelia wondered if this wife had suffered, as she had. Perhaps she'd sacrificed her pride in the interests of her family. Perhaps she was a better person.

Yelena came into the court room. Her dark eyes flashed fire at Ophelia and at the jury as she said yes, she had asked Mars to stay with her in Poland and he had dismissed her 'quaint little hut'. He always wanted the best for his family, she spat, although he preferred not to spend too much time with them. Her eyes rested maliciously on Angelica, who looked as though she had been punched in the stomach. Ophelia turned to see how Mars was taking this and his face retained that tolerant, patient look which he'd worn as he talked of Yelena's problems with her mother, but the reality of his relationship with Yelena was palpable now. It had become inescapable as soon as he'd mentioned the invitation to the Black Mountains. Now love was an issue, she could use it to show how unhinged Yelena had become.

'Miss Karpovska, would you accept that you criticised Mr Mars for things other people would be happy about?'

'What? I am not unreasonable. It is he who is the worm.'

'You complain, in your witness statement, that he gives you Joy perfume for Christmas?'

'My God, the man has no imagination.'

'It is good quality perfume, is it not?'

'It is rubbish and he knows it is rubbish. The same thing, every year, as though I was his aunt.'

This was enough. If she hated him for his presents, the level of her spite was immense. Anything more and the jury might start to wonder at him for keeping her as his secretary for so long.

'No more questions.'

The prosecutor summed up his case but the jury weren't looking at him. They were indifferent to his words. They were looking at Mars and his wife, trying to work out the story for themselves. When Ophelia stood up there was a flicker more interest but no one smiled at her.

'Mr Mars has unlocked this case for you, members of the jury. He's shown you Miss Karpovska's true reason for bringing this complaint. You remember how it came to him, mid-sentence: "…perhaps she hoped for more in our rela-tionship. Perhaps she wanted me to be more than just her boss…" The simple lack of a pay raise wouldn't have been enough to make her invent this story of his assault. But her story is obviously untrue. The prosecution case, that Mr Mars, out of the blue, one day turned from family man into sexual predator, is obvious nonsense. Frustrated passion is the key to this case, members of the jury. It's all about a young secretary who was obsessively and unrequitedly in love with her boss.'

She felt the jury warming to her. The old man in the tweed jacket at the back smiled and nodded his head. The anorexic young woman in black pursed her lips and frowned in concentration. She felt, between herself and this random group of people, an easy, strangely reciprocal flow of thoughts. Her words came in regular cadences, almost in iambic pentameter, and her thoughts followed so swiftly after one another that now she put aside her prepared speech and improvised, hesitating when she saw someone making a note, speeding up when another leaned forward impatiently. She talked about the intimacy that could grow between two people 'no more than a rubbish bin away from each other', the tiny details each would know about the other's life, the opportunity for Yelena to admire, to fixate on the charismatic and charming Mr Mars. She talked about the speed with which frustrated love could turn to anger, about the fury in Yelena's eyes, legs, words. 'It is he who is the worm,' she quoted, 'the man has no imagination.' 'Who,' she asked, 'says these things about a casual philanderer? This is the language of a would-be lover, not the victim of a random grope…'

It felt as if she was telling them a familiar story, one they'd heard before and could nod over and mumble at. It felt as if no one wanted the chapter to end. But she knew better than to try to stretch this out. With a last deft flourish she sat down. She saw that some of them were still looking at her when the judge was summing up, and she was pleased.

The judge rehearsed the evidence tersely. He said it was a classic jury case, one person's word against another, as though this sort of case held little interest for him. He repeated, several times, in the stilted manner of someone reciting a formula that has long since lost any meaning, that they should not convict unless the prosecution had satisfied them so that they were sure of the defendant's guilt.

Jeremy seemed happy enough to talk to her now, while the jury were off deliberating. Mars and his wife clearly wanted nothing to do with them, so Ophelia and Jeremy went to the canteen together. As they drank their coffee and ate a sandwich, Jeremy said, 'Nice speech, Miss Dormandy.'

'Oh good,' she said, hoping he would elaborate.

'You been working with Samuel long?'

'Since I started. Sixteen years.'

Jeremy smiled. 'And I've briefed him for the last forty-two, since he was a pupil and I was in articles. He's always been the best.'

'Yes.' Ophelia put aside her vanity and relaxed into this shared affection for her mentor.

Jeremy talked about their early wins, about Samuel's charm and his guile, about how Samuel and he had decided that bright ties helped their dozier clients to remember who they were in a crowded magistrates' court, about how, later, Samuel had inspired almost tribal loyalty in a whole generation of armed robbers. When the tannoy called them into court, Ophelia felt she was being dragged helter-skelter through the decades.

This time when they took their seats, the jury seemed to look around the court with a new confidence and enjoyment. It was their turn now. Some of them nodded to her, some nodded to Mars in the dock. The foreman entered their not guilty verdict so loudly that the ushers smiled at each other. The judge dismissed them quickly. He seemed keen to be gone. It was three o'clock, so he was safe from being given a new case for the day.

Outside court, Mars and his wife came up to her together. He looked exhausted. Only Angelica looked pleased. But they were undeniably a unit. Mars had his left arm wound tightly around his wife's waist as he extended his right hand for Ophelia to shake. She took it firmly and saw in his eyes a frank admission of something, though exactly what it was, she couldn't say. Perhaps he was acknowledging that she'd been right about his defence, or right to have kept away from his embrace, that his life was complicated enough as it was.

'Goodbye, Miss Dormandy. Thank you.' She saw him squeeze his wife's waist as he said this, prompting her to give Ophelia a distant smile.

She said, 'Thank you, Miss Dormandy. You must get so tired of the nonsense people talk. I hope I never, ever, come to a place like this again.' She sighed and looked down at her immaculate vermilion nails. 'The prosecutor was so silly and that woman…' She reached a hand up to her husband's face, her red nails flashing in the fluorescent light, and caressed his cheek so vigorously that she could hear the rasp of acrylic on stubble and see a red line appear on his cheekbone. Ophelia remembered that anger herself, but she hadn't wanted to scratch Patrick's face. She'd felt he was already too far away.

She blushed as she remembered that she too had felt Mars's cheek, and that it had been soft then, with no trace of stubble, though their meeting had been in the afternoon. He must have shaved specially. He must have planned her surrender. If his wife knew about it, would those red nails reach for Ophelia's eyes?

Angelica looked around the waiting area with undisguised distaste. Her voice was at its softest, most lisping, as she said to her husband, 'Darling, let me take you home before our car is stripped by one of these defendants.' And then she started walking away from them, with Mars still attached. He seemed to have lost all independence and he barely nodded a goodbye to Jeremy as she propelled him to the lifts.

Jeremy, indifferent to the wife's rudeness and relaxed now the job was done, said, 'Come on. Time for a drink.' Ophelia wanted to get away from this case, but she thought a drink might wash away the bitterness at the back of her throat and anyway, refusing Jeremy would be professional suicide. She agreed to meet him at the door when she'd got out of her robes for 'a quick half'.

The pub was full and very smoky and the bitter taste in her mouth seemed to get worse rather than better with every sip she took.

'So, tell me the real story then,' she said.

Jeremy smiled. 'The bike storage was their den. When I went in there, the floor was thick with cigarette stubs and there was a pile of cushions in one corner. He didn't tell me, but it was obvious that the affair had been going on for a long time and that he'd ended it, probably on the second of June. You were quite right about his defence, of course, but he simply couldn't own up to the affair. He came as close as he could in court. His wife is a toughie. She doesn't even let him smoke. Her father would have chucked him straight out of ABM and he might not have found it so easy to get a new job. American-run banks take a dim view of this sort of conduct. Mars was lucky Yelena didn't have anything more against him. The tattoo was a problem. Moral of the story: never get a tattoo.'

'Do all your stories have morals, Jeremy?'

'Unlike my clients,' he said, twinkling at her.

They finished their beers and Ophelia sensed that they both felt that nothing good would come out of talking over this case any more. She was glad to have won, but she didn't like to think about it. It didn't feel over. She wondered about asking Jeremy's advice on her separation, but that too felt unfinished. She thanked him for the drink and started to walk back to chambers.

Her telephone rang.

'Hi, Miss Dormandy, it's John here.' He sounded troubled. Still, it was important for her to get out her good news quickly.

'I've just finished in the Bailey. Mr Mars was acquitted.'

'Good. I'll tell Mr Slidders. Um, I've got a Helen Fennick on the line for you. She says she was at Bar school with you but she's ringing about the case of Kalpanichandran. You did a hearing in June and sentence was deferred until next week. She says she's been briefed by the family.'

This didn't sound good. 'Oh. OK.' she said. Then there was a click.

'Hi, Ophelia, you may not remember me. It's Helen, Helen Fennick, you know, from the vocational course? Chair of the croquet and debating clubs? Anyway, I'm ringing you about Mrs Kalpanichandran. You represented her at St Albans in June this year.'

'Yes. That's right.' She didn't want to get drawn into any pally stuff. She could tell this was going to turn nasty.

'Well, I've been briefed by the husband's family. They are concerned that she pleaded guilty without meaning to. There could be an application to vacate her plea so she can enter a not guilty. I know this is very annoying, but I wonder if you could send me a copy of the endorsement on your brief about the change to guilty, because the original instructions were, I believe, that she was innocent of the charge.'

Taxis roared by and Ophelia could only just hear. She could picture the brief: the name of the case and the location, the solicitor's name and address, and hers, all typed in bold font on the right-hand side of a thick piece of cream paper, leaving room for her to write everything that happened on the left-hand side. As the judge gave his sentence she'd written it down and signed and dated it, but there was no denying the blank space above. She simply hadn't written out what she should have written: *No pressure has been applied to me to make me change my plea. I accept I am guilty of the charge.* She hadn't got Mrs K to sign this or anything. Of course, there'd been too much to do and too little time, but so small a formality could have been done in a trice. Was the truth of it that she *had* applied pressure to Mrs K? She'd been so sure it was the right thing that she had told her what to do. And poor Mrs K was always being told what to do. When Ophelia was there, she'd agreed with her, but when she was with her in-laws, clearly, she'd agreed with them.

Ophelia gritted her teeth. She'd persuaded Mrs K to plead guilty with reason and gentleness. She'd gained Mrs K's trust. If she'd presented the declaration for signature, she'd have spoiled that feeling. But this had left her exposed. She'd treated her client too much as a friend and too little as a defendant. Now that one moment of restraint, that procedural failure, could undo her completely.

Still, she wasn't going to give anything away.

Ophelia turned into a blind alley to get away from the noise and said, studying the dirty brickwork, 'As far as I've heard, I am still instructed by Mrs Kalpanichandran. Any communication between her and me is, as you know, covered by legal professional privilege. I can't send you anything. The family, your clients, agreed to pay back the money she stole so she could get a suspended sentence. If they don't, she faces a substantial prison term. I take it, from what you have said, that they haven't paid a penny?' Poor Mrs K, she thought. Maybe it was a girl baby and they didn't care about her any more.

Ophelia put more steel in her voice and went on, 'Have you actually read the papers? The prosecution case is overwhelming.'

'Ophelia, I know this is difficult and embarrassing, but I do have my professional duty to perform. I wasn't asking you for a lecture. I was asking if you could send me a copy of something on the *outside* of your brief. If you are going to be difficult, so be it. I'll get the information elsewhere.'

'OK. Goodbye,' Ophelia said quickly, hoping not to betray her beating heart. She had to walk for a good ten minutes before she felt calm enough to speak to anyone. Then she rang her solicitor in the case, Paul Simms.

He sounded pleased to talk to her. 'God, Ophelia, I've just had the most awful bloodhound on the line. Some woman called Fennick. She was asking me for our notes. I told her to mind her own business. As far as I know, Mrs K is still instructing us on legal aid. She hasn't told me otherwise. Of course, I don't actually have any notes about the change of plea as my clerk was late, but I guess you'll have your brief endorsed.'

A bus was passing. Ophelia held her phone towards the roar so whatever she might have said was quite inaudible. She brought it back to her mouth.

'It does suggest the family haven't paid up, doesn't it?'

'Yes, which means prison for our client. I'm going to phone up that horrible family and tell them they'll be in contempt of court if they don't pay. I'll just have to hope they get frightened and don't take advice on the point.'

'Yes, maybe you could also say it is contrary to the regulations for them to pay privately for a barrister when the defendant is already receiving legal aid. Say if they aren't careful they could be investigated by the Legal Services Commission.'

'You know me, I'll say anything,' Paul said cheerfully. Maybe he'd pull it off. He was good at persuading people, when he tried. He just didn't try very often.

Ophelia didn't like to think about the consequences if he failed. It would be bad for all of them, not just Mrs K. She needed a career, not a hearing in front of the Bar Standards Board and a possible suspension.

She looked at her watch. It was only two. She felt as

though the day had gone on for a week already. She needed comfort. She needed a friend. She dialled Flora's number.

'Fancy a cup of tea?'

'Yes! I've just finished a meeting and I'd love to meet. I've got something to tell you.' She sounded happy.

'Usual place in ten?' It was Mars's phrase. Why had she left out the 'minutes'? Well, she'd get over it soon.

'Yes.'

Flora was at the counter ordering tea and waving her hands around when Ophelia came in. She got one for Ophelia too and they went back to the seat they'd had last time, in the window. Outside, Ophelia saw two pigeons fighting over a slice of tomato. She looked back at Flora.

Flora looked different. It took Ophelia a little while to work out why, because it had been subtly done, but she was *wearing make up*. It gave her fresh face a slightly harder edge, a paler hue, more defined eyes. Flora was holding herself still, waiting for comments.

'You look great, Flora, but make-up? That was never your thing. And are you sure it doesn't contain contraband whale blubber or pigments extracted by strip mining?' She arched her eyebrows teasingly and Flora gave a small hoot of laughter. The man at the counter looked over and smiled.

'You're right. I haven't looked into this enough. And it feels as if I've got a layer of clay drying on my skin. It's horrid, but you see I've got to go to this smart drinks party with my new man and…'

'Hey, Flora, whoa. New man?' This was also what was different about Flora: a secret glow beneath the chalky veil.

'I know it's ridiculous. I went on a retreat to get closer to the spirit world and I came back with a boyfriend who feeds me caviar. I call him my *international man of mystery* because I don't know what he does, except that it involves taking a lot of planes and he wears sunglasses on the back of his head.'

'The strangest things can be attractive.' Ophelia smiled ruefully, more to herself than Flora. 'But I'm not sure that all this mystery is a good idea. He might be dangerous.'

'I don't think so. He is funny and has curly blond hair on his forearms like a teddy and he is healthy and American.'

She couldn't help it. Seeing Flora's excitement, a little jealousy came to pique her mood. She looked out of the window. There was only one pigeon with the tomato now. Ophelia wanted to change the conversation.

'So long as he doesn't like sticking pins into butterflies, like the last client I represented,' she muttered.

'You do know that your clients aren't exactly representative of the general population, don't you?'

How irritating. Flora was patronising as well as in love. Ophelia felt herself frowning.

The waitress brought them chipped mugs of strong tea and Ophelia held hers under her nose, letting the steam rise over her face like a purifying treatment.

'Are you OK?' Flora said. 'You look troubled.'

'Well, I did get into a flirtation with a client and that was a mess, and I'm still missing Patrick like hell and Alex says he wants us to leave London and he's spending too much time with that boy Edward, the thirteen-year-old you didn't like the look of. And I might have a problem at work too and I'm just feeling desperately alone.' Flora was looking at her so anxiously that she added quickly, 'except here with you.'

Flora smiled and then folded her hands on the table and spoke slowly and clearly, like a professional giving her expert opinion. 'Don't worry about things you can't do anything about, like stupid Patrick and your clients. Concentrate on the main thing. Keep Alex away from Edward. I don't like it when I see older boys spending too much time with boys younger than them. It usually means they want to use them in some way. A four-year age gap is too big for them to be genuine friends.'

It made Ophelia shrivel inside, the thought that she'd been neglecting Alex, letting him go to Edward's so often, and not getting to the bottom of why. Tonight, when she got back, she'd tell him he couldn't go there any more. Still, she felt mortified at the dismissive way Flora spoke of Patrick and her clients. Flora was probably right, but it was painful nonetheless. Ophelia gulped at her tea, uncomfortable with her friend who had all the answers.

Flora seemed to sense that Ophelia didn't want to talk about these things any more. She started to describe her weird weekend in Scotland and the strange drink they'd drunk, called *ayahuasca*, made from some tree in South America, which made you feel at one with the world and each other.

Ophelia laughed and said it sounded better than white wine and would Flora please get her some soon? But the mood between them stayed tense, and after they finished their cups of tea, they both got to their feet and said they had better get on.

Ophelia walked back to chambers thinking how strange it was that Flora should like a man who reminded her of a teddy bear. It just didn't sound sexy, but then what had she found exciting about Mars? Skin like an orchid? A desire to re-make paradise? People were all weird, not just her clients.

There were no cheques in her cheque drawer but there was something intriguing in her pigeonhole. There was a small rectangular box wrapped in yellow paper. It had no label, although it looked as though it had once had one because there was a thin claret-coloured loop of string attached to the top. It must be a present, and the only person it could be from was Mars. She swept it into her arms, a little ashamed at her delight, but pleased to be appreciated.

John came through the room and saw it.

'Present from an admirer, Miss Dormandy?'

'Present from a client, I think,' she said proudly. How gratifying to be able to prove her success so naturally to her clerk. She decided to unwrap the box here. What was the point of going upstairs with it? This was the opposite of a secret, after all.

She pulled off the dot of sellotape on top and the paper fell away. It was a yellow box of perfume. *Joy*, it said. She put it back in her pigeonhole and walked out.

Samuel was flicking through an auction catalogue. His face looked a little pale but there was a flush on his cheekbones and his eyes were bright with mischief. His shirt was the same purple as her mother's favourite rose, the Cardinal de Richelieu.

'Ophelia returns in triumph!' he said with a twinkle.

She flopped onto one of the hard chairs. 'Can you guess what Mars has just sent me, as a gift?'

Samuel looked at her intently, his mouth curving at the edges, waiting to be amused.

'Tell me.'

She said it slowly: 'A bottle of Joy perfume.'

Samuel looked away, embarrassed. 'Oh dear. I am sorry about that, Ophelia.'

So she'd been right to take this badly. He understood the important things, Samuel. He wanted to cheer her up, so he pointed at something that had obviously made him feel better. 'Look.' He pushed a Christie's catalogue towards her. 'It's a bergère like mine, but not as nice, and the estimate is five hundred pounds more than I paid for it. Perhaps I should give up barristering and become an antiques dealer.'

He'd never talked about retiring before. She looked at him sideways and he smiled.

'You can't retire on me. We've got this case of Godwin to fight,' she said, mock-stern.

'I know, my dear. I know.'

Chapter Nineteen

Walking back to her office, Ophelia's phone beeped with a text.

Can I see you now?

It was from Matthew Mars.

No good would come of this, but maybe he had something to explain, some mitigation for the Joy perfume present, some transforming gesture. She wanted to believe in the best of him and she wanted to feel something other than shame as she thought back over his case. Perhaps if they met she would find some small sign of grace. She could tell him how well he'd performed in the witness box. But then he probably knew that already. She texted back:

See you in the Holborn Wine Cellar in ten.

'In ten' again? This was becoming a bad habit. She went to the newsagent's and bought some football cards. Alex didn't have Theo Walcott. She hoped it wasn't because he hated him. Anyway, it would be something to sweeten the pill of her telling him he couldn't see Edward so much.

Back in the Holborn cellar, she took the seat she'd sat in last time she'd met Mars, and the same music rippled soothingly from the speakers. The same Chablis would be waiting behind the bar. It was her round this time. She went up to the heavy wood counter and ordered a bottle and two glasses. She'd save money on nibbles. No one ever *needed* an olive. She carried the bottle and glasses back to their table and poured herself a taster. This had been a long day, for both of them. She thought of Angelica Mars-Bingham's fingernails sinking into Mars's cheek and wondered what other parts of his flesh they had strafed since then. How strange: was she jealous of his wife now? Ophelia could remember the brush of Matthew Mars's lips on the down of her cheek, his hand pressing between her shoulder blades, his tongue reaching for hers. Everything about him spelled two-timing, narcissistic, bad news, and so, of course, she wanted him. She grasped the beading bottle in her hand. She was afraid. She was in danger of becoming a furniture-kicking lunatic like Yelena here…

She took a small sip to steady her nerves and studied the barrel table, half-expecting to see the previous occupants' names scratched there, like at school. She almost got out a pen. She felt that transgressive.

A shadow fell over her and she looked up quickly. But it was not Mars who stood above her, looking down. It was his wife.

Ophelia studied her in silence, taking in the finely woven houndstooth suit, the tan leather gloves, the Hermès scarf and the small perfect features of Angelica Mars-Bingham seized in awkward rigidity.

'You weren't expecting me, were you?'

'No.' Ophelia tried to keep her voice steady, straightforward, if not at ease. She felt her cheeks flush and hoped Angelica would not notice. 'Can I offer you a glass of Chablis?'

Angelica twitched her one out-of-place hair back into the

sculpted blond swirl at her ear and sat down carefully, as though she'd never been in a bar before and she doubted its cleanliness.

Ophelia tried to be calm and reassuring. She wanted to be the host, not the delinquent. 'The chairs are a bit hard, I'm afraid. But please, have a drink.'

Angelica said nothing, but folded her arms across her thin well-tailored body and fixed her eyes on a midpoint in the barrel between them. Most of her skin was covered in tweed or silk or suede or sheer powder, but next to her right eye Ophelia saw that Angelica had a slightly protruding, visibly pulsing vein. She felt the beat in her own veins, hammering at her brain. She knew Angelica's pain. She'd been there. Keeping her hand as steady as she could, Ophelia poured a glass of wine for Angelica and handed it to her. 'Did *you* send the text?'

Angelica nodded and then reached suddenly for the glass. She took a big gulp. Ophelia did too, and there was a kind of comradeship in that. Then Angelica looked at her and the comradeship waned. Angelica's eyes studied her intensely, but from a distance, as though she was examining a specimen under a microscope, adjusting the focus, her pen ready to compile the data.

'I'm sorry to trick you. I just had to know what was going on between you and my husband. I saw your name in his diary and I found a little envelope with your name on it which looked as if it was meant to go with a present.' When she spoke there was hardly any trace of the little girl lisp that had muffled her voice at court; now it was crisp and clean.

She paused and Ophelia waited to see how far she would go with this. Angelica waited too, hoping perhaps that Ophelia would give herself away. Behind the counter Ophelia could see the barman putting clean glasses away on the shelf.

There was no one else here. No prospect of rescue.

Angelica frowned and sipped at her wine, as though she was decoding a message there too. Then she put the glass down and sighed.

Angelica's chin trembled slightly as she said in an angry whisper, 'In the last few hours I have discovered that my husband has had two extramarital affairs. I just need to know whether to make that three.' Then she swivelled her eyes back onto Ophelia's with a pitiless, penetrating look. She wanted facts, not understanding. She didn't blink.

Ophelia was speechless, torn between wanting to comfort the wronged wife and wanting to defend herself in the face of hostile attack. She could see Angelica swallow behind the expertly knotted scarf and she felt how parched her own mouth was and how her head throbbed.

'You are asking me if I had an affair with your husband?'

Each word seemed to stick on its way past her lips. She needed to push them out one at a time with her dry breath.

'Yes, that is what I'm asking. I'm sorry if it sounds rude.' Angelica didn't sound sorry. She was cool and sprung, like a hunter near her quarry. Her revenge would be cold and effective.

But Ophelia wouldn't let herself be caught, not like this, on charges that couldn't be made out, even if she was guilty of something. She took a sip of wine and said simply, 'No. I haven't had an affair with him. If you have a note for me I would like to see it.'

Angelica bridled and frowned but she reached into her bag and brought out a small yellow envelope. It had a little hole in one corner, as though for a string, which was torn through to the edge of the envelope. It was the same colour yellow as the Joy perfume box. Ophelia extended her hand to take it and she could see Angelica hesitate. She saw that the envelope was still sealed and she wondered at Angelica's delicacy in not opening it.

'Don't worry. I'll tell you if it's important.' That made Angelica colour a little. Ophelia saw then that the seal was crinkly. Angelica must have opened and resealed it. She tore the envelope and read:

> *Please go to the orchid house whenever you want. I have named a new specimen after you. Paphiopedilum dormandis has bright white petals that make you feel clearer-sighted, just looking at them, and it has a slipper with light blue veins, like your hands. I've put a label in front of it so you can't miss which one it is. Thank you. Matthew Mars.*

She shook her head and looked up at Angelica. 'You needn't worry about that. It's just a thank-you note.'

Angelica looked puzzled, wrong-footed and annoyed that the conversation was slipping out of her control. 'Did you have a private relationship?'

Ophelia stood up, smoothing out her skirt. She didn't want to be cross-examined. She might have said, 'I know what you are going through. This happened to me. I left my husband', but now she saw Angelica as her prosecutor. An instinct of self-preservation kicked in and she said, with dignified finality, 'What happens in a conference between lawyer and client is privileged. I was his lawyer. Nothing else.'

Angelica got to her feet quickly and held out her hand briskly, as if to take back the initiative and to confirm that the interview was over with honour on both sides. 'Thank you, and the wine was very nice too.'

Even without the girlish lisp, Angelica seemed very young, with her small bones, her small voice and her sense that things had to go her way. Her conventional neatness made her look as though her mother had dressed her. She seemed more like a precocious fourteen-year-old than a mother of three, and Ophelia felt sorry for her all over again.

'I find a glass of wine often helps,' she said confidingly and picked up her glass, holding it high for a belated toast. Angelica lifted hers too. 'Bottoms up!' Ophelia said, and they touched glasses and poured the wine down their throats together. Then Ophelia gathered up her things and, with one last rather formal wave, hurried away before embarrassment or rivalry could rise up and disturb this provisional truce.

Chapter Twenty

There was no escaping it. She was not so much better than Patrick after all. True, she'd split up with Patrick by then, but what had she been doing flirting with her married client, meeting him for what could never have been a professional purpose, before his trial had even happened? Vanity, curiosity, lechery… she had these sins too. She dug her fingernails into the fleshy part of her palms as though she could squeeze the badness out of herself, and she felt a little better. She was glad not to despise Patrick any more. It had seemed so much against her nature.

She imagined Patrick in the orchid house, telling her she looked nothing like the flower that was named after her. She thought of her mother's walled garden in Suffolk, and how Patrick's head had suddenly appeared over the top of the brickwork just as she hitched up her skirt to brown her legs. She remembered his delighted laugh, his dangerous, graceful jump onto the busy lizzies, his lack of repentance at their destruction, his hand on her goose-pimpled thigh…

But that playful, teasing, celebrating Patrick had made fewer and fewer appearances, until he'd dematerialised altogether. The man who had taken his place was a mystery. Perhaps it would have helped if she had read his last letter… Flora had told her not to contact him, but one little text couldn't hurt? She couldn't resist typing:

See you tomorrow

How compromising was that? It was just admin. She was checking he was taking Alex out as usual. That was allowed.

She checked her answerphone and her heart quickened as she heard a message from Patrick. He must have called while she was with Mars's wife, and this thought too made her blush.

The message held no comfort for her.

'Just me, Patrick, to say I *did* get the Hackney job after all, so is it OK for me to give Alex pocket money, as that's what he wants?'

She didn't know about a Hackney job. That must have been what was in the letter she'd been so desperate about, just stuff about work and money.

Money. For all the time she spent worrying about it, it had never interested her. Sometimes she wondered if this meant she was still something of a child, missing out a necessary stage in her development. When she'd been with Patrick, he'd been so much worse with money than she had that she'd felt adequate enough. But now even Patrick was engaging with the subject, talking about money, not love. What clearer sign was there that everything was irrevocably over between them?

She got off the bus and walked up her street. Alex would be waiting for her, probably cross. If she'd been a different, better sort of mother, she'd have been at his rugby match that afternoon. He'd asked her to come, even though he knew she was in court, which showed it was important to him. If he played badly he'd feel it was her fault. Like with his concert.

She heard the taps running as she opened her front door. The bathroom door was ajar, as if inviting her in, so she left her bag and slipped quietly upstairs on the carpet, hoping

Freia wouldn't pop out of her room with questions.

Alex was in the bath with water halfway up his chest, his big toe in the tap and thick bubbles everywhere. His eyes lit up when he saw her, but she'd seen they were flat as wet slate a second before.

'I'm sorry I missed your match. How did you do?'

Alex picked up a big handful of bubbles and applied them to his chin to make a long beard, which he stroked contemplatively before answering. Ophelia noticed that his arms, where the bubbles had been, were bruised black and scratched.

'They won 14-6.'

'Never mind. Did you get hurt?'

He shrugged his shoulders as if to say, 'maybe, but what does it matter?'

'Were you pleased with your game, at least?'

Alex looked down into the mess of rainbow-streaked spheres. 'I *got on with it,* if that's what you mean. I nearly scored a try.'

She'd have expected him to look more pleased at this. Maybe a coach's harsh words had made him hate the whole thing.

'Well done!'

'So, did you win your case?' He looked her straight in the eyes. She felt he was trying to establish an equivalence in their activities, an equality between them.

'Yes. Thanks. My orchid-collecting businessman was acquitted in spite of telling lies to the court. He came up with something almost true at the end, and he was just charming enough to get away with it.'

'At least one of us has done well.'

He grinned and she gave him a half-smile back. Yes, they were a team, but she was the one with parental responsibility.

Flora's warning was fresh in her mind.

'What games do you play, with Edward?'

'He's got some cool computer games.'

'What do you like about him, apart from the games?'

'Mu-um, what is this? He's just my friend, OK?'

'Well, it's just he's four years older than you, so it's a bit unusual.'

'And you're Miss Normal?'

That made her wince. She wasn't any good at his. She wasn't getting anywhere.

'I just think such a big age gap isn't a good idea.'

'But we're friends, aren't we? I mean, you tell me all about your cases, like you'd tell Flora. You don't think we have too big an age gap for that. I feel different from the kids in class. It's not my fault you made me so grown up.'

She felt like he'd punched her.

'No, Alex. It's not your fault. But I'd like you to stop hanging out with Edward just now, OK?'

His eyes widened and his chin, still slightly bubbled, quivered. 'No! You can't just decide that. That's mean and not fair.'

She bent over him and kissed his freckled forehead. 'You always seem out of sorts after you've been with him.'

He pulled away from her and stood up in the bath. The line of his swimming trunks was still visible, proof of their long summer at the beach, but now he was covered in bruises and scrapes and he seemed so fragile. She held out a towel and he grabbed it roughly. She could see they weren't going to be friends for some time.

'Can I put something on your cuts?'

He shook his head and drowned out any further talk with the grind of the electric toothbrush. She decided to leave him and try a chat in the dark later. But when she came back up, after two glasses of wine and half an hour, his light was already out and he was, or was pretending to be, sound asleep.

After one more glass of wine, she felt strong enough to call Patrick.

'Hi.'

'Hi.' He sounded tense. Almost as tense as she did.

'I told Alex I don't want him to spend time with a boy four years older than him and he said it was my fault that I'd made him too grown up for his class. Have I done the wrong thing?' It was too long a sentence, too jumbled up and with no lead-in. And she an advocate. Shame.

He sounded stilted but gentle. 'It's my fault that I'm not there. I'd support your decision, Ophelia. Who is this older boy?'

But what about the other point? she wondered. Had she made Alex grow up too much? 'Edward,' she said.

'OK, I'll talk to him about it.'

There was a silence.

'Thanks,' she said. Her head and hands ached. She hated the silence and the miles between them. When he said it was his fault he wasn't here, did he mean that it was his choice, that things would always be like this? She couldn't face asking.

'I've got to go,' she said.

'See you at ten.'

She finished the bottle.

———

If only she'd slept. Her eyes looked puffy and her skin lifeless even before she put on the light over the mirror. Patrick was coming. What would he see? A mess... She covered herself in a fine veil of powder. If it had been summer, she'd have put on sunglasses. Today she wanted a screen.

She was putting on a red dress when the bell went and she heard Alex open the door. 'Hi, Dad! Whassup?' she heard him say brightly, much happier than he was with her.

Then she heard Patrick, 'Just been making a buck.' She remembered she'd never answered his question about the pocket money. It was ridiculous: she wanted to talk to him, but she didn't talk when she could, she threw away his letters and cowered upstairs when he came round. She had to do *something*. She clattered helter-skelter down the stairs.

Even Patrick, usually so laconic, looked taken aback. She was just going to throw herself in… though what that meant she couldn't say. She went towards him, waving her arms to make up for the gaps in her words, just about getting them under control when she saw him look at her with increasing puzzlement.

'Hi, Patrick. It's me…' Who else was it going to be? 'I mean, I'm sorry I wasn't feeling very… well. And yes, whatever you think is best about pocket money. I've been wanting to ask… um, if you did write me a letter I lost it, um, with the wine which was very nice of you and I should have started with that, sorry. It was nice of you to think of me. But I lost the letter, before I read it. If there was a letter.'

He looked very uncomfortable. 'Well, there was one, but it just said stuff… like how I'd like to spend time with you both.'

How wretched to be reduced to this. And in front of poor Alex. Every bit of her ached. She wanted to look into his soul and cross-examine his thoughts, but she felt exhausted, overwhelmed by awareness of her failures and all she had lost.

'OK, right. Well, I hope you have a good day together.'
'Are you alright?'

Was he just being polite again?

'I have a case...' The awfulness of having to defend Godwin on Monday seemed to stop up her throat. But Patrick didn't wait for her to finish. He cut in angrily: 'We need to get going... Ready, Alex?'

And so he chafed that old wound, her inability to communicate outside work about anything but work. They stared at each other in awkward silence for a moment. Then he wished her a good day and removed Alex, her only companion, leaving her with only mess.

It was much later, when she was tucking Alex up in bed, that she learned that Patrick lived in as much wreckage as she did. She was drawing Alex's curtains while he lay still in his lamplight, looking at the swirls on the ceiling, when he said, with a faraway voice, as if it were a fable, 'You know Dad lives in his office. He left Caroline two months ago and he's been sleeping in the office ever since. He washes in the kitchenette.' The image of Patrick trying to fit bits of his body into the small, round sink in his office kitchenette, and the relief at discovering her rival gone, made Ophelia laugh long and free. Alex went on, enjoying her reaction, 'He keeps it a secret from the others. He leaves work at seven and goes to the pub for an hour before sneaking back in. He sleeps in a sleeping bag in the stationery cupboard.' He'd always had a thing about stationery cupboards.

'Did he tell you this, as a secret?' She stroked his hair gently.

'No, or I wouldn't be telling you.' He was right, but wounding.

'Did he ask you to tell me?'

'No. I just thought you'd think it was funny and, well, maybe a bit sad.'

'Thank you.' She kissed him on the forehead and

turned out the light.

'Should we help him?' Alex's soft voice seemed louder, in the dark.

'Let's think about it,' she said, not knowing what to think. 'Did he give you money?'

'Now that *is* a secret,' he replied in an American accent and sniggered.

Secrets. Alex had them. Patrick had them. She had them: shameful secrets like her father's crimes; like her flirtation with Mars.

Her eyes itched and her nose tingled and she thought of Patrick cradling a lonely pint in the Deptford Arms, half-watching football, half-watching the new owners of riverside apartments eyeing the bar menu and shaking their heads. Patrick would be scratching a spot she'd noticed on his forehead, thinking about home perhaps, and wondering in which part of this pub Christopher Marlowe had been murdered.

Chapter Twenty-one

As Ophelia walked to chambers, a light south-westerly breeze lifted the hair from her neck and a teasing Indian summer sun tickled her cheeks. The black roads were printed with gold and brown leaf patterns and she realised she was feeling more cheerful than she expected to be on the morning of this difficult case. There was always something exciting about the first day of a trial, even a depressing one. The freshly starched tabs on her lace collarette, like an ironed tablecloth in a restaurant, raised an expectation of performance, and the uncertainty as to where everyone would sit and how they'd behave was like a first day at school. And then there was the suspense as to how the trial would go, what unpromising arguments would suddenly gather momentum, who, in spite of the odds, would actually win.

Samuel was in his room wearing a fine black wool suit, flapping his hands and fussing like a cartoon hen that kept losing her chicks. 'Now *where* did I leave my coloured pens? I have to have my coloured pens. Ophelia dear, do *you* have any coloured pens?' He was picking up and putting down everything on his desk and table, auction catalogues, letters, ink well, photographs of Marcia and his daughter, and then starting at the beginning again.

'Might they already be in your bag?'

'That was the *first* place I looked.' Still, he went over to the big bag by the door and unzipped the top section.

'Well, here they are! How extraordinary. And where did I put my gloves?'

'I think I can see them poking out of your coat pocket. Shall we start walking to court? We can talk about everything on the way.' The longer they spent in his room the less ready he got.

'Good, yes…' He started opening his bag anyway, getting things out of it, putting them in again.

'Are your robes at court?'

That seemed to decide him. He zipped up the bag and pulled its handle up. 'In my locker. Let's go.'

She'd imagined them walking slowly and chatting, letting the fresh autumn air into their lungs as an antidote to the dusty heating and orange lights of the Bailey, but he hailed a cab.

Usually he would chat continually in taxis, as careless of confidentiality as he was of seat belts, but this time he just sat and stared out of the window in front of them as though he were exhausted already. The cab drew up outside the Old Bailey. Samuel patted his pockets. 'Sorry, Ophelia, can't find my wallet…'

She hopped out and paid. Samuel got out of the cab slowly.

'You run along and talk to the client. I may be a little while.' He was checking the pockets of his bag.

Ophelia got into her court robes but didn't go to the cells. After their last exchange she couldn't face Godwin alone. She waited outside court, hoping the solicitor would fill her in.

Jane Gilhooly, in a vivid blue jacket, approached her with a smile.

'Good morning! Is Samuel here?'

'Yes, he's upstairs changing. How's Mr Godwin?'

'Looking forward to the cross-examination of Betsy. That's what's been keeping him buoyant in prison.'

'Did the Peakes lose their surety money?'

'No. No one's bothered to follow that up.'

'Good.' Ophelia had been feeling responsible for talking Mrs Peake into that ill-advised arrangement.

Jane Gilhooly obviously felt awkward with nothing to do. After looking up and down the concourse she said, 'I'm just going to sort out my papers in court', and disappeared through the swing doors.

Neither Samuel nor the prosecutor arrived until the tannoy called them into court, and Ophelia knew that they would have been talking in the men's robing room. Men seemed to spend longer getting dressed here than the women did. It might be partly because they had those impossible stiff collars to struggle with, but she suspected it was mainly because their room was bigger and didn't smell of gravy. Or maybe they just liked time away from women. Samuel and the prosecutor sauntered into court like old friends.

The fifteen men and women from whom the jury would be selected were shepherded into court, stepping on each other's toes, bumping handbags, unsure where to stand. The clerk picked up their name cards. They were small enough to fit in her hand. She read out the names portentously, as though mustering an army from a group of reluctant conscripts.

When all the jurors were sworn in and the extras despatched, the judge put on a special folksy voice and told them not to talk to their families about the case, however tempting it was. Then, rather stiffly, as though he resented anyone other than himself talking in his court, he called on Mr Wynn, the prosecutor, to open the case.

Mr Wynn was not an eloquent man, but the story he told

was compelling enough and Ophelia noted how the men, especially, winced as he described Mr Godwin's casual seduction of his disabled fifteen-year-old stepdaughter. Samuel, as always when a prosecutor told the jury his side of the case, appeared to pay absolutely no attention, and fiddled conspicuously with his files.

Betsy York was the first witness. She walked proudly into court dressed all in white – like Samuel's 'innocent' files – and she wore her name conveniently stamped in large cursive letters of gold around her neck. Gold hearts bobbed from her ears. Her hair was long, worn high and black, her face taut and pointy and her lips protruded, as though she'd had plastic surgery.

'It was hard,' she said, 'when my husband went to prison. I had no money and no one to help me with my daughter Trish. Robert Godwin was nice to me. He bought me jewellery and he had a good job. Scaffolder. Cash in hand. He said he loved me but maybe he was just interested in Trish. He liked to spend time with her doing boring things. Trish loved the attention, poor kid. No one else looked at her after she got beaten up.'

'When was that?' the prosecutor asked.

'She was twelve, so it was just after I met Robert. She was assaulted by a boy at the bus stop. After that, she had a scar and walked funny and wouldn't look you in the eye. She didn't learn good either. Trish was in a sorry state and that was what Robert took advantage of.'

'What did Robert Godwin do?'

'When she was twelve he played stupid games with her and they laughed like idiots. When she was fifteen I started to leave her with Robert cos I had a job in a hair salon and Trish scared the customers. Then last September Trish started to beg me not to go. I didn't catch on till January, when Trish told me everything.'

The prosecutor drew out the details. Betsy said Trish had said it started when she was fifteen. Robert had made her watch porn and made her have sex in nylon tights… She gave a whole catalogue of sordid details.

Samuel got to his feet. He laid traps for Betsy quietly and with such a minimum of fuss that she didn't see them coming.

'Were you an attentive mother?'

'Yes,' Betsy smiled and ran her finger to and fro under her necklace.

'And Trish was your only child?'

'That's what I said.'

'It was you who nursed her after the bus-stop incident?' Samuel's voice was full of understanding and encouragement.

'Yeah. I was up all hours.' She was pleased to talk about her sacrifices.

'And you got her to wear a special high shoe.'

'I did.'

'And you filled in all the forms and did all the work for the compensation hearing.' Samuel sounded impressed.

'Yes. It took me a year.'

'But it was worth it. You did well?'

'I got ten grand.'

'Where is that money now?' He asked the question without inflexion.

Betsy looked annoyed and confused. 'It's in an account.'

'Where?'

'In a bank.'

'Which one?'

'I dunno. Judge, what's this got to do with anything?' She turned fuming to the judge.

Samuel whispered to Ophelia, 'She used it to do her face, didn't she?'

Ophelia smiled at his shrewdness and nodded.

'You are coming to the point, I hope?' the judge said, raising an eyebrow at Samuel.

'Of course, My Lord.' Samuel winked at the jury and some of them smiled back. Samuel turned back to Betsy. 'Mrs York, you took care that Trish always wore those shoes, didn't you, for two years before making the claim?'

'I did.' She was proud of this.

'Trish didn't like it but she did as she was told?'

'I made sure of that.'

'As you always do,' Samuel said, more a comment than a question. He looked at the jury to make sure they'd heard this exchange. Betsy's words resonated with an edge of menace in the space Samuel had left for them.

Betsy, sensing her position was slipping, put in, 'I'm a good mum.'

'Yes,' Samuel said. 'It was you who kept the birth certificate and all Trish's papers?'

'Of course, I had sole care.'

'And you gave them to the police?'

'Yes.'

Samuel asked for the birth certificate to be shown to the witness.

'Do you see the year of birth is smudged? It looks like it's been changed. Did you make a correction on the birth certificate, to fit with your case that she was only fifteen when you started work at the salon?'

Betsy slammed her hands down on the wooden ledge in front of her. 'Are you accusing me of forgery and not knowing my baby's date of birth? Of course not.'

Samuel asked for the passport to be shown next. The jury

rustled in their seats, loving this. Betsy glanced carelessly at the passport.

'You see the date of birth at the back?'

She made heavy weather of finding the place.

'You see it's a year earlier than the date on the certificate, the date you tell us was Trish's real date of birth?'

She shut the passport with a snap. 'Well, it's a mistake.'

'Have you spent the compensation money?'

Betsy looked to the judge for help, but he just looked down at his notebook. 'What on God's earth would I do with all that money?' she asked Samuel.

Samuel said neutrally, 'Some women have expensive surgery to their faces.'

Betsy looked so angry it seemed she might burst into flames. A couple of women on the jury tittered.

Betsy said she wanted to leave, that the barrister was insulting her. The judge looked up from his notebook, as though summoned back from a faraway place. Ophelia reflected how little judges liked to argue with QCs, whereas criticising juniors was considered a perk of their job.

'Please avoid speculation, Mr Slidders,' the judge said.

Samuel went for the jugular, pointing his pencil at Betsy. 'Did you get your "obedient" daughter to make up the rape so you could have a pop at some more compensation?'

Betsy nearly stormed out, but then a more devastating idea came to her. She stared at Godwin in the dock, not speaking. After what felt like two minutes, she said, focusing just on him, though every eye in the room was on her, 'You are a pervert, Robert Godwin, a kid-abusing pervert. You've done it before and, if you get out of here, you'll do it again. You will rot in hell.'

Her words seemed to echo long after she'd spoken, as

if she were a prophetess.

Trish's evidence was all given by TV link, so her presence was shrunk down to a small head on a small screen. The evidence for the prosecution was just the pre-recorded police interview, where a police officer spent half an hour asking her about her favourite films (Trish couldn't remember what they were called and gave incoherent summaries of the plots). Eventually they got onto the allegation. 'There were afternoons on the sofa. Mum was at the salon. Robert made me have sex and watch nasty films. Maybe six times.'

That was it.

Samuel took off his wig and peered at her through the link with an avuncular expression.

'Was Robert nice to you, Trish?'

'Yes.'

'Did he say you should take off the funny built-up shoe your mother made you wear to see if you could walk normally?'

'Yes.'

'And you could walk properly then?'

'Yes. It was better then.'

'And he brought you comic books?'

'Yes.'

'And that was how he taught you to read, when you were twelve?'

'Yes.' She paused and then said, 'That is when it started to happen.'

Everyone in court jolted at that.

'But you told the police it happened when your mother was at the salon, when you were fifteen.'

'Yes.'

'Not twelve.'

'Well, I was twelve.'

'But the police officer asked you this same question, when did it start, and you said it was when your mother went to the salon.'

'Yes.'

'And you told the police officer you were telling the truth, didn't you?'

'I was confused.'

'And actually you were sixteen when your mother went to the salon, weren't you?'

'I don't know.'

'When you went to court before, for the assault at the bus stop when you were twelve, you repeated what your mother told you to say?'

'Yes.'

'And in your interview with the police this time, you said what your mum told you to say?'

'Yes.'

'You were seeing someone when your mum was at work at the salon, weren't you?'

Trish looked confused. 'Yeah.'

'But that was Ron, not Robert Godwin, wasn't it?'

Trish looked unhappy then, as though he had touched on something she couldn't admit. 'N-no,' she said.

'Robert Godwin never did anything to hurt you, did he?'

'No.'

Samuel nodded as though she'd just said Godwin was innocent. Which she hadn't, quite. Ophelia thought she seemed a very natural sort of witness, but the picture she sketched of Godwin's parenting made her shudder. He loved her, but everything about him was wrong.

The screen switched back to the prosecutor and he asked, 'You said you told the police what your mother told you to say. Was what you said true?'

'Yes.'

The prosecutor called some more evidence, but nothing became any clearer and when the prosecutor closed his case, Samuel asked for the jury to retire.

Samuel told the judge there was no case for his client to answer. The girl's evidence in cross-examination was totally at odds with the charge. The sex, she said, happened when she was twelve, not when her mother went to work in the salon. Betsy York went to the salon when Trish was fifteen, according to Betsy, who seemed to base her evidence on Trish's birth certificate. In fact, the birth certificate looked faked and it was at odds with the passport, so Trish would have been sixteen, and over the age of consent, at that point. Given the uncertainty about when the conduct was said to have taken place, and given the complete absence of any telling details or forensic material, a conviction in these circumstances would be unsafe. It was the judge's duty, he said, to direct the jury to acquit the defendant.

The judge did not agree. 'The girl is a little vague on her dates but the substance of the case is there,' he said. 'It is a matter for the jury. We'll hear from Mr Godwin tomorrow.' Court rose for the day and Ophelia's head and body felt as numb and swollen as if she'd been travelling all day in an aeroplane. Samuel also seemed to have none of his bounce.

They went, mechanically, to the cells to see Godwin. They didn't even exchange words in the lift, though it was empty.

Godwin too seemed unwilling to talk. When they asked him if he had any comments, he shrugged his shoulders.

'When you are in the box tomorrow,' Samuel said, 'just keep it simple.' Godwin nodded, as if he understood completely.

In the taxi back they still didn't speak. Ophelia worried about two things: Betsy's prophecy and Trish's shift in her evidence. Why had Trish said Godwin had abused her when she was twelve, unless it was true? It could not have been Betsy's idea. Ophelia couldn't think of an answer to this. Maybe Samuel would, but he looked like he needed a cup of tea before talking about anything.

As they got out of the taxi, Samuel said, 'Hang on, my dear. Let me pay and then I have a favour to ask you.' He even had his wallet.

He took her arm and walked, leaning into her, into chambers. He said, 'Ophelia dear, my daughter is coming to visit me and I would very much like you to meet her.'

She'd wanted to have a quick chat about Godwin and then get back to Alex. After her failure to make the rugby match, and their argument over Edward, she should be there. If necessary they could talk about Godwin in the morning.

'I'd love to meet her one day but today is difficult…'

Ophelia saw a shadow fall over Samuel's face, a disappointment with her and with the world, and she relented. 'Maybe a very quick meeting…?'

He brightened instantly. 'Thank you. You see, I think she'd make a brilliant barrister, if she set her mind to it. Because of me, she thinks it's a boring old man's job. But if she met you, she'd see what fun she could have!' He patted Ophelia's sleeve encouragingly.

She felt the irony of this: their case at the moment was very far from fun. She noticed also that Samuel was very animated now, and it made her realise he'd been distinctly lacklustre most of the day.

It was chaos in the clerks' room. Five o'clock was the time of day when cases came last minute into the list and there weren't enough bodies to throw at the crises. Papers had to be shifted out or swapped around and solicitors called to say it's not Miss Smith but Mr Brown who's doing your case, and

Miss Smith and Mr Brown had to be told too and everyone felt stressed, except for John, who seemed to find it thrilling, spinning so many plates at once. Samuel, impervious to everything, went and stood next to Bill's desk. He told Bill (though Bill appeared to be halfway through a phone conversation at the time) that his daughter was coming and could he *please* look after her and phone him straight away *and* find Betty to make some tea.

Bill, busy and senior though he was, interrupted his call to reply, 'Yes, of course, Mr Slidders. We'll take her right up…'

Samuel bustled around his room like an anxious host. He even plumped up the cushions on the blue chairs. He looked at his watch.

'Sara should be here any minute. I'll just go to the loo.' He went out.

A minute later there was a knock on the door and Bill's head appeared.

'Oh, hello, Miss Dormandy. I have Mr Slidders' daughter here for him.'

Bill opened the door and showed in a tall, large-boned young woman whose face was almost entirely hidden behind a thicket of orange hair. She wore a floppy green T-shirt cut wide at the neck with pinking shears, a patchwork skirt she might have made herself and wooden clogs. She was probably in her early twenties. All Ophelia knew was that Sara was Samuel's only child. Ophelia got up and offered her a hand:

'Hello, you must be Sara. I'm Ophelia. I'm often your father's junior, his assistant in a case.'

Sara shook her hand and swung the mass of hair off to one side, revealing a gentle face with large features rather like Samuel's, but fleshier.

Bill, in the doorway, cleared his throat. 'I'll be going then,' he said, and disappeared.

'I've heard a lot about you,' Sara said.

'Your father's been very excited about you coming. He won't be long. Come and sit down.' She saw Sara heading towards one of the blue chairs and she feared Samuel would feel let down if his daughter sat there. 'Try the bergère. It's his favourite.'

Sara giggled, rolled her eyes and sat down on Samuel's chair. And then Samuel appeared in the doorway, beaming.

'Sara, how good you've come. So you've met Ophelia, that's the main thing. Now, we'll have some tea together. I'll call Betty. Maybe see if she could run over to Bellamy's for some cakes.'

'Thanks, Dad, but I don't want anything. I thought we were going home quickly?'

'Oh, you must have a cup of tea at least. I'll call Betty.' And without waiting for a reply, he picked up the phone and ordered his usual and Earl Grey with lemon for Sara and normal tea with milk for Ophelia.

'So, do you like my room, dear? I'm glad you found the best seat!'

'Yes, it's actually quite comfy. Where did the rug come from?' She pointed a chewed fingernail at the silk prayer mat by the fireplace. Samuel looked embarrassed, as though he didn't like to show off to his daughter and didn't know how to answer her. No wonder Sara didn't think his job was fun. It seemed as if he didn't tell her things.

'It was a gift from a Saudi sheik.'

Sara looked intrigued. 'Really, Dad? You never mentioned him.'

Samuel shrugged.

Ophelia felt Samuel wanted her to do the talking, today. 'The sheik's son held up a bank in Kensington with a cigarette lighter that looked like a gun. He thought it was a great joke but he might have got six years. Samuel got him off with just a fine, isn't that right?'

Samuel, forgetting his hatred of the blue chairs, came and sat on one and stroked the bright silk weave of the carpet. 'I mainly remember the fees in those days,' he said. 'That was when Ivan was our clerk. He used to charge like a wounded rhino.' Sara smiled nervously and looked at Ophelia, as though checking for the right response.

Ophelia, in a stage whisper she'd learned from Samuel, added, 'And he was a misogynist bastard.'

Sara blushed and Samuel grinned.

'I'll have nothing said against the man. Without him, Sara, we mightn't have been able to pay your school fees.'

The curtain of red hair fell back over her face. Maybe her father had embarrassed her. Parents were always good at that.

'Dad,' a small voice came from under the curtain, 'we should go soon. Mum is expecting us.'

'I know. We'll have our tea and go. Can't disappoint Betty now.'

'Did you take your pill?'

'Damn it, I forgot.' Samuel stood up and patted his pockets, a familiar gesture. 'Maybe I left them by the kettle earlier...' He opened the door and saw Betty about to come in, carrying the tea tray. 'Oh, Betty dear, you didn't see a little pill bottle, did you? I just can't think where I put it... ' Betty shook her head and he held the door for her to come i   n with the tea things. 'Thank you, dear. I'll just go and see if maybe I left it in the loo. Talk among yourselves,' he added, gesturing vaguely to Sara and Ophelia.

Ophelia gave Sara her tea and took a sip of her own. A

quietness filled the room, pregnant with things waiting to be said. Ophelia asked, tentatively, 'Is he not well?'

Sara started talking all in a rush. 'No, and the doctors say he should stop working, but he won't listen to us. He says it's what keeps him alive. But it's killing him. His heart is failing and the stress of this job is too much.'

So this was the real reason Samuel had wanted her to talk to his daughter. It wasn't to persuade Sara into the law, but to persuade her not to force him out of it.

'Should I remind him to take some medicine?'

Sara nodded and burrowed hurriedly in her woven bag. She pulled out a chewed biro and a scrumpled leaflet and scribbled fast.

'Here's my number. Will you call me if you think he has got worse, please?' Sara's hand trembled as she held the paper.

Ophelia took it quickly. 'Of course,' she whispered.

The door banged open and Samuel stood smiling at them, waving his pill bottle in triumph.

'All done.' He'd combed his hair again and he looked determined to be well. He sat down at the table and took up his tea. 'Good tea, ladies?' he asked before taking a sip. They nodded and he drank.

'So, Sara, did you get a chance to ask Ophelia how she likes the job?'

Sara blushed. 'Not yet.' She turned to Ophelia and asked tentatively, 'Do you love it?'

'Of course, when I'm working with Samuel. He makes everyone laugh. Juries love him.'

Sara leaned a little further forward and asked, slightly stammering: 'B-but isn't it hard defending people when you know they're guilty?'

Ophelia spoke intently, as though she was answering this

question for the first time in her career. 'You almost never know, for sure. So long as they say they didn't do it you have to go with that, however improbable their story seems. Actually, it's far worse defending someone who might be innocent, who might get convicted for something they didn't do.' She looked over at Samuel and he winked.

Sara breathed in quickly. 'Has that ever happened to you?'

Ophelia turned to her. 'Nearly.'

Ophelia found it strange seeing Samuel in Sara's face. Samuel was so complete and fully realised. That was what happened if you spent a lifetime doing something you were good at. Sara was much the reverse, full of vague ideas and flashes of emotion and confusion. But that didn't mean, Ophelia told herself, that Sara was wrong about her dad. The law had been Samuel's life, but maybe it shouldn't be any more.

Samuel got to his feet. 'OK, Sara, we'd better go. Ophelia, see you here tomorrow at nine?'

Ophelia got up and left them together, feeling sickened. She should have guessed that he was ill. She'd had enough signs: his complexion, his tiredness, even his questions were not as sharp as they had been. She just didn't see things she didn't want to. It had been the same with Patrick. How low she felt. Samuel was the soul of chambers for her; its humanity and expertise; its fun and objectivity. She had to cherish him, and help him go.

She walked down to the river and stared across at the South Bank. The fairy lights along the river wall were missing odd bulbs, sometimes lacking power for a whole strip, like her father's Christmas lights.

Alex was waiting for her on the stairs.

'Darling, let me just get a drink,' she said. 'Go up and I'll come and see you in your room.'

But she didn't go straight up. As she was pouring her glass of wine, she saw a pile of unopened letters by the fridge. Admin seemed easier than talking tonight. Alex's school had given her another month to pay up. She filed the letters and threw away the rubbish, poured herself a second glass and then went upstairs.

He was sitting on his bed staring at the wall. 'That took a long time,' he said.

'Yes, sorry. Everything seems hard today. I just found out Samuel is sick and will have to retire.'

'Mmm,' he said, noncommittal.

'And my case is going badly. My client's wife just called him a pervert who would rot in hell and it sounded quite persuasive.'

'I thought all your clients were guilty? What's so special about this one?'

'I guess you're right. For some reason, I always want to rescue them anyway.'

'You care more about the guilty than the innocent?'

'No, I just meet them more often and they need me more.'

He nodded deeply, as if she'd said something significant. She rushed to change the conversation. 'So, school OK?' She guessed from the hunch of his shoulders that it wasn't going to be better than OK.

'Someone stole my rugby kit. I wasn't allowed to play.'

She did a quick calculation. That was about sixty-four pounds. 'How annoying and horrid. You did check lost property, didn't you?'

He frowned and let out an exasperated, 'Mu-um'.

'On Sunday I could take you to see some orchids a client of mine grew, if you like?'

He gave her a very disapproving look, as if to say, 'Why would you think I'd be interested in orchids?' The look might also mean: what are you thinking of, taking your son to a criminal's den? That would be a fair point too, she realised, wondering what had become of her judgement. Just because she wanted to show him something special, that didn't make it a good idea. In fact, it would have been an awful mistake. They might have bumped into Mars. Even if they didn't, the scene of her wrongdoing was sure to make her unhappy. No, she never wanted to go there again.

'You're right. Alex,' she said, kissing his forehead. 'I was being stupid. Again.'

He smiled up at her.

'Yeah, Mum, but don't beat yourself up about it.'

Chapter Twenty-two

Godwin went into the box. He couldn't keep his evidence simple and Samuel couldn't contain the volleys of fury his client felt bound to launch at Betsy, the police, even the judge. He was like a man possessed.

'No one cared for Trish like I did. I loved that little girl the moment I saw her. She was so lost. She turned away from you when she talked but she'd smile like the sun coming out if you were nice to her. Betsy never even kissed her. She used her to milk the system, that was it.'

'Tell us what you did with her when she was twelve.'

He spoke in an unstoppable rush. 'I got her to walk without those shoes so she wouldn't be a cripple. I got her comics and Disney films. I made her laugh. Betsy's jealous cos Trish loved me more. And last year Betsy went mental when she found out I was sleeping with another girl. That stuff about Trish and porn films and tights is all lies. Lies for revenge. It's killing me they got Trish to say that.' He balled his fists and rolled them in his eyes, as if to blind himself.

'Please, Mr Godwin, can you just stick to answering the questions?' Samuel said and the judge threw his pencil down on the desk. The jury were enjoying themselves. They sat on the edge of their seats, gripped by the bloodsport being played out in front of them.

Samuel tried to break down Godwin's account into

specifics but he always rushed into general blame and recrimination. He said what he had to say, as well as a lot of other stuff about Betsy's affairs and Trish's fling with Ron the builder and his own torrid thing with someone's sister. Life on the Kingston trailer park seemed a sinister saturnalia and Robert Godwin a man out of control.

At the end of his evidence, Mr Godwin said solemnly, 'I swear I am innocent, on my grandmother's grave.'

Ophelia remembered him telling her how fond he'd been of his grandmother. It seemed strange for him to drag her into this. It was as if Godwin felt the trial had become a battle for his soul and he wanted to invoke the power of his ancestor.

The prosecutor suggested he'd been nice to Trish only to get into her pants and he roared again, 'No, on my grandmother's grave.' This phrase became a refrain, his answer to every question, an incantation more than a reply.

By lunchtime, everyone was exhausted. The court broke early and Samuel said he was going to have a rest, if Ophelia didn't mind. She thought they ought to discuss speeches, but Samuel was an old pro, and he probably needed a rest more than any suggestions from her. Faced with the gloomy prospect of other barristers asking her how 'it' was going over a plate of soggy beef in the Bar Mess, she slipped away by herself, out into the streets of Smithfield.

The meat market was nearly closed. A few lorries were still drawn up by the ornately grand building and the streets were shiny from recent washing. There was a smell of bleach and fresh blood. Inside the purple and green gates, you could see rows of white chiller units, all empty. One or two men sauntered about pushing units back, rearranging meat hooks, shutting the great shiny clasps on the lorries, relaxed and cheerful after lugging animal carcasses through the night, knowing that their tasks were done now. She envied them.

She'd come here with Patrick once, after a party in north London. They had taken a long ramble afterwards, through streets which were dark and empty except when they came to club entrances where groups of young men and women gathered and hummed, like bees crowding in front of a hive. The strap on one of her sandals had broken but she'd limped, leaning on Patrick, ignoring the night buses that might have shortened their journey, happy to be together in quiet, night-struck London. And when they reached Smithfield, it was almost light and the hauliers were cheerful and loud and work-a-day and suddenly she'd felt hungry and, without consulting about it, they'd followed a group of men in bloody aprons into a brightly lit pub and ordered sausages and egg and beans, toast and tea, and they'd sat and eaten quietly in the midst of the men calling out to each other, buying pints and exchanging platitudes and it had seemed exotic and homely and delicious.

She returned to court with a heart as heavy as though it were her, not Godwin, who might be sent to prison. Samuel at least looked pleased to see her, and while the prosecutor gave his speech to the jury, he drew some dashes for letters and a gallows for a game of hangman. Mr Wynn's closing was more eloquent than his opening had been. The only consolation was that she guessed 'philanthropist' before the poor man on the gallows grew legs.

Samuel stood next and he almost worked his magic. He talked straight to the jury, making them sit up and feel their responsibility, and he relied on the mess of the evidence. 'How can you convict a man of something this serious when the witness doesn't even know when it actually took place? If this terrible thing had ever happened, she'd remember it her entire life, wouldn't she? Everyone remembers their first sexual experience. It would be all the more memorable if this was some forced act, if you had been, as the prosecutor suggests, groomed for this moment by your predatory stepfather…' He talked too about Betsy's cosmetic surgery and the missing money and Ophelia could see that the jury loved the mystery of it all, the chance to play Miss Marple.

He did not talk for long and when he sat down, she noticed that he sank lower than he had before.

The judge summed up for longer than either of the barristers; for longer, it felt, than the evidence had lasted, reading his notes of everything as he'd got it down. Eventually he stopped speaking and the ushers, Liz and Linda, according to their badges, held the Bible up high with their curling pink laminated nails and swore to keep the jury in some private and convenient place. It reminded Ophelia of a poem Patrick had read to her:

> *The grave's a fine and private place,*
> *But none I think do there embrace…*

The judge's voice cut into her reverie. 'Take him down,' he said as finally as if this was the end of his sentencing remarks, rather than a reminder that Godwin didn't have bail.

The jury only took twenty minutes to decide to convict Godwin. The judge gave him ten years. This time Mr Godwin made no sound at all.

'Shall we go and see him?' Ophelia asked Samuel as the jury filed out, not looking at them. It was a rhetorical question. They had to go.

Samuel sighed. 'My dear, I'm feeling a bit short of breath. I'd like to just sit here a while, if that's OK. Would you mind going alone?'

'Of course not,' she said, as lightly as she could. 'What shall I tell him about the possibility of appeal?'

'No appeal.'

She nodded.

———

The air in the cell was stale and smelled of hot dust and sweat and chewing gum. The chairs and table were screwed to the floor, so lawyer and client had to face each other head on with nothing between them but the chipped vinyl table.

Robert Godwin stared at it. Ophelia kept her eyes on his face. A vein pulsed in his temple. His mouth was set.

'Mr Slidders says we don't have any grounds for appeal,' she said.

He was silent and she waited, sensing something was brewing.

'I'm not guilty of those charges,' he said. 'I never had sex with her when her mum was at the salon. By then she was Ron's girl. Nothing to do with me. Though I loved her and I missed her. We were together before, but I never had sex with her after she was fourteen.' Tears hung in the corners of his eyes. 'I've lost her for ever now.'

Ophelia shuddered and kept her peace.

'I shouldn't have been convicted. There was nothing going on the time they said, and there was never any porn or funny business.' He turned on her. 'You and Slidders didn't put on a good enough show. You didn't scare Betsy.' His eyes were red and full of hate.

'She cursed me!' he shouted and his spit landed on Ophelia's face.

She kept her cool. 'Sometimes juries do rough justice. Trish said you had sex with her when she was under age. You admit that too. It might not have been on the dates on the indictment, but an indictment could have been drawn with those dates, with the same result we have now. It would have been the same offence and the penalty could have been worse.'

He stood up and brought his head within a few inches of hers. 'What do you know about rough justice? You've never had anything rough in your life. I'll give you rough justice.'

'Please sit down, Mr Godwin.'

'No. I will not sit down and listen to you telling me I got what I deserve. I will not sit down until I have made you understand, for ever, that you can't talk to a Godwin like this. The Godwins are proud and strong. We are the law, not you people in stupid wigs and bat cloaks. You, Miss Dormandy, understand nothing of justice, or of love.' He pointed a finger at her chest and his face was screwed up with fury and pain. 'I'll get you for this, Miss Dormandy.'

She backed away from him and banged on the cell door for the jailer to let her out. Godwin's mouth curled as he saw her fear and a gleam entered his eye. The jailer released her and she walked out of the cell without looking back.

Outside the court building, she turned on her phone. There were two texts. The first was from Paul.

Mrs K is on tomorrow. I told the family to pay up but I don't know if they will, or if you'll have to face Miss Fennick. Good luck. I'm in the Maldives.

The second was from an unknown number:

I know where you live. Godwin.

She felt anxiety bubble in her stomach and in her brain and her hands shook. Did Godwin have a hidden phone? It was possible. The jailers were careless. He'd have her number from when she tried to find him, when he broke bail. He was furious, but the real question was whether he was dangerous. He was in custody, after all. She could call Freia and tell her to watch out for strangers, but that was just the sort of panic Godwin was trying to create. No, the best thing to do was ignore him. Otherwise he'd won.

She went to find Samuel.

Chapter Twenty-three

It was dark when she got back to chambers and no light showed under Samuel's door. She was about to go when she thought she heard a faint noise, like a muffled sniff, from the other side of the door, so she knocked and pushed it open. The lights were all out but she could see the outlines of his furniture by the pale glow of ambient city light that fell over the garden and in through Samuel's generous windows. He was not at his desk or at the table. She thought she must have imagined the sound, and was about to go when she saw a slight hump in one of the ill-favoured armchairs.

'I'm here, Ophelia.' His voice was low and had a crack in it.

'Oh, good. I thought I'd missed you.' There was a long pause which she felt she should fill, but all she could think of was the threat from Godwin and she didn't want to distress him with that.

'I'm sorry, Ophelia. I lost that case. We could have won it, maybe, if I'd talked to you about it all more. I should have kept her on a tighter rein. I should never have left a gap when I asked her if Godwin taught her to read. It was obvious one thing would run into another.'

'But we didn't know there was an affair when she was twelve.'

'We should have known.'

'He has confessed it to me now.'

'Oh, I'm sorry about that. I should have come to see him with you afterwards. Now he'll want to turn you into his scapegoat.' He exhaled slowly. 'Defendants are so much trouble, aren't they? I think maybe my family are right. I'm too old and ill for this game now.'

Ophelia had to sit down. Her legs were failing under her, as though her heart were as weak as Samuel's. She felt it beating hard and fast. She dabbed at her damp eyes with her cuffs and put a hand gently on his knee.

'You were great, Samuel. There was nothing we could have done. You still have the magic, you know.'

He touched her hand lightly. 'Thank you, my dear. Now, will you help an old man with a bad heart get a taxi?'

'Of course, Samuel. I'd love to.'

He pulled himself up by her arm with a determined matter-of-factness, as though this was all quite normal. She didn't turn on the lights – he'd wanted to be in the dark – and they inched their way together to the door, Ophelia scanning the carpet for tripping hazards as they went.

Samuel went down the stairs in front of her and he didn't turn into the clerks' room to say goodnight. He pressed on out of the buildings to the railings in front where he leaned back, catching his breath.

It was raining, a fine drenching rain that found the gap between your neck and your coat collar, and came through your shoes, into your bones. 'Ughh,' he groaned, hunching up his shoulders and reaching for her arm.

On the main road, the cars' headlights made trails of gold on the wet tarmac, but no points of orange appeared above the numerous black cabs that sped away to the west, so she left Samuel by a lamp-post and crossed over to catch one of the cabs still heading east into the City, where everyone was wealthy enough, on a wet day, to hop into one without thinking what it would cost. A cab was bearing down on her fast, but suddenly she saw a man step out of an office up the road and run straight to the taxi as it began to slow. He put his hand on the handle and she bellowed at him, 'Nooo... we've been waiting for ages and the gentleman is sick.'

The man fell back instantly, chagrined. 'Oh, I'm so sorry.' She felt suddenly awkward too. Samuel could easily have heard her. Luckily, he looked surprised when the taxi turned in the road and pulled up next to him. She helped him in, doing up his seat belt, as if he were a child. She waved him goodbye with a cheerful smile. 'Safe home,' she said and then got out her mobile to text Sara:

Samuel in taxi home. Case lost. Morale low.

As she sent her message, more raindrops pearled on her phone screen and seeped up through her thin soles, soaking her nylon-sheathed toes. The wine shop looked bright, warm and dry and she stepped inside. She needed something to lift her spirits. There was a bottle of Spanish Albariño by the till, which reminded her of a long lunch with Patrick in Seville. She bought it and scurried to the bus stop, feeling the damp rising up her bones. When she sat down in the bus, she noticed that her wool suit smelled like an old sheep.

Chapter Twenty-four

Everything felt threatening as she got off the bus. The branches of the trees were so black they looked burnt and the tarmac glossy and molten as if it would stick to your skin. The cracks between the paving slabs were ominously wide and she remembered how, when she was a child, she thought that if you trod in such places bears would burst through and get you. As she walked down her street, she was surprised to see there were no lights on in her house.

She checked her watch. Five past eight. Alex should be in his pyjamas perhaps, but up and waiting for her. Freia should be getting herself ready to go out.

In her haste to get in she couldn't fit the key in the lock. She tried the bell. No one came. Eventually she got the key to work and switched on the hall light. There were two items on the floor, both white, both with writing on, and she found she didn't want to read either of them. She wished suddenly that she'd never learned to read, that she could just walk on ignorantly into her kitchen. But unfortunately, she could read, and once you knew how, you had to; it was just one of those things, a kind of curse. She picked up Freia's note first:

Alex has gone to Edward's so I am out with friends.

Just when she'd told him not to go there.

She picked up the second note. The envelope had nothing on it but her name. It must have been hand delivered.

My friend is watching your son.

She dropped the note, as if it burned her fingers. Who would send this, and who was the friend? It read like a threat. She felt herself falling through ice as, panicking, she thought, *Godwin.*

And Alex was not at home. She wanted to hold him to her and be sure he was safe. She'd told him not to go to Edward's and he'd ignored her. What else would he do, now he had broken his promise? With a predator like Godwin about, Fatima and Edward were no protection for him.

The house felt abandoned, as if its inhabitants had left in a hurry, fleeing some contagion or disaster. She felt it reaching for her too. She stuffed the notes in her bag and slammed the door shut, then turned and ran over the road. She rang on Edward's door. No one came. She rang again. And then again. A ghostly silver birch overhead shivered a confetti of yellow leaves around her. No sound came from inside the house, but lights burned on the ground floor and in the basement. She tried again.

Eventually Fatima came to the door. Ophelia did not even try to hide her agitation.

'I need to take Alex home now, please.' The words wobbled as they passed over her quivering lips.

'Alex? He's not here. Edward said they were going to *your* house.' Fatima was still and unemotional as a linen chest, and the boys were – gone! Ophelia could hardly speak.

'They aren't at my house. I've just come from there. When

did they leave, Fatima? When?' She was insistent now and Fatima was blinking at her.

'Maybe at seven?'

'That was an hour ago, at least! Fatima, they've been gone an hour! If they went to our house and found it locked, they would come back here. Could they have rung your bell here and you missed it?' She thought how long it had felt when she waited on the doorstep.

'No, I would hear. I am in my room downstairs.'

'But what did they say when they left? Where would they *go?*'

Fatima looked puzzled but not horrified. Maybe losing Edward didn't trouble her too much, but Ophelia felt she'd fallen off a cliff and the ground was spinning towards her.

'We must call the police. We must *search.*'

'You come in and use the phone?'

Ophelia nodded and walked in. There was a phone in the hall and she picked it up and dialled 999.

'Fire, police or ambulance?' She felt she needed them all, but she said 'Police.' There were some crackling noises and a voice gave her a reference number and asked her the problem.

'My son is missing. He is nine. He and his friend Edward who is thirteen have disappeared. A criminal is threatening me and he said in a note on my doormat tonight that he is watching my son. He is a paedophile. You must get him.'

'Where are you calling from, madam?'

'Camberwell.'

'We'll get the local police to contact you and we'll circulate a description. What do the boys look like?'

Suddenly she had no idea how to describe them, didn't even know how tall they were. 'Um, Alex Kelly, my son, is nine, brown sticky-up hair and quite tall, um, maybe four feet and blue eyes and freckles and big ears and chewed nails and his second toe is bigger than his big toe…' What was she saying? It was like she was talking to a morgue, the identifying features she was giving… 'and he was wearing – Fatima, what?'

Fatima looked stunned at being so suddenly addressed but she said, 'Both wearing jeans and hood jacket.'

'Jeans and a black hoodie. The other boy the same. He is older, thirteen, and taller. His hoodie is maybe grey. His hair is very short and he has a little diamond in his ear. And I'll give you my mobile so you can call me as soon as you find them…'

Ophelia stumbled over her number as she gave it, repeated herself, and found she was sweating and stammering as she asked when the local police would contact her. They told her to be patient. It would all be done soon.

'And the paedophile is Robert Godwin. He's just been convicted of child rape at the Bailey. He somehow got a message out here tonight. I want you to contact the Bailey and find out where he is and who his associates are…' Words failed her. How would they get to the bottom of this? She couldn't even tell them what prison he'd be taken to.

'Madam, this man who you think kidnapped your son is *currently* in prison somewhere?'

'Yes,' she said. 'But he may be in some paedophile ring. They stick together those guys.' She heard a reserved silence at the other end. 'They are always looking for fresh blood,' she added, desperately.

'Well, it will take some time to locate the prisoner within the prison service network.'

She wanted to scream but she knew there was no point. New prisoners often went missing in the system. 'Get them to call me as soon as they find him. And *get his phone!*

She hung up and stared wildly about her, confused about where she was and what to do. Somewhere out in the dark Alex was in danger, in greater danger with every minute that passed. She stumbled back out of the door, mumbling to Fatima to call her if the boys came back. And then she was in the dark in the shadows of the big trees, staring at dark shapes, hoping to see them move. Maybe Godwin's friend had lurked behind that camellia, watching the boys leave, following them.

She staggered down the road towards the pub. Had they gone there, perhaps? Alex always wanted a sip of beer if there was one to be had. His robot was an addict. The gentle-faced Irish publican might have taken them in. How she hoped he had. The closer she got, the more she persuaded herself that they were there, on old green leather seats under a chalky blackboard and dusty antlers, but the pavement cracks gaped at her and the lights seemed to sway and every shape she saw was suspect.

She almost fell on the bar. The publican, who always greeted her when she passed his pub, looked concerned.

A man at the bar touched her arm and asked, 'You alright, darling? Can I get you a drink?'

She shook her head vigorously and stared into all the corners of the pub. It was full of Londoners, art students and plumbers and teachers and men on their own with the crossword and women in pairs, chatting. Snatches of talk about politics and telly and family floated through the thick hot air, but there was no sign of the boys.

'I've lost my son. He and a friend are missing. You haven't seen two boys, nine and thirteen?'

The publican and the man at the bar looked shocked and edged away from her, as though her misfortune might be catching. No, they said, definitely no children had been in.

She staggered back on her heels, and the publican put a shot of whisky on the bar.

'Take it, love, on the house,' he said. She downed it, hoping it would steady her nerve.

'Thanks.' She replaced the glass on the counter and then tottered out uncertainly and stood on the street corner, looking at the passing vehicles and wondering, What if they'd been bundled into a car? They could be far away already by now. Her phone rang in her bag and she scrabbled for it.

It was the police; calm, trained, helpful. 'Miss Dormandy, we have three police cars in your area looking for the boys. We just need to ask you a few extra questions. You said there was a stalker?'

'Robert Godwin. I just represented him at the Bailey. He threatened me after the trial and then he sent me a text saying "I know where you live," and then I get home and there's this note on my doormat about watching my son, who is gone… Please, please follow up this lead. It's only a phone call.'

'Are you a criminal barrister?'

Did she, for a moment, detect a trace of amusement in the policeman's tone? Most police officers hated defence counsel.

'For my sins,' she said, and she meant it. She wished she'd never met anyone like Godwin in her life.

'Have you informed the boy's father?'

'No. I… I will now…'

'Is there any chance he could be with his father?'

'N-no.' Though how could she say?

'We'll put out a message to forces all over London, Miss Dormandy. Don't worry, we'll find them.'

How she wanted to believe in them! She'd spent her professional life picking holes in what they did, exposing their sloppiness, their dishonesty, and now everything rested on their eyes and ubiquity. She thanked them fulsomely, trying to make up, in that minute, for all the criticisms she had heaped on them for one and a half decades.

And then she called Patrick.

'Ophelia!' He sounded pleased and surprised and this made her feel seasick.

'Help me, Patrick. Alex is missing. He's gone out with his friend Edward and no one knows where they are. I'm at the green looking, but I can't find him and this horrible rapist I represented left a note at the house today saying "I am watching your son". He's in prison but he must have a friend... I don't know but maybe they've taken him, taken them...' She couldn't say anything else, didn't have the strength. She could imagine Patrick pulling at his long greying hair, his face contorted, his heart splitting, like hers, in the silence. But he was better than her in a crisis. He didn't speak till he was calm and sure of himself.

'I'm coming now, Ophelia. Don't worry, we'll find him. Have you told the police?'

She made a sort of agreeing noise through a sob and hung up. There was a shape in the doorway opposite which she had to investigate. As she drew closer it moved. It had a foot. And a can of cider. And a beard. She moved on.

In Wren Street she saw three boys in hoods sharing something out under the lamplight. She tried to make one of them Alex, wishing he were there, but the boys were bigger and they were black. A television set crashed out of a third floor window and a woman was screaming, 'Don't you dare bring her stuff in my house!' Music throbbed from a parked car with tinted windows. A man with grey hair and a stoop walked past. He was dressed from head to toe in grey camouflage and he had an unlit cigarette dangling from his lips. She passed on through the desolate shopping arcade, past the closing down pound stores and the long-gone bookshop. Only McDonalds was busy. She stepped into the orange glare to look around. More hoodies, but not the right ones, and mothers with small children. Shouldn't they be in bed? she thought and then wondered at the irony of her dictating mothering to anyone. She went to the crowded bus stop and hunted among the hunched dark figures, struck by their isolation. No one talked at bus stops, even when they came in pairs; lives suspended in waiting. Her life felt suspended too. She hardly felt she was breathing as she wandered, all eyes, north, west, east and then south again in the shadows, a soul in limbo.

Eventually her feet ached so much that she had to acknowledge them. She was at the green now, by a bench, so she let herself collapse down onto it and looked at her watch. She'd been ricocheting around the same streets for two hours without a clue. She stared at the sealed pebbles of the path beneath her and she thought of Alex on the beach in Brighton when he was four. How pleased he'd been with the wet glistening stones, all deep orange and blue with white flecks, how he kept picking them up with a cry – 'Oh look, pretty pebble!' – and putting them in his pockets until he could hardly move, and then putting them in her pockets too. He said he was going to start a stone museum and charge visitors a pound. He was going to add in the bits of plate he'd found in the mews so he had lots of things to show. But when they got home and the pebbles were dry they looked quite dull and he lost interest in the museum. She'd put them under the privet hedge in the front garden, in a small pile. They were still there, she guessed, like stones on a Jewish grave.

Her head was too heavy for all its grief and she cradled it in her hands, letting the tears run through her fingers and down the backs of her hands.

'Alright, darling?' A man with a can sitting next to her,peered into her face, like a nurse checking a patient for dangerous symptoms.

His face was pale but weathered, with eczema patches under his eyes and a fine tracery of broken veins on his nose and cheeks. His eyes were dark and haunted and his body smelled, as hers might if she stayed out like this for days and days, which, perhaps, she would. He raised his can.

'Only ninety-nine pence at the Green. I'd give you some, but it's empty.' He looked genuinely sorry not to help, and peered down the hole to check there wasn't a drop to offer her.

She remembered the Spanish Albariño in her bag and pulled it out. 'Have this,' she said.

He looked at it and then at her, as though she were a visiting angel.

'You *sure*? You first,' he said, gallantly.

Drunks were meant to lie and cheat for drink, not give it away, and yet here he was, offering her what was now, by rights, his bottle. He seemed pretty moved by his own generosity too. Tears balanced in the corners of his smiling eyes and he was rubbing his legs with anticipation. None of this was helping Alex, of course. She felt limp with despair. She could think of nothing to do but stay out on this strange vigil. So many people passed through the green every day that, by statistical laws, Alex must too and if she was here at the heart of the chaos, then whatever was happening to him would happen to her too. And so, she reasoned, in some way they were together, even now.

Except that they so obviously weren't. She found, as when she was trying to describe him to the police, that she could hardly call Alex's face to mind. He was becoming an abstract epitome of pure loss. She felt bestial for still breathing, sitting and responding to the kindness of this stranger.

The drunk made a jabbing gesture at the bottle, which she took to mean, *get on with it* and so she unscrewed the top and took one big swig, and then another. It made her eyes smart and her body tingle. She handed it over. 'All yours.'

And just at that moment, as the drunk took the bottle with a jubilant chuckle, she saw Patrick coming towards her almost at a run, his hair sticking out at all angles and his face white. She shot to her feet, blushing to think how Patrick was finding her. And then her despair washed over her again and she staggered back onto the bench. Nothing mattered now.

Patrick's hands closed around her, lifting her away, and she smelt his familiar slightly spicy smell. He was peering into her face, looking for answers to so many unasked questions. She felt she could hear them all and answer very few of them. She shook her head.

He let her go slowly, checking her stability, and asked-softly, 'Where have you been? I've been looking for you as well as Alex. Why didn't you answer your phone?'

Perhaps the police had rung too, perhaps her mobile had been ringing and ringing continually, muffled by the garbage she carried around with her and by the noise of the street. She dropped her bag on the bench as though it was on fire and reached in to hunt out the phone, hope quivering in her fingertips. She felt Patrick vibrating beside her like a tuning fork; she could hear the pitch of his anxiety; felt it vibrate in her sinews too. Three missed calls... all from Patrick. She shook her head again.

'Nothing from the police. I'll hold it in my hand now, so we can hear if...'

Patrick nodded and steered her away from the bench where the drunk had retreated with his bottle into the corner.

Patrick threaded his arm into hers, as he used to when they walked around London in happier times but this sort of comfort seemed wrong and she pulled away. Who was touching Alex's arm now?

'Tell me what has been going on.' He spoke firmly and clearly, like a parent, like she should have been.

She didn't look at him, but she pulled him by the end of his ribbed corduroy sleeve and began to say everything she could think of. She directed them along Church Street as she talked, looking in doorways and up at windows and letting the words flow out of her unchecked.

She told him about looking for Alex at Edward's house, and how she'd forbidden him from going there. She told him how Alex had said he wanted to leave London so he could have more freedom and how she'd said London would be a great place for adventures, when he got older, 'I said that we'd had lots of adventures here... Maybe I encouraged this?'

'No, Ophelia. Don't blame yourself.'

She held his arm to stop herself stumbling as she started to cry again. She sobbed so hard she was almost incoherent as she told him about Godwin and Betsy and Trish and all the threats and despair.

Patrick turned white at this, but he said nothing for a while. He directed her into a side road by the magistrates' courts, where there were quiet spaces and ill-tended gardens. Occasional passers-by hurried along the street, slightly hunched. No one lingered. It was cold now and her left hand, still gripping the phone, began to ache. Patrick cleared his throat and then paused, as if he was about to say something difficult.

'I think we should go with the simplest explanation, that he's just gone absent without leave.'

The chill that gripped her chest eased a little. Patrick went on, not looking at her.

'When I was a boy, even as young as Alex, I was often very bad. I took money from my mum's purse and sneaked out of my bedroom window to go to the sweet shop. At night, when I couldn't sleep, I would climb out. One night I broke the window of the post office with a half-brick from the lane. I didn't mean to worry anyone, but I wanted to know what it was like to do things I wasn't meant to. I wanted to work stuff out for myself. If I think where I'd go, if I were Alex, it could be… anywhere. And Edward? I don't know him. You said he's older? He probably has some plan. Alex will follow Edward. Does Edward do drugs?'

'Drugs?' She was stunned at the thought and at her failure to think it for herself. She squeezed his arm tighter.

'Where do they deal drugs round here? You should know. You probably represent them all. He'll have heard all about it from you.'

She shivered at this sharp side wind. He was making a fair point, but was he blaming her for the criminality of Camberwell, and corrupting their son?

'I thought you were the one who knew about what bad boys did?' she said, stepping away from him.

He took her hand gently, as if it was something delicate he needed to keep safe. 'I'm sorry, Ophelia. I didn't mean this was your fault. It's mine, if anyone's. But come on. Let's find him. I'm sure he's quite close. He doesn't like walking very much, unless as part of some sporting activity.'

She squeezed his hand very hard. It was probably all just old talk, but he was beginning to make her feel Alex might be almost safe.

'Let's head for Brixton,' he said and directed them south. She stared into the crowded late-night bakery on Coldharbour

Lane. It was like a family gathering in there, lots of people in a cheerful huddle, none of them remotely like Alex. Out on the street, two drunk girls were giggling and pushing at each other. If only Alex and Edward were just out enjoying themselves like them. Ophelia glanced at Patrick's face for reassurance, but the frown-line down the middle of his forehead was so deep he looked as though he might split in two. Maybe she looked like that too.

Once she'd felt that they were two halves made complete by being together, each with their own rough edges and defects corrected by the other's gifts. Except that they'd turned out not to be perfect halves and now it felt they were splitting again, not from each other this time, but from themselves, like cells mitosing under a microscope. There would be no original Patrick or Ophelia any more and their new, multiplied selves would act in various basically human ways, but there would be no reason for any of it, no soul. Without Alex, they were nothing. Suddenly she could see Alex, as she first saw him, his head pointy, his chin gently receding for better access to the breast.

'You remember the day he was born, how grumpy and old he looked?'

Patrick nodded and frowned deeper, if that were possible, and his eyes took on a concentrated glow, as though he were trying to conjure the boy back with an effort of the imagination. Ophelia went on, trying to conjure him too, 'He looked like my grandfather after discovering someone had drunk his best port, except that he didn't swear. Remember how he curled up his pink wrinkled fingers and jabbed at the air? And then he started to feed and became soft and smooth and plump as a baby.'

'Which he still is.'

'Yes – the way he tries out different voices, it's like he's still learning to talk. I'll never forget that language he used to speak that sounded like Russian, when he was one…'

'…And how he loved the stairs?' His hand reached for hers and she squeezed it, passing the memory between them, making Alex real again, an umbilical cord of parental love.

'And the moon,' she whispered, looking at it above the trees, round, solid and orange as a half of his birthday cake. And then she thought of his party, of all those boys who weren't very like him, and Edward, indifferent, passing through. Alex had tried to keep up with the jokes. He must have tried to keep up with other habits of Edward's. And now she thought about it, he had seemed spaced out after seeing Edward. Perhaps Alex's character, his dreaminess, his lack of confidence and clarity would make him vulnerable to the promise of a drug-altered world. She tried to push this thought from her mind, crunching Patrick's hand bones in hers as she had, so many years earlier, with the pain of labour.

The phone rang in her hand: a withheld number.

'Hello?'

'Miss Dormandy, we've found two boys matching your description but not giving the right names. Could you come down to Peckham Station right away?' Her heart leapt and rebounded. They were found – or weren't they? Alex must be there. She could picture him, blushing, unable to meet her eye, but quivering with relief at his rescue.

'Yes!' she replied and turned to Patrick. 'We've got to get to Peckham Police Station, now!'

They were just feet away from the main road and Patrick sprinted up to the line of traffic. A double-decker bus was pulling up at the bus stop, and behind it she could see that rare thing for Camberwell – a taxi with its light on. Patrick was doing his ear-splitting whistle and waving a desperate hand, but she saw the taxi accelerating out to get past the bus. She saw Patrick turn, almost in mid-air, and head for the front of the bus so he could cut off the taxi on the other side. He was fast, but the cars seemed faster. Patrick flung himself out into the road four feet in front of the bus stop, far into the outside lane, to where the taxi ought to appear, and suddenly it seemed as if a double disaster was going to befall them. She shut her eyes and heard the slow belch of a bus halting and the squeak of turning wheels, the tick of an indicator. She waited for whatever dull thud might follow. She looked up and there was Patrick holding open the door of the cab, flushed but alive, and she felt blessed, light on her feet, free in her heart. Alex and Patrick, both safe: what she had lost, found.

She jumped into the taxi with a coltish toss of her head and a cry: 'Yes!' But Patrick was staring at her, waiting for details and she had to shake herself back into the facts, into the reality that they didn't know for sure that it was Alex at the police station. 'They've got boys who look right, but they're giving the wrong names.'

Patrick clapped his hands. 'Well, what would you expect?' They didn't talk. They both looked forward, willing the cab on through amber lights, tense, hopeful of what the police station would bring them.

The irony of her position didn't escape Ophelia. She still remembered how she'd hated the detective constable who had arrested her father. They'd come in uniform, at six in the morning, with the national press. They hadn't waited for the door to be opened at their knock. Instead, they'd spoken through a loudspeaker, in case anyone in the street might miss the event, telling the Dormandys to open up in the name of the law, like it was some sort of period drama. Certainly it was a comedy, from the way they'd swaggered and crashed into things, the way they had told her mother they 'wouldn't say no to a cup of tea'.

'You've got to come with us now, but don't worry,' DC Hays had told her father, bleary from just waking up, hastily dressed, not yet sharp enough to see the trap. 'We've got a blanket here for you to cover your face so it doesn't get plastered over the papers.' Papers they'd tipped off, of course. He'd thanked Hays sincerely and stooped so he could droop that awful rug of shame over his bowed head and swiftly, before he could repent, they'd led him out into the flash of the cameras, a man ashamed to show his face, a man disgraced. This must have helped to kill him. The heart attack had been a month later.

Their cab stopped and Patrick was on the pavement, handing the driver ten pounds for a six-pound fare, saying, 'Keep the change, mate.' He even opened the police station door for her.

Chapter Twenty-five

Peckham Police Station was not designed for joy. There were a couple of benches along one wall facing a photofit image with the words 'Have you seen this man?' above a face that was far from human. A perspex cubicle ('Keep door shut to maintain privacy') imprisoned the first in line. A woman was at the counter.

'I don't know when I lost my phone. Somewhere at the train station. Please, can't you just give me a reference number?'

The policeman shook his head. He was filling out a form slowly, in capital letters. He spelled out his words aloud: 'AWARE OF LOST AT STATION.'

Ophelia could feel Patrick beside her, taut, waiting for her to take action. She stepped away from him and pushed open the door. The woman and the policeman looked at her angrily, united at last.

'Sorry, but I just have to know – did you find my lost child?'

The officer slapped his right hand down on the desk, like a film judge with his gavel.

'You should wait your turn, but if you give me a minute I'll get you the inspector.'

He had turned away before she could be grateful. A minute later he was back, this time with a man with even more shiny buttons and a long, lined face. His eyes twinkled when he saw Ophelia.

'Miss Dormandy, I presume? Do come with me.' He opened up the desktop and came into the cubicle, offering his hand. 'Inspector Brown.'

Ophelia nodded and gestured to Patrick, who joined them. 'This is Alex's father, Patrick Kelly.'

The inspector shook hands with them both and then led them into a long corridor. They passed interview rooms and a room showing CCTV footage, a canteen, shelves of dusty papers, tape machines, polystyrene cups. He showed them into a small office and offered them a seat and a chocolate biscuit, McVities, like in chambers.

'Have you got a photograph of Alex?' the inspector asked. 'We need to be satisfied of your connection with him.'

She had a passport snap in her wallet, all his colour washed out by the white light; a mugshot. She gave it to him. Patrick also reached inside his jacket and produced a photograph. His photograph was much better. It showed Alex, flushed and happy, wearing his new Arsenal strip and holding a football. The inspector grinned at them.

'Yes, we have your boy. He gave us the name Orlando Dormandy when we stopped him, and he's stuck to it ever since. Great sticking power, that boy has, and confidence. Said he couldn't be arrested because he was under the age of criminal responsibility. Made us look it up! But he must be older than nine? He's very articulate.'

Ophelia couldn't stop herself from jumping to her feet and reaching out her hands to the inspector. If Patrick hadn't been there, maybe she'd have embraced him. His deep -creased humanity made her regret all the bad things she had ever said about the police. Perhaps he understood some of this as he offered her his hand so she could turn her waving into an appropriate gesture.

Patrick was more dignified and knew what to say. 'Thank you, Inspector. Orlando Dormandy was Alex's grandfather. Where did you find him?'

'We found him on Coldharbour Lane with his friend. They were talking to a known drug dealer who ran off as we approached. Your son had nothing on him, except for something that looked like an emerald, which the arresting officer assumed was stolen.'

'An inherited fake,' Ophelia threw in cheerfully. 'But what sort of drug dealer was it?'

'Cannabis, madam.' As if he was offering her a dish. No, I think I'll have the kipper, thank you very much. Cannabis. And he was only nine.

Again the inspector seemed to take pity on her. He shook his head ruefully. 'Bad business, but we don't think it was for him. We've seen his friend around there before. He probably wanted to use your son to carry the stuff for him. Maybe your son had told his friend that he was below the age of criminal responsibility?'

Because she'd told him that.

'They are in the cells, separate cells, which will have put the frighteners on them. Have you got a name and contact number for the other young man's parents?'

Ophelia wrote on a receipt from Bellamy's and handed it over. The inspector raised his eyebrows and gave a half-smile as he saw the name of the famous model. She felt he was enjoying himself, that he was already turning this into an anecdote.

'Thank you, Miss Dormandy. I'll contact his mother now. And if you wait here I'll get Alex out for you.' He stood up and drew his heels together, giving her a quick, almost military, possibly ironical nod.

Ophelia and Patrick looked at each other and she saw in his face what she felt in her own: exhaustion and relief softening his eyes and mouth, melting the bones in his hands, which drooped longer than she remembered over his worn corduroy knees. His dark hair, now ragged to his ear lobes, was evenly scattered with grey, and his face too seemed to have lost some of its freshness, as if a pale gauze obscured the original Patrick. She reached her fingers towards his, because they had been there before and because he seemed to need some fresh surge of life, or because she did. But as the tips of her fingers brushed his, the door opened and they saw Alex blushing beneath the inspector's paternal hand.

'Here he is, Alex Kelly, aka Orlando Dormandy. His details will be retained on police files but for now he is not subject to any further restriction on his liberty.' The inspector raised his hand from Alex's shoulder and gave him a pat there, a sign of encouragement and dismissal. Alex shuffled towards them in silence with his back slightly hunched, ready for a cuddle. Ophelia took him in her arms.

'Thank you so much, Inspector Brown.'

He clapped his hands together briskly, as though it was getting cold and he needed to warm himself.

'My pleasure, Miss Dormandy and err, Mr Kelly.' He looked at Patrick questioningly, as if he was trying to work out where he fitted in, as if Patrick wasn't quite respectable. She took Patrick's hand in solidarity, without letting go of Alex and then they walked out, awkwardly interlinked, like a group of happy drunks.

They walked along the Peckham Road in silence for a while, squeezing each other's hands and shoulders. Alex moved his lips without saying anything, trying out his apologies, looking for one he could actually say out loud.

'I'm sorry, Dad, that I pretended not to be a Kelly.' He

blushed and Ophelia understood that he didn't know where to start with his apology.

'Hey, it was the right thing to do. Mustn't sully the honour of the Kelly name.'

Patrick's jocularity annoyed her. There were serious things they had to discuss and this was frivolous.

She cut in, 'A Kelly wouldn't *get caught*, you mean.' And then she felt ashamed of herself. Poor Alex had meant no harm.

'Was it awful, in the cells?' she asked.

Alex nodded. 'The smell. And the bench was like the changing room at school and the door was so thick.'

She pulled him tighter towards her. He must have been as terrified as her. 'So tell us what happened before you got there.' She noticed that they were all looking forward, as though it was too intrusive to look each other in the face at the moment of confession. Their feet, though, were in step with each other. The moon was the colour of old teeth.

'Well, Ed wanted to get some grass and we went over to Coldharbour Lane. He said he'd give me a drag, but if I wanted some I should buy it myself. I said I didn't have money and he said if I had something valuable the guy would take that instead. He said he'd done that with stuff of his mother's. So I thought I'd try my emerald. What was it called again?'

'A Chatham emerald. My mother wouldn't have them in the house. She said they were bad luck. Maybe she was right.'

Patrick shook his head. 'Come off it, Feely. Since when did you become superstitious? Go on, Al, tell us what happened.'

'So the guy was just on this street corner and Ed seemed to know him pretty well. He gave him five pounds and the guy showed him a bag, but he didn't give it to him straight away. He wanted to know what I wanted and I was showing him the emerald when the police showed up. I'm really sorry.'

They glowed orange in the street lights and Ophelia couldn't tell if he was blushing. '*Drugs*, Alex? Have you been *doing drugs?*'

'No, of course not! I am sorry. I was just with Edward… You know…' He waved his hand in the air, as if to show how easily one thing led to another.

Ophelia stopped walking and turned to him. 'Listen, Alex, this is very serious. I know you've heard me talk about drug dealers and criminals of all sorts, but that doesn't mean this world is OK. The people I deal with are broken, lost, often a little mad. Their lives are a mess and their crimes destroy their lives. Drugs make you stupid, dependent, unable to function. Gradually they take you out of normal life altogether. You are not to do this again. You are not to go on the streets without me or Patrick or Freia. There are people, bad people, out there who could hurt you.'

Alex nodded. There were tears in his eyes and she could see he was frightened and ashamed.

'And I don't want you to see Edward either. Do you understand?'

'Yeah, I'm sorry, Mum. It just felt like he was my only friend.' His voice quivered.

She hugged him tight. Not enough hope, she thought. She hadn't given enough hope to either of them, Alex or Patrick.

'Darling, you're lovely. Of course you have friends, and you'll make more, easily.'

Patrick, on the other side of him, ruffled his hair. 'Of course you will,' he said, matter-of-factly.

Alex turned first to one and then the other and smiled and nodded. She and Patrick exchanged a look of relief and Alex walked on with a straighter back and his feet pointed in the right direction.

Soon they were at the front gate. Patrick opened it for them.

'I'll say goodbye now.' His voice sounded very low.

It was Alex who replied. 'No, Dad. Please stay. Please, please stay. We've got a nice bath and everything.' Ophelia and Patrick stood frozen, close but separate, telophased. 'Mum, can Dad stay, please?'

She felt Patrick look at her, timid, hopeful, and she looked down at the gate, speaking at it, not hi.: 'Yes. You can have the sofa bed if you want.' She regretted her brittle tone, but she couldn't help it. There was just too much pain. 'Alex tells me you've been sleeping in the office,' she said, opening the front door and stepping into the dim hallway. Patrick didn't reply, perhaps because it hadn't really been a question. She walked into the kitchen. 'Can I get you a drink?' She opened the fridge door and reached for a bottle. She turned to look at him and blushed. He was looking at her as though she was naked, not in a sexual way, but as though he saw everything essential about her and any pretence was useless. She poured them each a glass of white wine and when he didn't take his, she picked up one of them and drained it defiantly. Then she turned to Alex. 'Sorry darling. What would you like? I could do you a hot chocolate?'

Alex beamed. 'Yumm…'

As she got the milk out of the fridge, Patrick said gently, 'Might I have one too, perhaps?'

She nodded, annoyed that he was making her feel like an alcoholic, annoyed that the boys seemed such a unit, annoyed with herself for being annoyed. Now should have been a time of joy, but everything was too messed up for that. She poured and stirred and heated their chocolate and drank the second glass of wine. The boys, meanwhile, were arm-wrestling.

They were endearingly delighted with their hot chocolate, and they sipped at it gingerly and exclaimed 'Mmm!' competing as to who was loudest. The smell of warm sweet milk made her think of Alex as a baby again and of herself, so happy to be so needed, as he sucked at her breast. She caught Patrick's eye then and saw he was thinking something similar, or rather that he seemed to know what she was thinking, and his wistful eyes seemed to add 'You are such a lovely mother. We should have had another baby'. And as so often before, she felt both drawn to his idea and infuriated by it. He wanted a spare, in case they lost Alex again. He wanted to feel himself multiplying. He wanted to wipe out his wrong by binding her more tightly to him. She stared fiercely at the golden bottle so as not to look at him, so as not to let him start to tease and talk her round. Then she turned to Alex, whose chocolate moustache was straight and dark and rakish, like Errol Flynn's.

'Have a look at yourself before you wipe that off. Once that was a fashionable look.'

Alex stood up and studied his reflection in the glass panel of one of the kitchen units and smiled Patrick's smile, with one corner of his mouth.

'A good look for a gem trader?'

She laughed. Inspector Brown was right, she saw. Alex was surprisingly articulate for a nine-year-old. It took something shocking like this to happen, to make her see him from the outside. She'd been wrong to worry about him being vague and unformed. He was just diffident, sometimes.

Patrick looked at her with raised eyebrows and shook his head. 'Pure Dormandy,' he said, slapping Alex on the back.

This time Ophelia didn't mind the implication. Maybe he was a bit like her father after all.

'Bedtime, my darling Alex,' she said. 'You've got school and I'm in court and it's midnight!'

'Will you both put me to bed tonight?' he asked, looking hopefully from one to the other. It was a few years since he'd had both of them in attendance at bedtime, Patrick reading a story and doing all the voices, Ophelia picking up socks, tweaking the curtains, joining in the laughter.

'OK, but quickly,' she.

'Come on,' said Patrick, making as if to hit Alex on the bottom and they ran upstairs squealing.

Ophelia followed them more slowly, leaving them to it in the bathroom. She could hear Patrick: 'No, Alex, that's not a freckle, scrub harder.'

Then Alex mock-misunderstood: 'It's my beauty spot.'

She gathered up the flotsam from Alex's table – empty ink cartridges, last week's RS sheet, a flyer for a cake sale at school – and the jetsam from his floor – mainly socks. She plumped up his pillow and studied the umbrella stand and wondered if part of this whole adventure hadn't perhaps been a plot to get Patrick back in the house with them.

Alex came into the room in his pyjamas. He insisted on receiving kisses from both of them, having them sit down on his bed and hug him, one after the other, and he wanted his door left more open so he had lots of light, as he had had it when he was much younger. Ophelia, who'd had first kiss, went to the door and waved stiffly to Patrick.

'Goodnight to you too,' she said.

She retired to her bedroom, leaving him to sort out the sofa bed and his jumbled emotions, whatever they might be, alone.

Chapter Twenty-six

Ophelia saw Mrs Kalpanichandran senior first. She was standing outside St Albans Crown Court holding a baby and making noises at it, completely absorbed. Ophelia didn't want to interrupt, but she knew this elder Mrs K would hold the key to the morning.

'Good morning, Mrs Kalpanichandran. What a beautiful baby!' It was. It had tiny features and a curl of black hair.

Mrs K senior looked up at Ophelia and then back at the child. 'I think she has my eyes.' There was no animosity and no reference to Helen Fennick. The money must have been paid.

'Is your daughter-in-law upstairs?'

'She is waiting for you,' she said, with an edge of criticism.

Ophelia checked her watch. She wasn't late.

Her client was sitting holding hands with her husband on the bench outside court. Their heads were inclined and slightly tilted towards each other, as though they were in quiet conference, and they had their feet in the same position, toes turned in. Ophelia was struck by what a unit they seemed. As she approached they looked up.

'Oh, Miss Dormandy,' Mrs K said, jumping to her feet. Her husband stood beside her, his hand round her waist.

'I've just seen your child. What a beautiful baby.'

They smiled proudly. 'Yes,' said Mrs K. 'We called her Asuntha. Even my mother-in-law is in love with her.'

'And the money has been paid back?' Ophelia wanted to get the question out of the way.

'Yes, and my husband is teaching now. I am just worried all the young girls will fall in love with him!' Mrs K said teasingly and looked up at him from under her eyelashes.

He shifted his weight awkwardly from one foot to another. 'Tell your lawyer about the letter,' he prompted.

Mrs K dived into her bag and drew out an envelope. 'Here, Miss Dormandy,' she said and held it out.

The envelope was not sealed. She reached in and drew out the letter.

Your Honour,
I am writing to ask you not to send Mrs Kalpanichandran to prison. I consider myself her dear friend. I know that she stole from me but I understand the reasons and I have forgiven her. All the money has been repaid. Mrs Kalpanichandran is a young woman of exceptional qualities. If I had not had her help the florist shop would have failed as soon as I started it. I know how hard things have been for her in the last year. She has suffered already for what she has done. If she goes to prison I will miss her very much. I would like her to come back and help me in the shop whenever she is able.
Yours faithfully,
Bethany Letts

If this was genuine, and there was no reason to suspect it wasn't, getting Mrs K her suspended sentence would be Ophelia's easiest job in years.

It all worked. The judge nodded appreciatively over the letter, Mrs K junior looked pretty and contrite. Mrs K senior looked distinguished and generous. The husband paced up and down outside with the baby. Mrs K got a year's imprisonment suspended for two years. She was free.

Afterwards, she came up to Ophelia in tears and drew her aside. She talked fast, as though she was frightened of being interrupted. 'I can't thank you enough, Miss Dormandy. It was all going so wrong when we met. Everyone hated me for what I'd done. And you know I didn't even want the child? I got pregnant hoping it would be a boy and that would save us. But then I had the scan and I knew it was a girl and no one was going to be pleased with that. When you said the child could bring us together I began to think again… And then they didn't want to pay, but the solicitor frightened them. I thought of what you said and I brought Asuntha to my in-laws. They loved her! They were even prepared to pay then. You saved my life, Miss Dormandy!' She wrung her hands and sobbed. Her husband came up and handed her the baby, who was also beginning to bleat. The mother and child gazed at each other and quietened together.

Ophelia slipped away.

Chapter Twenty-seven

On the train back to London, Ophelia switched on her phone. She had a voicemail from the police confirming they'd located Godwin and confiscated his phone. She smiled, feeling that today good outcomes were possible.

Ophelia didn't go back to chambers. She needed air and the feeling of daytime London around her, benign and bright. She wandered into the National Gallery to remind herself how blue the angels' dresses were in the Wilton Diptych and thought how like Alex they looked, except that they didn't have freckles or big feet and their hair went down, not up. She stared in the windows of shoe shops, trying to want the sensible shoes, but ended up trying on some kitten-heeled slippers.

She found a narrow arch beneath a building which seemed to lead out into a bright green space. She'd passed here often but never noticed it. In the autumn sunshine on the other side, late-blooming roses stood in billowing rows of pink and red on raised grassed beds. Enclosed by buildings on all sides, it was a secret, urban garden leading to a big, flat-faced church, like a barn. A few benches with occasional singletons reading books lined the paths, adding to the cloistered feel of the spot. It seemed far removed from the glut of shops and street performers and general hysteria the other side of the arch. It was a perfect place for a tryst, and yet everyone here was alone.

Ophelia sat on a wall beside a row of roses and reached out to feel the fallen petals next to her. They were soft and velvety to the touch but they tore easily. Absently, she picked and shredded them into handfuls of confetti, soft and light as goose down in her palm.

She thought of Patrick, too at home on her sofa. He'd be lounging lazily and leaving his mark; probably filling the kitchen cupboards with his bloody curry powders and depositing his hairs in the bath. Her skin felt as though ants were running all over her.

Then she thought of Patrick with Alex in the kitchen, chatting and wrestling like they were last night, and this made her feel better. At least he'd keep Alex away from trouble. Perhaps home wasn't so bad after all, she thought, getting up and walking to the bus stop.

An hour or so later when she opened the front door, she heard a strange noise coming from the dining room. 'Hi!' she called out.

A preoccupied-sounding 'Hello' came back from Alex.

She followed the voice and saw that the dining table had been turned into a table tennis court. There was a net clipped over the middle and the flaps were extended. At either end of it, Alex and Patrick hopped from one foot to another, flushed and bright-eyed, waving bats.

'I'm just making a comeback!' Alex said.

Patrick's possessions sat in a black bin bag on the sofa, as if he'd just been let out of prison. He had the slightly strained energy of someone who can't remember how to fit in. He blushed as she looked at him, as though he thought she might not be that pleased to see him. She turned back to Alex.

'Good. Keep it up.' She went upstairs. Only when she was

running her bath did she realise that for the first time in weeks she hadn't gone straight to the fridge for a drink.

Her phone beeped at her. It was Flora.

In the pub at end of your road with new man. Join us? x

She had so much to resolve, but she felt a strong urge to do what she'd always done in a difficulty: to go away and concentrate on something else. Except, of course, that when everything went wrong at home she lost the ability to concentrate elsewhere.

She washed and changed into jeans and a figure-hugging jumper, boots, lipstick, eye make-up. Whatever the night held, she'd be ready for it. She went downstairs to see what Alex and Patrick were doing.

They were sitting on the sofa together, giggling and talking, some language she couldn't understand.

'What's all this?' She couldn't help feeling left out.

'Retsiger perp!' Alex exclaimed, pointing at his prep register. 'Retsiger Perp rof erutangis!' and then he made signing gestures and pointed at the homework book again, and she suddenly understood the words were back to front.

'KO' she said, gamely, and signed the book. They didn't react to her at all. They'd moved on to a new face-pulling game. Tonight, she thought, it might be best to leave Alex to his father.

Freia appeared in the doorway looking puzzled and a funny orange colour. Ophelia gestured to Patrick and back to Freia to effect an introduction.

'Freia, I guess you've already met Patrick today? He's staying on the sofa at the moment.' As she said this, she realised that they'd never agreed on an end date for Patrick's stay and she blushed. Freia nodded at him, uninterested, making Ophelia feel how old they both must have become. Patrick had always been so attractive to women, and yet Freia didn't even notice him. She just saw someone as old as her father.

Freia was animated by something else. 'Yes, yes. You like my tan?' She pulled up her sleeves to show a greater expanse of orange.

Alex stared at her. 'Are you that colour all over?'

Freia didn't seem to think this was rude. She seemed pleased to get a reaction.

'Everywhere except my bikini line, see...' And to Ophelia's surprise, Freia pulled her top wide open at the neck to show the line of a bikini strap over her shoulder. Maybe she was trying to catch Patrick's attention after all. 'And tonight I lighten my hair, so it is a summer-all-over look.'

Ophelia nodded. 'Of course. One wouldn't want an autumn head with a summer body.' She added, ' So if I went out would you be here if Patrick needed something?' And then she thought maybe that sounded like Patrick might make a pass at her. Who could know what impulses Patrick might have? This was excruciating.

'Yes, I can babysit,' Freia said impassively.

'Thanks,' said Ophelia. 'Also, Freia, in the future, can you keep a closer eye on this boy? I don't want him disappearing, like last night. He's got to stay next to you when you are out together. He mustn't go out on his own or with a friend. I'm not saying it's your fault, but we must all be more careful.' Ophelia felt she couldn't be very angry with Freia given that she had been so remiss herself.

Freia nodded and returned to her room.

Ophelia heard Patrick shift his weight on the sofa and she knew he was embarrassed and unsure of his postion. He was asking her, mutely, whether she wanted him to babysit, whether she might invite him to join her, or whether she wanted to get rid of him altogether. His soft eyes were overhung by such furrowed brows it was like peering into heavily gabled dormer windows.

'I'm meeting Flora and her new man,' she said, rather offhand, and then added, 'You'd be welcome, but Alex needs you.'

Patrick looked at his shoes. It was Alex who decided the matter.

'Go on, Dad. Buy Mum a drink. She'll need one.'

Ophelia looked quickly at Alex, catching his jibe, catching something else too: a mischievous determination to throw his messed-up parents together.

Alex shrugged as if to say, 'You know you do. Why pretend?' He looked from one to the other, revelling in the discomfiture he'd caused. Then he gave them both a big grin, planted a kiss on each of their cheeks and took himself upstairs, saying, 'Goodnight, Mum and Dad, I'm putting myself to bed tonight', with provoking assurance.

'Seems like he knows what he wants. What about you?' Ophelia said, turning to Patrick with a challenge in her eyes. She didn't want him to think he could just flop into this arrangement.

He held her look steadily. 'Yes, please. I would like to come out with you very much. That's something I've been trying to say to you, but not saying very well.'

Her heart beat so hard she was not sure she'd heard him right. She didn't know what he meant by it. 'Shall we just go then?' she hazarded.

He stepped to the door and opened it. 'Yes, let's go.'

Ophelia called to Freia as she walked out, 'Alex is putting himself to bed. If you could check on him in an hour…'

Ophelia couldn't even walk down the street with him

calmly. She knew she was being silly but she couldn't stop herself from saying, 'Why don't you ever wear anything but black T-shirts and corduroy? You look like an academic.'

Her irritation seemed, oddly, to make Patrick more relaxed. 'Because the last time I thought about clothes was when I was at university. Anyway, what's wrong with looking like an academic?'

'It just suggests you don't care what people think of you.'

He put his hands in his pockets and shrugged his shoulders. She knew he was right to ignore her jibe. There was nothing he could say on this subject that would make her feel better. What she wanted to talk about was their relationship, but she didn't know where to start and that made her angry. They walked side by side with a quivering space between them, like magnets held the wrong way round, repelling instead of attracting.

As she got closer to the pub, her discomfort increased. She remembered all too clearly how she'd collapsed on the bar here and downed a shot of whisky without a word. She wobbled and walked faster with sharp little steps. Patrick kept pace easily with long, loose strides and he opened the glazed door for her.

The publican was behind the bar and he met her eye with a gentle, inquiring look. She gave him a thumbs-up sign and he smiled back with relief and jollity. She felt that the evening might be a success.

Flora was lounging on the sofa by the fireplace. She was wearing a long piece of Indian silk around her waist and a scarf of the same turquoise at her neck and her hair cascaded down from a comb in the shape of a chilli pepper. She looked, unusually, almost languorous. She jumped up as she saw Ophelia. The man she was with stood too and Ophelia was struck by how open-faced and clean-cut he was, but not boring, looking. Not at all.

'Ophelia, this is Brad. And Patrick, what a surprise!'

Flora was so naturally effusive that, if she had reservations about Patrick, they weren't obvious. Patrick kissed her on one cheek and looked away. Ophelia and Brad eyed each other quickly. Brad looked at her as though she was an extraordinary creature and he was trying to categorise the particular oddness that he observed.

His scrutiny made Ophelia a little light-headed. She arched her eyebrows. 'Hi, Brad. What do you drink? I've got to go and talk to the publican so I might as well get everyone a drink at the same time.'

'A beer, thanks. *Lager.*' He put on an English accent for that. He was obviously East Coast American.

Ophelia turned to the others. 'White wine for you, Flora, and a pint of best for you, Patrick?'

They nodded and she hurried back to where the publican was wiping the counter with slightly puffy, psoriasis-spotted hands. He looked up quickly when she came, ready to hear the story, if she wanted to tell it. She spoke softly, so only he would hear.

'Thank you for everything the other day. The police found the boys on Coldharbour Lane. You were so kind to me. I don't know what to say. Um, have a drink on me, won't you? And I need some drinks for my friends...' He nodded his thanks and his face flushed as he got a pint glass ready. 'A pint of best, please, a pint of lager and two white wines. Oh and some salt and vinegar crisps,' she added.

As she brought the beers to the table, she heard Flora pumping Patrick for information. 'So when did you move out of Caroline's, then?' She turned to go back for the wine, as though she wasn't listening at all, but she strained to hear him. She thought that he said two months, but she couldn't be sure. She collected the wine and crisps quickly, but the talk seemed to have moved on when she got back. Patrick was speaking about Alex now, about how determined he could be in defence, and Ophelia thought how she would never have known that. When it came to football, she just didn't know the right questions to ask.

Brad thanked her for the beer and asked her if she'd been friends with Flora since 'way back'. He was looking at her with a curiosity that made her want to baffle and tease, but what she wanted most of all was for Patrick to notice her and feel jealous. She hated herself for this petty revenge, but it seemed necessary somehow.

'Well, we're both too young to have a "way back" obviously…' Brad showed some very white teeth as he grinned in response. She went on, 'But yes, I've known Flora since the long, gone days when we scavenged for treasure on the beach and fell in love once a week.' How long did that habit last? Till she'd met Patrick… She could tell from the set of his shoulders he was listening, too, even if he appeared to be talking to Flora. He was probably wondering what she meant by saying she'd fallen in love every week, and when she'd stopped, if ever…

'What happened to you? You couldn't stand the pace?' Brad was studying her beauty spot now and she made it disappear in the dimple of her smile.

'I never found anything valuable enough in the shingle. I decided to concentrate on getting qualified instead.'

'That sounds even worse. Qualified for what?'

'Wearing a silly wig and talking a lot.'

'Oh, I thought that was your natural hair.' He winked and she giggled, looking at Patrick to check he was still close.

She went on the attack, but with her head tilted to one side. 'What about you? No one has any idea what you do.'

'You mean Flora didn't tell you how important I am?'
Brad pulled up the sleeves on his jumper. His forearms were
indeed like a teddy's.

'Oh, she told me *that*, of course.'

Brad looked over at Flora proudly. 'I expect she would.'

Ophelia looked at her too. She was smiling so freely, more
freely than ever seemed to come to Ophelia. Patrick was
looking troubled, sincere, as though he was telling Flora
something important and true. Ophelia wondered what this
was, whether it was about her or about Alex. Ophelia said,
almost to herself, 'But then she's very nice about everyone she
meets…'

'Nicer than you?' Brad was eyeing Ophelia curiously
again.

She smiled. 'Much nicer.'

Brad beamed and put his head on one side, imitating her.
'And you feel you haven't had all the data about me that you
require?'

'Precisely. I can't have my best friend hanging around
with a man of no fixed abode.' She pulled a mock-stern
frown.

Brad righted his head. 'You should be locked up.'

'No, that's what happens to my clients.' If she couldn't be
happy, like Flora, at least she could be quick.

'Well, you probably spend too much time with them.'
Brad, she guessed, was also pretty quick.

'That's the first thing you've said that I agree with.'

He shook his head. 'You need a drink.' She agreed with
that too. She needed another glass of wine and a break from
this banter. She needed to see Patrick. As Brad went off to the
bar, Patrick broke away from Flora, but he avoided Ophelia
as she turned to him.

'I'll give Brad a hand,' he said, moving away.

Flora came up to her excitedly. 'So, what do you think of Brad?'

'He seems good fun.'

They looked over at Patrick and Brad collecting the drinks. Flora nudged Ophelia and whispered. 'Patrick loves you very much, you know.'

Ophelia felt everything shake a little, as though a heavy goods lorry was passing outside, but it was inside her that she felt it.

The men were coming back. She strained to hear their conversation. Brad was saying, 'You should do some work in the Middle East. They're building like crazy out there and they can afford to get it right. If I was in your shoes I'd go out there like a shot. I can fix you up with some meetings in Dubai, if you like.'

Ophelia stared into the dark mesh of shadows under Patrick's eyes and wondered about her own man of mystery, wondered whether he wouldn't, after all, like to try something grand and new, to develop his talents; whether some great ambition might not rise up in him, now he had experienced freedom from his wife and child.

'Thanks,' he said slowly, as though he was chewing it over, but not jumping at it, not pleased. And then he darted a look at her, knowing she was watching him, probably knowing exactly what she was thinking. He came up and gave her her drink.

'Any news of Mr Godwin?' he asked.

'Yes, sorry, the police left me a message saying they had found him and taken his phone away. I don't think he'll do it again. It would jeopardise his chance of ever getting parole.'

Patrick looked down at his drink and moved so he blocked her line of sight to Flora and Brad. She sensed he didn't want to lose her to some other conversation again.

'And what about Samuel Slidders, your favourite leader? How's he these days?'

Patrick had met Samuel once at a chambers dinner and Samuel had told him he was a very lucky man. Patrick had told Samuel that husbands received far less attention from their wives than leaders did from their juniors. Samuel, evidently pleased, had given Patrick a manly clap on the back and forgotten him instantly. Patrick had remembered him ever since.

Ophelia found herself talking and talking to Patrick about Samuel, about his health and his daughter, about how she'd told Godwin to brief him and how the brief had come before she knew he was ill, though she should have known, if she'd been looking properly. 'I just don't see things when they're painful, do I?' she asked and he gave her a forgiving smile. She realised then that she'd been talking too long, ignoring Flora and Brad, whom she'd come to see, and not even letting Patrick speak, though she wanted more than anything to know what was passing through his mind. She was just too frightened to ask. She fell silent and turned back to where Flora and Brad were standing.

Patrick tried to make up for Ophelia's sudden awkwardness. He talked interestingly about how everyone hoped the housing market in the Thames corridor east of the City would take off but how Plumstead felt like a plague pit, and he tried to tease more out of Brad, but Brad had turned monosyllabic and Ophelia guessed he preferred the company of women.

After a while, Ophelia said she had to get home and what a treat it had been to meet so spontaneously on her doorstep. Flora and Brad were effusive. Brad was livelier now he knew he'd be alone with Flora again.

Patrick gave Ophelia a sideways, questioning look.

'Patrick?' she said, offering him her hand. They kissed her friends goodbye and went to stand together just outside the door of the pub, bracing themselves against a sharp north wind and feeling the turbulence between them.

It felt as though they were both stuck, neither of them knowing how to start the conversation that hovered between them. Ophelia was more used to having to speak, but she felt incapable of being other than oblique.

'Thank you for coming with me tonight. I was glad you were there. But I felt maybe I talked too much to you.'

'Too much? Impossible. Not enough…' He put his hand around her shoulder and drew her away from the doorway and the shaft of light that came out through the etched glass into the street. 'Listen, Ophelia, I'm so sorry for hurting you. I was an utter fool.' His face looked pale and drawn in the shadows.

'Yes,' she said, leaning into his body.

'I love you.'

She watched him cover his face with his hands now, full of pain and shame.

'Yes,' she said. Inside she was a tumult of churning thoughts and aching longing, but the numbness she'd cultivated over the last months stopped up her channels of expression. She felt as helpless, perhaps, as he did. All she could say was 'Yes'. She touched his hand gently with hers, drawing it away from his eyes. She looked into the mystery of them, exchanging mysteries, but she said nothing at all.

And then she found something to say: 'We'll talk tomorrow.' It seemed like a promise, that by then she would know her mind. Right now she wasn't there at all.

He nodded. 'Dinner together then?'

'Yup.' Like it was some sort of contract.

They walked in silence through the gate, into the house and up to the foot of the stairs. She stopped there. Her room was upstairs. His was down.

'Thanks,' she said.

His voice was low but resonant as he said, 'Goodnight.'

She paused, relishing the sound of his familiar voice, then turned and went upstairs.

Chapter Twenty-eight

She crept out of the house before anyone was up, too unsure of her feelings to know how to greet any of her family. Still, she peeked in on Alex, who was curled on his side like a large baby, and Patrick. She stood a second longer than she needed to, checking he was asleep and noting that he was wearing his watch, that his strong hairy calf was clamped over an errant cover, that a mess of black and grey hair covered his eyes but not his soft, partly-open mouth.

She bought herself breakfast on the way and arrived at the door to chambers at the same time as John.

'You're early today, Miss Dormandy. Though we didn't see you yesterday, did we?'

He was some years younger than her but he didn't feel shy of reminding her when she hadn't done what she ought. She should have called in after Mrs K's case.

'We got the suspended sentence we wanted,' she said brightly.

John turned off the alarm and switched on the lights in the clerks' room. 'A cheque came for you yesterday,' he said.

She had to force herself not to run to the cheque drawer. It rolled towards her as she pulled it and her folder, squeezed by so many others, jumped to her hand. She reached in and found a cheque for defending Mars.

'Thanks, John. That's exactly what I needed.' It would pay

the term's school fees, and a little more too.

'Glad to be of assistance. I might have another junior brief for you coming up soon,' he grinned.

'With Samuel Slidders?' she asked.

'No, he's taking it a bit easy at the moment.'

So it was official. He wasn't taking work. She nodded and trudged up to her room. She sipped coffee and tidied up the old papers that had to go back to solicitors. She tried to think about her career, about how pleased Paul would be to find Mrs K out of prison, and how he'd surely send her a new case, and Jeremy Schwartz too. But she found herself thinking more about her broken family, wondering if all their love for each other couldn't glue them back together, wanting to try. Perhaps they could have a holiday at half-term to make up for the summer. If it was somewhere hot it might feel like summer… She spent the morning looking at hotels in Egypt, Spain, Libya, places with buildings for Patrick and sand for Alex, until she felt numb with choice and a sense that this was all utterly remote and irrelevant. Her phone rang and called her back to the present.

'Come to my room for a Samuel's Special, won't you?' He sounded more buoyant than he'd been for ages.

'Just a minute!' she said and ran downstairs.

The sandwiches were on plates and there were glasses of water ready for them too.

'Did you send Betty?'

'I did, and you know what she told me? They've finally got my Special up on the board! They'll be running out of the smoked mackerel pâté soon. We may have to think up another one.'

'I knew they'd recognise your genius,' she said and took the plate.

Samuel beamed.

'The clerks tell me you're taking things quietly at the moment?' she said.

Samuel frowned. 'Well, my family have insisted on a short break. Actually, I feel better than ever. The pills are marvellous. I've come in today because I've got a late-night licensing hearing tonight. Unless you'd like to do it? It's awfully well paid and there's nothing to it. You just need to sound respectable and call the club manager to give evidence his bouncers are registered.'

He was tapping a thin pile of papers on his desk. She thought of Alex expecting her after school and her dinner date with Patrick. If she cancelled them now it would seem she didn't care and had learned nothing from all they'd been through.

'Very kind of you, Samuel, but I'm busy tonight. I'm sure the clerks could find someone, if you'd rather not?'

Samuel peered at her, puzzled. 'What's this, Ophelia? Busy? Are you putting your private life ahead of your work at last? Extraordinary!'

She felt a little constriction in her chest at the criticism. 'Well just this once.'

'Good.' He patted her hand. 'You need a strong sense of boundaries to be much use in this job. Let yourself get pushed around and no one respects you.' He took a bite of his sandwich. 'Though I, of course, will think you're great whatever you do.' There was a new softness in his voice that made Ophelia feel embarrassed. She changed the subject.

'You were right about Godwin. He regretted confessing to me. He sent me threatening messages, and then an apology.'

'You were too straight and open with that man,' he said. 'With someone like that you need to fail gloriously. More theatre, less empathy.'

'Thanks, Samuel. I'll just try to be like you.'

'You won't go far wrong then,' he said.

As she travelled home that afternoon, she wondered what she would find. Alex seemed happier and more extrovert with Patrick there. He did more playing and less thinking. Ophelia realised she was frightened of being left alone with Alex now. Her old methods had been found wanting.

And what of Patrick? He said he loved her, but that wasn't the same as wanting to move back in. Perhaps he wouldn't want to stay in the household that had banished him three months earlier.

And what of her? She couldn't even fathom her own desires. Her thoughts there seemed to fail and hang suspended.

As she passed through her gate, a cat scuttled into the privet hedge that separated her from the neighbours. Just where it disappeared, she noticed some rubbish that had blown under the bush, a stray takeaway leaflet or something dropped by the bin men. On another day she might have left it, but today she'd decided to make the best of things. She reached down and retrieved the paper.

But it was not rubbish at all. It was what she had been looking for a week before. Here was the brown paper bag with Patrick's writing on it and inside, where once the bottle of wine had nestled, she found a letter. It was a little damp and the ink had run in some places, leaving irregular blue tidemarks where the water had pooled.

Dearest Ophelia
I hope your birthday goes well. You are [blotch]. I am a complete and utter mess. I have been such a fool. I lost everything with you. I'm nothing now but knobbly knees, greying hair, with only a few measly possessions in a stationery cupboard. Yes, I am back sleeping next to the

photocopier [blotch] your photo in a black beret [blotch].
I left Caroline [blotch]. And now I am living in the
interstices of my old life, in the few parts of it I can still
reach.

 At least I am working harder. I'm putting my all into
a pitch for a new school in Hackney. You'd be surprised. If
only I could make you proud of me [blotch] meantime I
hope I'll soon have a bit more money to help pay for Alex.
I should be able to take something of a salary this month.
But what I'd love most would be [large blotch] might
forgive me and [medium-sized blotch].
All my love,
Patrick

She felt a flash of heat, like a blast from an opened oven door, and she stuffed his letter in her bag with a deep breath. She wanted to keep it close to her, to tease out every word and absorb his meaning. He'd already succeeded in one of his wishes, she thought with a half-smile. He was out of the stationery cupboard. But what had he meant when he said 'what I would love most?' What did he propose? The crucial parts of the letter were missing. Perhaps she knew them already. Perhaps he'd told her enough when he said he loved her the night before outside the pub. She could ask him to fill in the gaps – but the more she thought, the more she realised that she liked it as it was. The blue blotches were appropriate. They reflected the real mystery of their connection, of any human connection. They were like windows onto a blue sky, promising a fine day. If Patrick's meaning had been set out in words, she'd have worried over the sentences, construing them, debating and contradicting them. Like this, she was full of eagerness and hope. He was probably on the sofa, waiting for her right now. Her legs went weak and she propped herself up on the door jamb, hoping to slow a racing pulse, listening for the sounds within.

She heard Alex shout, 'Let.' Table tennis...

'Yes.' It was a voice she didn't recognise, a boy's.

Here was something new to defer the moment of truth. She breathed deeply and let herself in. There was no sound from Patrick, just the high-pitched ping of a hard white ball bouncing on a bat and a flat pong as it dropped on the old pine table.

She walked into the dining room. Alex was flushed, jiggling about on his toes, holding his bat poised. On the other side of the net was a boy she hadn't seen before, smaller than Alex and neater in his movements, wearing the same school uniform.

'Hello,' she said.

'Hi, Mum, this is Jonah. It's match point.'

'Hi, Jonah. Do carry on.'

Jonah nodded and served an un-returnable serve which ricocheted around the room.

'Well played,' Alex said, and her heart swelled to see what a good sport he was, and a good host.

'Well done, boys. Now come into the kitchen and let me give you something to eat.'

They followed her, polite and pleased. There was a news-paper on the table with pictures of almost-naked girls in bikinis, but no sign of Patrick. It made her heart contract, thinking of him sitting at her kitchen table ogling all that teenage flesh.

'Dad's in the bath,' Alex said.

She took a pineapple out of the fruit bowl and began chopping it. Sticky, sweet-smelling juices ran over her trembling hands, and she felt she might keep slicing, right through the heart of it, into the top and then on up, slicing her retaining hand, and her arm. She shook herself to stop the image settling in her mind. She handed the pineapple to the boys and picked up the newspaper. She held it above the bin, about to drop it, but something made her stop and put it once more on the table. She looked at it, and looked again. And then again. There was something about the girl in the purple bikini... It was Freia!

She felt Alex watching her.

'Yes,' he said grinning, 'it's my au pair. She's gone out to celebrate with Giulia. She says the photographer said she is "more funny than most British". He did the last bit in her accent.

Ophelia found herself bursting into unstoppable giggles, as she used to in the school library. Waves of relief and remorse at her own silly jealousy engulfed her and rolled her in laughter. She would have liked to be more dignified in front of Alex and his friend, but she couldn't hold herself back, and she began to feel all the freer for it, as though laughing purged her unhappiness. Alex and Jonah were laughing too, though whether they were laughing with her or at her she couldn't say, and didn't particularly care.

The doorbell went and she pulled herself together, drying her eyes on her sleeves. A tall woman with greying hair and two little girls at her trouser legs stood anxiously on the doormat.

'I'm Jonah's mum. I hope he's been good?'

'Hi, I'm Ophelia,' she said. She felt it was important to keep her name, even in motherhood, 'He's a great table-tennis player, your Jonah. It was fun having him.'

Jonah had come up behind her and he seemed gratifyingly reluctant to go home.

'Mu-um, can't I stay for a sleepover?'

'Not now, Jonah. Come on. Alexandra and Ellie need

their baths. Thank you so much for having him. Alex must come over to ours soon.' And then, with some groaning and hunting for shoes and bags and waving goodbye, Jonah was gone.

Alex gave her a look that made her feel all too understood.

'So Daddy's taking you out for dinner tonight?'

'You don't mind?' she asked hastily.

This would be the second nightt in a row she was out. Usually he minded if she went out once, and he'd just run away to get more attention, after all. But nothing about him looked as though he minded. In fact, he looked as though it was entirely his idea. He smiled.

'No.'

'Jonah seems nice,' she said, embarrassed and keen to see whether he had, already, made a new friend.

'He's clever and good at drop shots.'

Well, she thought, not bad life skills to have.

Alex was looking at her with that appraising look again. 'You like clever people, don't you, Mum?'

'I suppose I do.' An irrepressible urge to hug him came over her. 'You know me a bit too well.'

'No, Mum. Just right.'

Alex was definitely more grown up than she'd thought. He'd grasped something that she was still reaching for.

'Yes. It is best to understand each other,' she whispered.

He grinned triumphantly. He was loved and he was right. What more could he want? He squeezed her so hard she could scarcely breath, so hard that all their secrets would pop out of them both.

She saw Patrick watching them from the landing with a benign tolerance which was faintly irritating. She blushed and kissed Alex's forehead before letting him go.

Patrick's hair was brushed away from his handsome lined face, his naked legs were strong and slender, his knees not really very knobbly, his robe slipping at the front, showing curling dark hairs on his chest. She felt her irritation with him slipping too.

'Hello, Ophelia,' he said. 'Just getting myself respectable enough to take you out. Your page-nineteen model will be back soon to babysit.'

He walked down the stairs, so naked, so close. She felt as nervous as though she was about to sit an exam. He spoke quite naturally. 'There was a call for you from the governor of Wandsworth Prison. He was very apologetic about the security lapse over Godwin's phone. I asked him to monitor Godwin's visits and he agreed. They will also keep a record of the complaint for the parole board.'

Patrick had got far more out of the governor than she would have. Ophelia had already forgiven Godwin the threats. He hadn't harmed Alex, after all. But Patrick was clearer-sighted than she was and he could get people to do things, if he tried. He was right to keep Godwin under surveillance, and he hadn't even heard Betsy's evidence. She gave Patrick an awkward pat on the back, swallowed hard and ran up to her room.

It was a mess in here. Her dressing table was thick with lengths of barrister's pink tape, train tickets for her tax folder, photographs of Alex, and cards from him.

She saw the birthday card he'd given her the week before and picked it up. That seemed a long time ago and she hadn't been concentrating then. This time she studied it carefully and she saw not just the players, and Alex scoring a goal, but also a supporter on the touchline. It was a woman with short yellow hair and high heels – it was her! She had a speech bubble with the words 'Pure genius!' inside it and her stick arms waved chaotically above her head. She was wearing a blue and white spotty dress. Ophelia had forgotten that dress. It was a year at least since she'd set fire to it, leaning too close to a candle. Once she'd worn it all the time. It had been one of Alex's favourites. And yet she'd forgotten she ever had it, forgotten she'd ever worn spots at all. She smiled as she realised she was one of the 'spot-wearers', along with those other exuberant lawyers, Samuel and Jeremy. She sank down on her bed thinking about them both, and about how their clients came back to them. She wondered if her clients might start to come back to her, not as revenge, as she'd imagined with Godwin, but as a sign she was appreciated – and proof they were recidivists…

She woke with a start and reached for her clock. Nine o'clock. Patrick would have been expecting her downstairs an hour ago. She sat up abruptly and blinked, feeling dizzy. She listened to the sounds of the house. She could hear the swell of Freia's film music below her. And Patrick – would he be annoyed? She tried to imagine him and she realised she knew exactly what he would be doing. He'd be sitting at the kitchen table reading the *Architectural Review* and occasionally scratching his balls. He'd be getting hungry and wondering whether to break into the salami in the fridge or whether there was still a chance of her waking up and joining him for dinner. She opened her door a crack and called down, quietly so as not to wake Alex.

'Sorry, I just woke up.'

She heard his voice coming up from the kitchen, as she'd expected, but warmer, friendlier: 'No hurry.'

She chose her prettiest underwear, her finest stockings, her tightest skirt, her softest blouse; blue as the velvety night. She fussed at her face with make-up brushes, trying to find some perfect self, failing. She felt shy as she tiptoed downstairs in vampish boots, but when she stepped into the kitchen, he had his eyes almost covered with his hands and he peeked out at her through the gap and made her giggle.

'I'm so hungry I could eat you up,' he said, getting to his feet.

'Well, hurry, let's go. To the Chinese, then?'

'Oh, not the Chinese. We're going somewhere special tonight.' He smiled a wonky smile, revelling in some undisclosed plan.

She wiggled her head from side to side, as if considering the proposition. 'OK, so long as you let me take you somewhere else afterwards…'

'Not dancing?' A look of mock horror crumpled his forehead.

'No. Somewhere quiet and urban, but floral.' He skewered her with his look. She smiled back, with what she knew was a version of his own uneven smile. 'A little secret,' she added.

Patrick gazed at her with frank admiration. His look made the back of her scalp tingle and her legs shake with each step she took towards him. 'Are you ready to go?' His voice was freighted with hope.

She nodded, put on her coat and slid her hand around his arm. He drew her in close, so the backs of her fingers pressed against his chest, and he flicked open the lock on the thin front door.

The bare, trailing branches of the great plane trees opposite swayed across cones of street light and cast bifurcating shadows on the pavement. Ophelia breathed in sharply before stepping with Patrick into their web.

Clare Jacob was brought up in London and New York. She read English at Oxford and became a barrister because she loved John Donne. After years of defending clients accused variously of bomb-making, hiding cocaine in coconuts and stealing underpants, she decided to capture the lunacy and mystery of it all in a novel. She is married with three children.